RECLAIM

ALY MARTINEZ

RECLAIM
Copyright © 2020 Aly Martinez

All rights reserved. No part of this novel may be reproduced, distributed, or transmitted without written permission from the author except for the use of brief quotations in a book review. This ebook is licensed for your personal enjoyment only. If you would like to share this book with others please purchase a copy for each person. This eBook may not be re-sold or given away to other people.

RECLAIM is a work of fiction. All names, characters, places, and occurrences are the product of the author's imagination. Any resemblance to any persons, living or dead, events, or locations is purely coincidental.

Cover Design: Hang Le
Editing: Mickey Reed
Proofreading: Michele Ficht and Julie Deaton
Formatting: Champagne Book Design

RECLAIM

WARNING: This book may contain triggers for some readers.

PROLOGUE

Nora

CHOICES.

Everyone makes them.

From mundane and monotonous to life-changing and unimaginable.

But regardless what that choice may be, life is lived in the consequences.

People want to believe that decisions are weighted. In theory, "What should I have for dinner?" should fall on the opposite end of the spectrum as "Should I swallow this bottle of pills?" But in reality, even the smallest decision can change the trajectory of your entire life.

"Oh God!" Ramsey yelled, scrambling across the dirt road on all fours. I watched in the rearview mirror as he paused, hovering over the bloody and lifeless body, not sure which broken part to touch first. "No. No. No."

I wanted to care. I wanted to be flooded with guilt and regret. I just wanted to fucking feel something again. Anything.

Instead, I sat there, stunned and utterly numb.

My brother's mouth moved, fast and sharp, but I couldn't hear him over the ringing in my ears. With shaky hands, I tried to open the car door twice before I was successful. My chest vibrated as a barrage of emotions ricocheted inside me, none of them able to escape. All of them slicing me to the core of my soul.

Or maybe it was only the remnants of my soul, because the rest of it had been destroyed long before that starry night.

I swung my legs out, my head swirling with the high of adrenaline, and I struggled to find even one breath of oxygen.

My brother was seventeen, but he looked like a man as he started chest compressions and rescue breathing. Curiously, I wondered where he'd learned that. Then I immediately wished he hadn't.

It was pointless though. He was dead. I didn't have to be up close and personal to know that.

"Come on, come on, come on," Ramsey chanted, never giving up, just like the hero I knew him to be. "Breathe."

That asshole didn't deserve to breathe. He didn't deserve anything. He'd already stolen it all from me.

"Stop," I forced out.

Ramsey's panicked gaze swung my way. "What the fuck happened?"

How much time did he have?

Wood splintering into my back.

Blink.

His fingers digging into my flesh.

Blink.

The welcomed darkness that swallowed me as my only way to survive.

Blink.

Thea.

Thea.

Thea.

"Let him die!" I roared so loudly that it scorched my throat.

RECLAIM

But at least I felt that.

The sound of people talking in the distance interrupted my echo, and my brother's panic skyrocketed. Ramsey quickly abandoned his attempts to revive him and raced in my direction, but just seeing him lying there, alone and lifeless the way I would always feel, gave me a sick sense of pleasure.

I should have been crying.

Why wasn't I crying?

I'd spent two years living in fear—nightmares, sobbing until I physically passed out, hiding behind a smile for fear people could see the filth behind it.

Maybe there was nothing left of me to give. Not even tears.

The voices got closer, and Ramsey stepped into my line of sight, blocking out that monster the way I would never be able to do.

"You gotta go," he barked. "I'll take care of this, but you gotta go before someone sees you here."

"I'm not leaving."

He grabbed my shoulders and gave me a hard shake. "Listen to me. You have to leave. I'll get the car and meet you back at the house. If anyone asks, you haven't seen me. Tell them I've been with Thea all night."

I could hear the words coming from his mouth, but I was struggling to process what he was saying. It was like an optical illusion: I could see the picture in front of me, but none of it felt real.

I glanced around and his car was still running, the front end smashed and covered in blood. "What if they see your car?"

"I'll...I'll... I'll tell 'em I hit a deer or something." He looked over his shoulder as three silhouettes appeared at the end of the Johnsons' driveway. "Please, Nora," he hissed. "I promise you this is going to be okay. But you can't be here. If they find out what he did to you, they'll know this wasn't an accident. I can't risk that. Okay? You weren't here. Nothing happened. It was a terrible, terrible accident. End of story." He palmed each side of my face and pressed a shaky kiss to my forehead.

That might have been more jarring for me than running over a man.

Ramsey wasn't the most affectionate brother. We hugged on occasion, and when I was little, he'd always ruffled my hair or pinched me playfully on the side.

But he wasn't a forehead kisser.

"Ramsey," I choked out, the adrenaline starting to ebb from my system, a hurricane of emotions moving in.

"Please," he whispered, his desperate and pleading brown eyes sparkling with unshed tears in the moonlight. "Just run home and get in bed. I'll meet you there. Everything's going to be okay."

Okay. That was a word I recognized all too well. Not *good.* Or *great.* Or even *fine.* Just simply *okay* was a state of being for us.

Besides, Ramsey had never steered me wrong before.

So I squeezed his hand, and like a coward, I ran.

Choices. Everyone makes them.

But mine would ruin us all.

ONE

Nora

Three years earlier...

THINGS I HATED:

 The sound of Styrofoam squeaking.

 The seeds in strawberries and therefore strawberries in general because the seeds were too tiny to pick out.

And bugs. Every shape. Every size. Every color. I hated them all.

Ramsey told me I was crazy because I would carry frogs around in my pocket when I was younger and trap lizards in old shoeboxes. My brother thought that was "way more gross." But if I so much as crossed the path of a grasshopper, it might as well have been a hitman. It didn't matter how many times he told me that dragonflies wouldn't hurt me. Or how often my teachers tried to convince me that butterflies were kind and gentle. One flutter, hop, or squirm and it would push me past the point of all reason and straight into hysterics.

Clearly, hunting earthworms was the obvious career choice for me.

Well played, Karma. Well played.

"Ew, ew, ew," I whispered, using my fingers to rake through the dirt. It was going to take all night to get my fingernails clean.

My long, brown hair fell into my face, the purple glitter barrette Ramsey had given me for my birthday failing me. I should have grabbed a ponytail holder before I'd left, but sprinting from the house and pulling on my shoes before my dad went on a tirade about who'd eaten the last of the cereal was something of a priority.

"Oh, God." I fought a gag when a fat earthworm rolled out of the dirt. "It's just a worm. That's not even a real bug. It's more like a snake." I paused my pep talk and shivered. "Crap. Okay, snakes are bad too. This is not like a snake. Not at all." Using a stick, I transferred its slimy, squirming body into the coffee can my employer, Mr. Leonard, had fashioned into a bucket.

Sweat dripped down my forehead as the sweltering Georgia humidity curled around me like a suffocating wet blanket. It was only the first Sunday since school had let out, but I was already sick of it.

Ramsey and his girlfriend, Thea, were off sitting under their tree as usual. The invitation was always open for me to join them, but there were only so many googly eyes a girl could witness before losing her lunch.

Don't get me wrong. I loved Thea. She was super cool and fun, a little too tomboy for my taste, but my brother didn't seem to mind that his "Sparrow" had an aversion to makeup and nail polish. She lived two doors down from us, so we hung out a lot. Honestly, she was as close to a sister as I would ever get. But those two were getting grosser by the day.

For the record, collecting earthworms for Mr. Leonard was still worse by a million miles. It was a paying gig though, so I'd pounced when I saw the sign posted at the end of his driveway. My father was worthless, and with Ramsey's lawn mower out of commission until he could afford to fix it, I was responsible for earning the grocery money. My brother had told me not to worry about it and he'd figure it out, but I liked the idea of helping for a change.

Although I had zero experience in the worm-hunting industry, I was the star employee in the running-away-from-worms-at-any-and-all-costs industry. At twenty cents a worm, I figured even if it gave me nightmares, I could still make a pretty penny.

Or so I'd thought. The meager four worms I'd collected over my first three hours on the job said otherwise.

I scooped another handful of dirt while the rushing stream echoed off the surrounding trees. It had been a rainy week, so the creek was swollen and the usual hum of the flowing water had become a dull roar.

It was exactly why I didn't hear him walk up.

"Catch anything good?"

"Crap!" I startled, knocking my bucket over. "Crap!" I repeated, quickly righting it before any of the creepy crawlers had a chance to escape. When I was sure my bounty of disgustingness was safe, I snapped my head up to make sure I wasn't about to be murdered.

A boy around my age was standing a few feet away, wearing khaki slacks, an ugly striped button-down, penny loafers—the kind with the actual penny tucked in the slit—and a smug grin that did not bode well for my quiet afternoon alone. Especially since he was holding a bucket that matched mine.

Rising to my feet, I put my filthy hand to my eyes to block the sun cascading through the trees. I'd only lived in Clovert for four years, but it was a small town, so I'd met or knew of just about everyone.

Everyone except this sandy-brown haired boy with the most incredible baby-blue eyes I would ever see.

"Depends. Who's asking?"

He laughed and his short, curly hair ruffled in the breeze. "I'm Camden."

"Camden like the city?"

The amusement on his face never left as he twisted his lips. "Well, no. It's Camden like my dad. Who was named after his dad. Who was named after his dad. But *his* dad might have been named after the city." He lifted a skinny shoulder in a half shrug. "Anyway, I'm Camden Cole."

Camden Cole? What the flippity flapping kind of snobby, rich kid name was that?

We didn't have many wealthy people in Clovert, but old Southern money sometimes came home to retire or raise their family away from the big city. Though we didn't have a private school, so none of this explained why I'd never seen this kid before.

"How old are you?" I asked.

"Twelve."

Hmmm, only a year older than I was. I definitely would have remembered those eyes if I'd seen him at school.

"Where do you live?"

"Alberton."

I almost choked on my tongue. Ohhhh-kay. So probably *not* one of the rich kids.

Our little farming town with all of two stoplights and one grocery store was bad enough, but Alberton was next-level awful. It was over three hours away, but I'd been there a couple of times. Back when my dad had been a trucker—and occasionally sober—he'd make hauls out there. Being young, dumb, and desperate for his attention, I'd thought it was fun to ride along, but there was absolutely nothing in Alberton but a papermill, poor people, and the stomach-churning aroma of rotten eggs.

RECLAIM

My dad had told me it stunk because of the papermill, but that town looked like it was less than a week away from a zombie apocalypse, so I had my doubts.

"What are you doing here, then? Are you a hitchhiker? Serial killer? Circus performer?" Tipping my chin up, I gave him another once-over.

He looked harmless enough. Scrawny. Preppy. Dorky. I might have been small, but I'd grown up with a brother who thought tickling me until I peed my pants was an Olympic sport. I probably could have taken this kid if he tried to start anything.

Camden shook his head, a bright white smile splitting his mouth. "Nah. My parents sent me here to spend the summer with my grandparents. I think I'm supposed to be helping them out around the house, but I just make my grandpa mad all the time." He set the bucket down at his feet and shrugged. "I figure, if I tell my parents I got a job, then they can't be too angry I skipped out on gardening with Grandpa." He leaned forward and took a peek in my bucket. "So anyway, detective. If you're done with my interrogation, I'll repeat… Catch anything good?"

My shoulders sagged. I hadn't, and the dollar signs I'd been hoping for were fading by the second. "Not really. If you're after money, you'd be better off going back to Mr. Leonard and asking if he needs help in the fields."

"Then what would I do with all these?" He smiled, tipping his bucket so I could see inside.

Sweet baby Jesus, there must have been at least a hundred worms in there.

I lunged toward him. "Where'd you get all those?"

"Depends. Who's asking?" He quirked his brow mischievously.

Rolling my eyes, I muttered, "I'm Nora."

He sauntered over to one of the large rocks next to the water and thoroughly brushed it off before sinking down on top of it. The reflection off his perfectly polished penny loafers nearly blinded me. "Last name?"

"Stewart."

"You related to Mr. Leonard?"

"No."

"How'd you get this job?"

"Jeez, who's the detective now?" I fired a scowl in his direction. "I saw the sign and knocked on his door."

"Was anyone else here when you got here?" He looked up and down the creek to see if we were alone.

There was a solid chance my eyes were going to roll out of my head. Where the heck was he going with this?

"No."

He blew out a ragged breath and dug into his pocket to retrieve a crumpled piece of paper. "Good. It's just the two of us. That'll make it easier." He tossed the paper and it landed at my feet. I didn't have to pick it up to see that it was Mr. Leonard's *help wanted* sign. "Are you a rat, Nora Stewart?"

I crossed my arms over my chest. "I'm not a rat, but I do have an older brother who will kick your butt if you don't tell me where the heck you got a bucket full of worms without so much as a speck of dirt on your stupid, fancy clothes."

His grin stretched wide. "Promise you won't tell anyone?"

My patience was slipping fast with his trivial game, so my voice was louder than I intended as I replied, "Tell anyone what?"

"Jeez. Someone woke up on the wrong side of the bed today."

He was wrong. As far as I knew, my bed only had one side.

RECLAIM

The side where I woke up, fought with my dad, hated my life, and crawled right back into it every night, knowing that the next morning was going to be exactly the same.

I let out an aggravated huff. "Just tell me where you got the worms."

"Okay, but first, did Mr. Leonard tell you why he needs the worms?"

More. Freaking. Questions. And yes, I did understand that my frustration was a tad hypocritical. But he was the new kid. My questions were fair. His were just annoying. And nosy. And wasting my worm-plucking time.

"Well, duh. The whole town knows why he needs the worms. He and Dale Lewis have been feuding for months. They can't even be in the same parking lot without the cops getting called. I don't know how it started, but Mr. Leonard won't be caught dead near Lewis Tractor Repair, Bait, and Booze. Which means he and his sons have nothing to fish with. Which means he hired *me* to find them bait. Which means you better start talking right now about where the heck you got a whole dang bucket of worms, because I was here *first*." My chest heaved when I finished.

I was usually pretty good about hiding my emotions. Screaming and acting out didn't fix anything. Going with the flow was a huge part of staying in the shadows so no one realized what was really going on at home with me, Ramsey, and our messed-up dad.

But I was sweaty.

I was dirty.

I was eleven and had spent all afternoon hunting for nasty, gag-inducing worms so my brother and I could have something for dinner. Meanwhile, this kid—who probably wasn't loaded but definitely had enough money to use spare change as decorations in his shoes—had just shown up with a full bucket.

It wasn't fair. It wasn't right. And I was done. Utterly. Completely. All patience gone.

Unfortunately, Camden Cole was only getting started.

"You weren't here first," he stated.

I took a giant step toward him. "Yes, I was! I've been here for hours."

Abandoning his coffee can, he stood up, his smile finally morphing into a scowl. "Oh yeah? Well, Mr. Leonard hired me at noon!"

"Liar! The sign wasn't even there at noon."

With another step, he closed the distance between us. "I know because I ripped it down. He must have put it back up when I had to go home for lunch. I was late, which royally ticked off my grandpa, so he made me go back to church for seven hundred hours, and now I'm here, answering a million questions and listening to some girl I don't even know call my clothes stupid and yell at me. So shut up. Okay? I get enough of that shit from my family." He stared at me for a long second, a shadow passing over his dazzling eyes, but I didn't let it snuff my fire. This kid did not want to go toe-to-toe with me in a who-has-the-crappiest-parents competition. He would lose every time.

"Blah, blah, blah. You *still* didn't tell me where you got that many dang worms!"

"Who cares!" he roared into my face. "You know what?" Turning on a toe, he snatched his bucket off the ground. "Here. Take the damn worms. I don't care anymore." Tipping his can by the end, he dumped half of them at my feet. He pinned me with an icy, blue glare that only minutes earlier had been heart-stopping. Now, it was downright murderous.

RECLAIM

"I don't want your stupid worms." I kinda-sorta lied. I did want them. I just didn't want him to *give* them to me.

"Well, you got 'em. Now, leave me alone. Tomorrow, I'll take the other side of the creek."

Was that where he'd gotten them from? Was there a mound of earthworms ripe for the picking over there? No way I was going to be the dummy who let him have them all.

"I want the other side," I snapped.

"Fine!" he exclaimed.

Crap. He'd agreed to that way too easily. If his goldmine was over there, he would have at least argued. "No, wait. I want this side."

"Whatever!" Shaking his head, he stomped away.

Double crap! Was this some kind of reverse psychology? Thea had told me all about it. It was how she'd gotten Ramsey to agree to wear the friendship bracelet she'd made him. Was I falling victim to Camden's mind games?

"Never mind, I do want the other side!" I yelled at his retreating back.

He kept on trucking, calling over his shoulder, "Sure. See if I care!"

It was a hike from the creek to Mr. Leonard's house, but it was mostly flat, so I could see him the whole way. I smiled when he tripped. Then I groaned when he managed to stay on his feet. Only after he'd disappeared around the side of the house did I look down at the pile of worms at my feet.

There had to have been at least ten dollars' worth wiggling around. That would have been enough to feed me and Ramsey like kings. I could pick up burgers on the way home. Maybe even splurge on Cokes and fries. Heck, if I ordered off the dollar menu, I could afford to get some for Thea too. God knew she fed us enough to be owed a burger or fifty.

But as good as all of that sounded, it wouldn't be my money.

I was a lot of things: Broken. Sad. Angry. Confused.

But a thief wasn't one of them. Sure, he'd given me those worms, so it wasn't like I'd stolen them or anything. No matter how much it sucked, they were his.

There was no way I was showing up the next day owing Camden Cole anything.

Sighing, I grabbed my bucket, laid it on its side, and used a stick to scrape up the pile. I couldn't keep them, but there was no point in letting all his hard work go to waste. I'd cash them in and give him the money tomorrow—assuming he showed at all.

The rest of the afternoon was quiet. I found a few more worms in the dirt and then hit the jackpot around an old tree stump. I assumed it was somewhere similar to where Camden had gotten lucky earlier in the day.

I mean, not that I thought about Camden or anything. That would have been stupid. He was probably never going to speak to me again. Which was fine. I didn't need friends. I had Ramsey and Thea—by default, but whatever. There was also a girl who occasionally wore mismatched shoes and always stared at me on the bus. I didn't know her name, but we were practically BFFs.

Okay, so I could have used a few friends, but it was something I could worry about later. For the summer, I just needed a job, a paycheck, and not to lose my mind.

Nothing more. Nothing less.

TWO

Camden

"**C**AMDEN COLE, GET YOUR ASS BACK IN HERE!" my grandpa shouted as I took off out the door.

The screen door slammed behind me, and even with as mad as I was, I flinched. I'd pay for that later.

Dear God, I'd only been there three days and my head was already about to explode.

Camden, sit up straight.

Camden, real men look you in the eye when you talk to them.

Camden, don't forget to wash behind your ears.

I swear my grandma acted like I used my ears as a second set of feet. How my mom had survived her youth without throwing herself off the barn roof, I would never understand. The only thing that boggled my mind more was why my parents had thought it was a good idea for me to spend the summer with these people.

Oh, right. The fight.

The fight I hadn't started. The fight I'd had no interest in having when my Neanderthal cousins had come to our house for a weekend. Coincidentally, the very same fight I'd lost.

Yet, *I* was the one who'd gotten sent to my grandparents' house for the summer in what had to have been the family equivalent of boot camp. Yeah. Made *perfect* sense.

"Camden!" Grandpa roared again.

I didn't let it slow me. He was going to be mad no matter what I did. At least this way I could get some space to clear my head before listening to an hour-long lecture on what a screw-up I was.

When I'd finally made it through the grass, the toe of my sneaker caught on the pavement. The height of my athleticism was my ability to sometimes remain upright. If I'd really thought about it, that was possibly my biggest problem of all. My dad, a six-foot-four, two-hundred-and-fifty-pound former college athlete who had worked at the papermill since he was old enough to sign the back of a paycheck, was not the type of M-A-N who had a kid who tripped. It didn't matter if the sidewalk was broken, cracked, and a total safety hazard. I was Camden Donald Cole's son; I should have been born with hair on my chest and a football in my hands.

Instead, I liked books, science, and taking apart old electronics just to see how they worked. That last one would have been great if I liked putting them back together. *Fixing shit*, as he called it, would have been a worthy hobby for his son. But the tedious process of finding parts and making repairs wasn't nearly as interesting to me. I did it sometimes though because I could sell whatever clock, radio, or DVD player I'd been working on to make enough to buy more books, supplies for my science experiments, or more junk to pry apart.

Mom used to help me sneak stuff into our garage when Dad wasn't looking. She wasn't all too thrilled about having a scrawny klutz for a son, either, but she was much more tolerant than my dad, so we got along okay.

Grandpa continued to yell from the porch, but I kept going. The destination didn't matter as much as getting the heck

RECLAIM

out of there, but when a brightly lit sign from the grocery store appeared at the end of the road, it felt like a beacon guiding me home.

Grandma had made liver and onions for dinner. It was exactly as disgusting as it sounded, but I'd managed to hide the majority of it under my rice and green beans. With my worm money burning a hole in my pocket, I headed inside for a Coke and a candy bar. My parents would have shit a living, breathing turkey if they knew I was eating junk while I was gone. But, hey, that knowledge would only make the Snickers that much sweeter.

I was still perusing the drink cooler, debating between Coca-Cola Classic and Dr. Pepper, when I heard her voice. It was quiet and shy, not at all that of the rude girl from the creek.

"Oh, um… I thought it was going to be three ninety," she said.

Leaning to the side, I peeked around the cooler. Long, brown hair, tie-dyed tank top, and muddy white canvas shoes.

Nora Stewart in the flesh.

And wasn't that just fan-freaking-tastic.

Groaning, I sulked back behind the cooler with hopes that she wouldn't notice me. She was already checking out, so with some luck, I could avoid her completely.

"You gotta account for tax, honey. It's four seventeen," the clerk replied.

"Dang it." She sighed. "I always forget about tax. I, um, well… I only have four dollars."

My eyebrows shot up. That was impossible. She should have turned a crazy profit for the day. I'd dumped almost ten bucks in worms at her feet before I'd stormed off.

Which, by the way, was not my smartest financial move. But, fine, I wasn't great under pressure. She was bratty—albeit cute—and had gotten me all flustered asking questions and I hadn't known what else to do. I'd regretted it pretty much immediately, but I'd been too proud to go back. Especially after I'd almost busted my butt on an old stump in the ground.

Curiosity killed the cat, and I once again leaned around the corner.

"Can I put something back?" She crinkled her freckled nose as she took inventory of her purchases: a loaf of bread, the tiniest pack of ham I'd ever seen, a bag of chips, and pack of watermelon gum.

I twisted my lips. My parents were strict about making me pay for anything extra that I wanted, but I'd never had to buy my own dinner.

The cashier offered her a sad smile. "If you put the gum back, you'll have enough for the rest."

Nora shook her head. "No, that's a surprise for my brother." She grabbed the chips and handed them to the clerk. "I don't need those. Do I have enough money now?"

"Yep. That'll work."

Her shoulders sagged and a sharp knife of guilt stabbed me in the stomach. I had more than enough money in my pocket to cover the bag of chips—all of her groceries for that matter. However, after the way she'd yelled at me, I didn't figure she liked me all that much.

Still, I could have helped.

But I was twelve, and she was a girl, who was probably just going to shout at me again, and if she didn't holler at me, offering to pay for her groceries would probably embarrass her. And if it embarrassed her, it was sure as heck going to embarrass me.

So, like a fool, I stood there and did nothing.

I watched the cashier bag her groceries and pass her the change.

RECLAIM

She thanked the lady and tucked the money into her pocket. Then she took her bag and headed for the door.

"Hey!" the gray-haired man in line behind her called out, bending over to pick something up. "You dropped this." He extended a hand toward her and there it was: a perfectly folded ten-dollar bill.

My eyes narrowed as confusion rocked through me. If she'd had a ten in her pocket, why'd she say she only had four dollars?

The older man shifted gears into lecture mode. "You need to be more careful with your money, kid. You can't let it fall out of your pocket like that. A different kind of person might not have given it back."

She stared at him for a beat, sporting the fakest smile I'd ever seen. "Right."

What she said next changed the entire course of my life.

I didn't know it then, but with three words, the universe kicked the first domino that would ultimately form the sprawling path of my future. A path I would struggle to travel. One that would collapse under the weight of my regrets and eventually knock me to my knees, but I'd never stop getting up and forging ahead because it would forever be the only path that led me back to her.

But in that moment, they were just three infuriating words.

"Freaking Camden Cole," she muttered, taking the money from the man. "Thanks."

Freaking Camden Cole? What had I done? I'd given her that money. Which she obviously needed. And now *I* was *Freaking Camden Cole*? How was that fair?

"You want those chips now?" the clerk asked, but Nora just shook her head and shoved the money into her pocket so roughly that I'd have sworn she was mad at it.

Suddenly, I was furious at it too. I was dealing with enough crap that summer from my family without some girl who didn't know me at all dishing it out too.

Even under her breath.

In the middle of a grocery store filled with more strangers.

In a town where nobody knew me.

All of which were minor formalities to my mounting anger.

As she left the store, I abandoned my candy bar and followed her. She could yell at me all she wanted, but I'd done nothing wrong. If she wanted to be pissed off about the money, I'd gladly take it off her hands. No sweat off my back.

Nora was a girl on a mission though and moved fast as she stomped away carrying a bag in each hand. She beat me to the parking lot, and I tried to play it cool as I passed a few locals on their way inside, smiling and waving so as not to look like a creepy stalker as I chased after her.

Less than a second later, when she hit the sidewalk and started ranting to herself, a creepy stalker was exactly what I became.

"Freaking Camden Cole, with his pretty blue eyes. I mean who actually has eyes *that* blue? What are they, night vision goggles or something?"

My brows shot up and my jaw hung open so wide I could have caught flies. She thought my eyes were pretty. My mom had always told me that, but she was required by DNA to think it.

Nora Stewart was not.

And just like that, *Freaking Camden Cole* didn't sting as bad.

I dropped back a bit so she didn't hear my footsteps, but she kept right on ranting loud and clear. In a ridiculous tone that sounded nothing like my voice, she mocked, "Hey, I'm Camden Cole. Have some worms. I have a bazillion." She groaned and flapped her swinging arms. "I don't want your worms! I want my own damn worms. And maybe more than four dollars' worth." She let out a frustrated growl but just kept marching. "I bet Camden had chips with his dinner. He probably even got dessert. Eating chocolate cake in his stupid shoes and fancy shirt."

My whole body jerked, and I stopped in the middle of the sidewalk as if I'd hit an invisible brick wall.

Oh, God.

Oh, *God*.

She thought I was rich. That was the kiss of death.

She didn't know I'd had to buy those shoes myself. And yes, I knew exactly how ugly they were, and given the opportunity, I would have thrown them in a bonfire. But my dad didn't bitch at me when I wore them to church and that alone made them worth their weight in gold.

My breath caught when suddenly she cut into the woods. On the sidewalk, I could have pretended to be out for a nightly stroll. She didn't own the whole town. But if I got caught following her into those woods, it would have been far past the realm of coincidence.

I clenched my teeth as I watched her disappear on that dark, moonlit trail. I should have gone home. I should have left her alone, given up on the worm thing, and spent the rest of my summer trying to become the man my parents and grandparents were so desperate for me to be.

But even knowing all that, my feet didn't budge.

My heart thundered in my ears, and I stood at a crossroads. She was a complete stranger, yet my draw to her was like the moon pulling in the tides.

Years later, I'd still debate why I'd followed her that night. I wasn't mad anymore and she'd gotten far enough ahead that I couldn't hear her ramblings—good or bad. But for reasons I'd never be able to explain, my feet slid into her footprints on the dirt path.

She was a good bit ahead of me, but I did my best to keep quiet just in case. The woods weren't as thick as I'd assumed, and before long, porch lights from houses on the other side of the wood line illuminated our way. I wasn't tall by any means, but my legs were longer than hers, so I gained ground quickly. More than once, I slipped behind a tree for fear she'd heard me.

Through it all, she just kept walking, her eyes forward and her brown hair swaying across her back.

Stalking aside, it was nice and peaceful on that trail.

That all changed when the sound of a man's voice boomed through the silence. I froze, my brain struggling to figure out which direction it had come from, but Nora took off at a dead sprint.

I darted after her, and with every step, the shouting grew louder. Slurred cuss words soared through the air like wobbly arrows, escorted by an off-pitch symphony of grunts and grumbles. My feet pounded against the trail, sticks cracking and leaves rustling, but she never looked back.

Nora exited the woods first, her plastic bags looped around her wrists, smacking her legs as she ran across a yard of unkept grass straight toward a small ranch home with paint peeling off the crooked shutters. There was a broken windowpane covered by plywood on the front of the house, and the crack in the front door was visible even from yards away.

For a brief second, the night fell silent, so I ducked behind a tree to watch her while I caught my breath. I found no oxygen because no sooner than Nora reached the door did it swing open, nearly cracking her in the face. A man with messy, brown hair and a beer gut stumbled out, crashing into her. His hands snaked out, but not to catch her. He pushed her hard, sending her small body sailing.

On instinct, I lurched from behind my tree, but a boy, who I assumed was her brother because he looked just like her only *a lot* bigger, plucked her off the ground and dragged her behind him.

"Don't you ever fucking touch her again!" the boy yelled.

The disheveled man used the back of his hand to wipe his mouth and slurred, "I should gut you both. No wonder your mom left you ungrateful pieces of shit. You ruined my whole fucking life." His fist sailed through the air, landing hard against her brother's face.

I gasped and slapped a hand over my mouth as he fell back against the house and sank to his butt.

The man once again advanced, but Nora jumped between them, crouching low like a lion ready to attack. "Dad, no!"

Holy shit. That was her *dad?*

A blast of panic hit me, stealing my breath all over again. I had no idea what to do. If her brother, who was twice my size, couldn't take this guy, I would have been next to worthless.

I could get help though. Surely someone else must have heard the chaos. Frantic, I spun in a circle. Multiple porch lights were on, but my hopes fell when I saw bent blinds with shadowy figures lurking behind them. Bile crawled up the back of my throat. People were just watching like this was some kind of sport.

By the time I turned back around, her brother was on his feet again, his murderous gaze locked on his father.

"Get to Thea's," he barked at Nora.

She tugged on his arm. "No. Please, Ramsey. Come with me.

It's not worth it. He's not worth it. Please. Please. Please!" she screamed through her tears. "Daddy, go away! Leave him alone!"

Hearing her call that monster "daddy" felt like the tip of a dagger raking down my spine.

He slurred something I couldn't quite make out and then spit at them before finally stumbling to a beat-up truck. After he climbed inside, it rumbled to life like a fork in a garbage disposal.

I couldn't see Nora's face, but I didn't take another breath until his taillights disappeared around the corner.

As soon as he was gone, the door a few houses down swung open and a girl with flowing, brown hair, darker than Nora's, came running out barefoot. "Ramsey!"

"Shit," he mumbled before calling back, "I'm okay." He pulled Nora into his side and hugged her tight. "We're both okay."

The girl stopped in front of him and pressed up onto her toes to check his bleeding nose. "I hate that man!"

"Me too, Sparrow. Me too." Ramsey laughed. Like a real honest-to-God chuckle. And if I hadn't already been stunned into silence by what I'd just witnessed, I would have been shocked that he could still remember how to laugh after an actual fistfight with his dad.

Nora stepped out of her brother's arms and wiped the tears from under her eyes. "I got you some gum."

He had blood smeared across his face, but his grin was massive as he peered down at her. "How did you know I was on my last piece?"

"You're always on your last piece," the girl he'd called Sparrow smarted.

Nora giggled. And just like her brother's laugh, it was so real that it transformed my stunned silence into outright, mouth-gaping confusion.

RECLAIM

Who the heck were these kids? I was still shaking, and I hadn't even been involved in the fight. Sure, my dad yelled at me, but he'd never hauled off and *punched* me. Or pushed me. Or spit on me. Or told me I'd ruined his life. Jesus Christ, what kind of dad did that to their kids?

I couldn't even begin to wrap my mind around how I'd ever smile again after something like that.

But Nora did.

Guilt slapped me like a cold wind in the middle of winter. I'd treated her like a jerk at the creek, simply because I'd been mad that I had to spend the summer with my grandparents. My grandparents who had never once put their hands on me. Who supplied me three home-cooked meals a day, and every now and again, my grandma would sneak me an ice cream sandwich.

Jesus, I really was *Freaking Camden Cole.*

They walked inside together, and in an act only slightly creepier than following her home, I sat in the edge of woods and stared at her front door for a long while. I wanted to help, but I had no idea how. Before she'd blown up on me, I'd been planning to let her in on my worm scheme. That would at least put some money in her pocket. But if her mom was gone like her dad had said, she needed more than just a few bucks a day.

I debated telling my grandparents, but they really enjoyed turning a blind eye even within their own family. I couldn't imagine they'd leap into action for a stranger.

I could call my mom. She might have been willing to make a phone call if she thought kids were in danger. But would Nora want that? Once alarm bells were sounded with the police, it was hard to silence them. And what's to say the cops would have done anything anyway?

By the time I left that night, her dad still hadn't come home.

Her brother and the Sparrow girl were sitting on the porch, holding hands, and talking, but Nora was nowhere to be seen. She'd appeared all fine and dandy when she'd gone inside, two grocery bags still wrapped around her wrists, but I had a sneaking suspicion she wouldn't be getting any sleep that night.

God knew I wouldn't be.

THREE

Nora

Ramsey woke me up just before eight to see if I wanted to spend the day with him—and, of course, Thea. Our dad had miraculously made it home overnight, and my brother flat-out refused to leave me with him after the way things had gone down the night before.

It wasn't all that shocking, to be honest. My dad and Ramsey's brawling was pretty much business as usual.

We didn't talk about it.

There were no words left to say.

It was horrible and awful and wrong on so many levels.

But that inescapable hell was our life.

I hated that Ramsey had to worry about me so much.

But most of all, I hated that I needed him to.

While I washed my face and brushed my teeth, I filled him in on my newfound job at Mr. Leonard's. He laughed his butt off when he learned I was collecting worms all day.

I strategically didn't mention *Freaking Camden Cole*. My spending the day with a boy he didn't know would have no doubt led to a million questions—none of which I had the answer to. Besides, after the way we'd left things, I wasn't even sure if Camden would show up again.

When Ramsey and I got to the kitchen to make breakfast,

we found the bread left open and stale, the ham sitting on the counter for who knew how long, and my father passed out in his recliner, a half-eaten sandwich sitting on his chest.

It was only four dollars' worth of food, but the devastation of seeing it wasted was staggering.

It didn't matter how often he'd done it to us; it felt like a betrayal each and every time. Tears welled in my eyes, but I held it together, knowing Ramsey was beside me. It wasn't his fault, but he'd still spend the day feeling guilty if he knew I was upset.

While he made promises to bring home dinner that night, I slapped on a smile and toasted two pieces of the stale bread, smearing the last bit of peanut butter on them before passing one his way.

It was just another morning in the Stewart household.

Camden wasn't at the creek when I arrived, and the wave of disappointment that washed over me was startling even to myself. With a fresh set of patience, a boatload of guilt, and a set of piercing blue eyes on my brain, I realized I had no right to be mad at Camden. If the roles were reversed, I wouldn't have told him where I'd found my secret stash of a million worms, either. After all, I was his competition.

Mr. Leonard's feud with Old Man Lewis wouldn't last forever. But until it ended, Camden and I would be spending every day across the creek from each other. Having someone to talk to might make that miserable job slightly less horrible.

While I pondered the least humiliating way to apologize to Camden, a beetle big enough to have been related to squirrels ambushed me from the side. A scream tore from my throat, so loud that the echo off the trees alone was enough to deafen anyone in a five-mile radius.

Ducking and weaving, I ran to the edge of the water and frantically unwound my hair. I'd learned my lesson the day before about forgetting a ponytail holder and put my hair in a braid that morning. A freaking braid my attacker had gotten its gag-inducing feet tangled in, and now, I was seconds away from peeling out of my skin and living the rest of my life as a skeleton.

"Get off me!" I shouted, violently slapping at my hair. My panic skyrocketed when I heard the buzz beside my ear.

My freaking *ear*.

My exposed, open, and inviting ear the flying monster could crawl inside.

I'd have had to die.

Right then and there.

If that beetle got into my ear, someone would have to put me down like they had Tiffany Martin's dog last year after it was hit by a car.

Frantic and lost to all logic, I made a choice. I'd be wet and miserable the rest of the day, but beetles couldn't swim, right?

That part of the creek was shallow, but I lunged forward, submerging my face. Scrubbing like a wild woman, I washed my thick hair with both hands. The rocks were hard beneath my stomach and chest, but a few scrapes and bruises were a small price to pay to be bug-free.

Still unconvinced I'd gotten it out of my hair, I started to roll to my back. Two arms suddenly wrapped around my middle.

"Stand up!" he barked, lifting me as best he could, which admittedly was only to my knees. "Just put your feet down. It's not that deep."

Freaking Camden Cole. Of course. I was flailing around in the water like an idiot. What more embarrassing time would there have been for him to finally arrive?

I had zero time to worry about what he thought while there was a living, breathing insect. In. My. *Hair*.

"Stop! I'm under attack!" I yelled, continuing to splash water into my hair and on my face.

"Would you stand the hell up and stop trying to drown yourself?" he snapped, dragging me to the bank. Unceremoniously, he dropped me on the dirt and then collapsed beside me, panting and heaving.

He looked different than he had the day before. His short, sandy-brown hair was the same and those blue eyes were just as bright as ever, but his cutoff jeans and black T-shirt with the sleeves ripped off was a far cry from his khakis and button-down. Thankfully, with dirty knock-off Converse shoes replacing his stupid penny loafers, he looked like every other kid from Clovert.

I might even have gone so far as to say he looked like one of the cute boys who were so few and far between. Yeah, okay, fine—I definitely would have said it. And dang, wasn't that inconvenient considering I was soaking wet, covered in mud, and still unsure if we were even speaking.

He brought his knees up and rested his elbows on top while he caught his breath. "Jesus, Nora. You scared the crap out of me. I ran all the way from the road when I heard you scream. I thought you were being attacked by a coyote or something."

"Well, it was close," I said in all seriousness. "There was a bug in my hair."

"A bug?" It was as much of a question as it was an accusation. "What kind of bug? Bee? Wasp? Yellow jacket?"

"I think it was actually a beetle. I didn't stop to check though."

His head cocked to the side. "You just had a seizure and almost drowned because of a freaking beetle?"

His lack of concern was insulting. "I don't like bugs, okay? They're gross and they have these tiny eyes, and I don't even know where their nose is. Plus, they have extra legs and stuff. I mean seriously, who needs that many legs? Can you even imagine the sound of that thing in your ear?"

Horror contorted his face. "Holy crap, it went in your *ear?*"

I snapped my fingers and pointed at him. "No, but the point is it could have. You don't know what it was thinking. Bugs are unpredictable. They don't have to bite or sting or even crawl on you with all four million useless legs. All they have to do is see an open mouth or ear and you're done for."

He shivered and shook his head. "Jesus, how do you make a beetle sound so scary?"

"Welcome to my world." Shrugging, I stood up and walked over to the creek. I washed my hands, and since I was already soaked, I splashed water on myself and tried to get the mud off my black athletic shorts. They were a hand-me-down from Thea's horrific tomboy collection. I'd had to get creative with tie-dye and a pair of scissors to make the shirts not look like I'd stolen them from my brother, but they were at least useable.

"If you're so scared of all things creepy and crawly, why did you get a job collecting worms?"

"I need the money." I turned around and found him taking off his wet shoes and socks. Well, if you could call the one on his left foot a sock at all. It had so many holes it was more like a tube he wore on his ankle for decoration. Hmm, okay. Maybe Camden Cole *wasn't* one of the rich kids after all. Those were Alberton socks if I'd ever seen a pair. "Oh, that reminds me." I reached into my pocket, pulled out a soggy ten-dollar bill, and extended it in his direction. "Here."

He stared at my hand, his baby blues sparkling in the morning sun while a single drop of water hung on a perfect curl in the middle of his forehead. "What's that?"

"Your money for the worms yesterday." I shoved the cash in his direction again, and he leaned away as if I were trying to hand him a grenade.

"Why are you giving it to me? You just said you need the money."

"Uhhh, because it's *your* money? Don't worry. I took all the credit with Mr. Leonard. He told me if I kept doing such a good job he'd give me a two-dollar bonus each week."

That got his attention. "Two dollars? He didn't offer me anything extra and I had the same amount you had."

I batted my eyelashes. "Yeah, but I'm a girl. I'm not allowed to play football or pee standing up, but every now and then, it pays off."

"That's ridiculous," he muttered.

"I know. I think I would be really good at kicking field goals too." When he made no move to take the money, I bent over and tucked it into his discarded shoe. "Anyway, I'm sorry for yelling at you yesterday."

Barefoot, he stood up, his wet shirt clinging to his bony chest. "You don't need to apologize. I did my fair share of shouting too."

I dropped into a squat and got back to work, momentarily forgetting that my ears were once again at risk of kamikaze beetles. "Yeah, but you only shouted after I yelled, so I think it's still my fault. Anyway, it was a rough day and I kinda took it out on you." I kept my head down as I finished with, "Sorry."

His toes shuffled into my peripheral vision. "Why was your day bad? What happened?"

"I'm currently blaming it on a mild heat stroke, but I did have to spend the day touching worms. So maybe it was a real stroke too."

RECLAIM

"Today any better?"

I sighed and kept scooping and sifting tiny piles of dirt. "I survived a heinous beetle attack, but I'm soaking wet now, so I'm not sure yet."

"What about now?" His bucket suddenly appeared in my line of sight. And Holy. Cow. Worms. All the freaking worms.

My breakfast hadn't even digested yet and he already had like twenty bucks' worth.

I tipped my head back to catch his gaze. "Where do you keep getting all these worms?"

His smile nearly split his face. "Promise you won't tell?"

"I told you I'm not a tattletale."

"That sounds exactly like what a tattletale would say before running off to tattle on me."

"Look, I gave your ten dollars back. That has to mean something, right? Give me some credit. I could have easily kept it."

"You *should* have kept it. But okay, fine. I believe you." He sank down beside me, crisscrossed his long, skinny legs between us, and began stripping a leaf from its stem. "So, fun story, on my way home from church yesterday, I found a ten-dollar bill on the sidewalk." He stopped and looked up at me. He was so close I could see the dark flecks of sapphire peppered through his baby blues.

He stared at me for a long second, smiling like I should be able to magically read his mind.

Completely unnerved by the fact I could feel his exhales, I prompted him with a drawn-out, "Okay?"

He plucked another leaf off the ground and slid it between his fingers, stripping it bare. "Like, what are the chances? I was on my way back here to work, to hopefully make ten bucks and there it was just sitting on the sidewalk, begging for me to pick it up. I'm not really religious or anything but I did manage to make it through Reverend Lyon's sermon without falling asleep, so I feel like maybe this was God's way of paying me back."

What in the actual *hell* was this kid talking about?

"Uh huh," I said instead of what I really wanted to say, which was: *Get to the damn point.* I forced something that I hoped resembled a smile. "I'm not sure church works like that. God probably has bigger fish to fry than paying you for staying awake. But okay, sure. Can we get back to the worms now? It's supposed to be four thousand degrees this afternoon and I'd really like to catch at least a few before I melt."

"Oh, you can't catch any worms today."

"What? Why not?"

"Because Mr. Leonard said our limit is around five hundred a week and he doesn't want us out here on the weekends again." He lifted his bucket in my direction. "We've already got a hundred for today."

Now, normally, I would have shot to my feet, balled my fists, and screamed in his face that it wasn't fair because I'd been hunting all morning and this included a near-death experience with a beetle. But he'd said one key word that kept my temper in check. "What do you mean *we* already have a hundred?"

That wide, toothy grin reappeared on his face. "You ready to listen yet?"

I clamped my mouth shut, but so help me sweet baby Jesus, if he tried to tell me God was now paying him for staying awake in church with earthworms, there was a solid chance I was going to do more than just yell at him today. But he did, in fact, have my attention, so I gestured that my lips were sealed with a zip across my mouth, and then I threw away the key.

"Anyway, after I found the money on the way back from

church, I almost skipped out of coming here. But then I got an idea. And not fifteen minutes later, I walked out of Lewis Tractor Repair, Bait, and Booze with a hundred worms and met you. The end."

It should be noted that Camden Cole was officially the worst storyteller in the history of storytelling because, while it took him a solid five minutes for him to tell me all that, his version of nonsense events only left me with more questions than answers.

"You *bought* a hundred worms from Old Man Lewis?"

He nodded. "Oh, and a Coke. But I drank that before I met you. I'd have brought you one if I knew you were here. Next time though." He pointed a finger at me and clucked the side of his mouth.

I blinked at him too many times to count. This kid was not working with a full box of rocks. "Um…*why?*"

He shrugged. "I don't know. I guess to be nice. Why? You want a Sprite instead?"

Even annoyed, I was in no position to turn down a free soda. "No, Coke is great. But why would you buy worms just to sell them back to Mr. Leonard?"

He had the audacity to look at me like *I* was the idiot. "Uh, because the bait shop sells 'em for ten cents apiece and Mr. Leonard is paying twenty."

My head snapped back so fast it was a wonder it didn't fly off my neck.

He swirled his finger in front of my shocked face and smirked. "Oh yeah. You're following me now."

And I was. Because good Lord, that was brilliant. Turned out, *I* was the one who wasn't working with a full box of rocks. Freaking Camden Cole was a genius, and I didn't know why but it seriously annoyed me.

I stood up and glared down at him with my hands planted on my hips. "You can't buy worms from the bait shop. Mr. Leonard will lose his mind if he finds out he's fishing with cursed Lewis bait."

"How's he going to find out? You said you weren't a tattletale."

"I'm not! But..." I trailed off, knowing that what he was doing was wrong but not quite able to formulate a response through my absolute jealousy that I hadn't thought of it first.

"But nothing," he said, rising to his full height. He glanced over his shoulder up at Mr. Leonard's house, and then lowered his voice. "Look, he's not going to find out. Nobody knows me in Clovert, so I told the guy at the bait shop my name was Cam and I just moved to town. I made up a whole story about fishing with my brothers and told them we needed a lot of worms. It wasn't a total lie." He paused and looked up at the sky, deep in contemplation. "Okay, not true. It was mostly a lie. A little white one. I don't have any siblings. *But* I did some asking around at church and Mr. Leonard has a lot of brothers and five sons, who each have at least one more son, who each have, like, four kids who all like to fish, which equals..." He lifted his hand to start counting off on his fingers only to give up when he reached ten. "A lot of people, okay? And none of them are allowed to use the bait shop anymore. So over coffee this morning—"

"You had coffee with Mr. Leonard?" I asked rudely, which I was learning was the only tone I had when it came to Camden Cole.

He scoffed. "No. *He* had coffee and I helped myself to the hard candies from his wife's crystal bowl." He paused. "By the way, I still have a few of those left in my backpack if you want one. But warning, only the nasty butterscotch are left."

RECLAIM

Drats. Butterscotch was my favorite, but I feared, if he got distracted with getting me candy from his bag during this story, I'd never find out what the heck he was talking about.

"Thanks. I'm good."

He shrugged. "So anyway, I asked Mr. Leonard his limit. He said around five hundred a week because whatever his family didn't use he was going to set up shop down by his driveway and sell them to Lewis's customers, even if he had to take a loss."

Wow. Otis Leonard was a savage.

Camden continued. "I'll buy 'em for ten bucks. Sell 'em to him for twenty, and I'll show up here every day, pretend I'm collecting 'em, and get to avoid my grandpa for eight hours. Win. Win."

Okay, so maybe he wasn't the worst storyteller after all. That covered the majority of my questions, but not the majority of my jealousy.

"He's never going to believe you find a hundred worms *every day*."

"I know, which is why it's good that he hired *you* too. The two of us could easily get fifty worms in a day. All I ask is that you give me half back so I can buy more worms."

I once again clamped my mouth shut. Math was not my strong suit, but I was no dummy, either. If he was buying ten dollars a day in worms, that would have left ten dollars in profit. And he was going to split that with me? A girl he didn't know, who yelled at him a lot. Guaranteeing me five dollars a day? Twenty-five dollars a week?

One *hundred* dollars a month?

All without having to touch one single worm?

"Why would you do that?" I asked suspiciously. "You didn't even have to tell me, ya know? You could have just turned in your fifty worms every day and made five dollars. I'd have been clueless."

The frustration faded from his boyish face. "And let the other five dollars go to waste?"

"Sure. Why not? You don't know me."

He turned his gaze to the ground, his nearly constant smile slipping away with the uncomfortable shuffle of his feet. "I might know you better than you think, Nora."

A wave of unease skated down my back. "What's that supposed to mean?"

He shook his head and looked back up. "I know you don't like hunting worms. I saw you gagging as I walked up yesterday. I know you're the kind of person who returns ten bucks even when they need the money. And while I don't know if you would have included me in your plans if you'd thought of it first, I believe maybe once we became friends you would have."

I wouldn't have. I would have been scared that he would have told on me and that I would have gotten in trouble and lost my job no matter how much I hated it.

I looked down at my muddy sneakers, doing anything to escape the guilt churning in my gut. Outside of Ramsey and Thea, I didn't get a lot of sweet in my life. And coming from a friendly boy with pretty blue eyes, who had absolutely no reason to give it to me after the way I'd treated him, the weight of that guilt became suffocating.

"But above and beyond that," he said, "I thought it might be nice to have someone out here with me every day. Like a partner in crime or something. This could be our little secret, but if you're not interested—"

My head popped up. "I'm interested."

"Yeah?" The way he smiled slow and shy, like I'd given *him* a gift, only made my guilt multiply.

"Yeah. It'd be a win-win for me too if I got to spend the day away from my house. My dad screams a lot. I might have gotten it from him."

His eyes flashed wide, and for a blink, I swear his face paled. He quickly covered it with a grin. "Soooo, what are we gonna do today?"

"I don't know. What do you want to do?"

"Slapjack?" he suggested, holding his hands out in front of him, palms up.

"Oh please. Don't make me embarrass you."

He laughed, loud and rich. "Okay then. I brought some books and stuff to draw with. I almost brought my radio, but the batteries are dead."

"What kind of batteries?"

"C. But I need, like, eight of them and those things cost a fortune."

"I'll bring some tomorrow. I've got a whole case. They randomly gave them to my dad at his last job." Truthfully, Dad had stolen them from his job stocking at the grocery. The drunk dumbass thought they were double As he could use for his remote control. Not surprisingly, he was fired the next day.

I'd always been a crappy liar, so my cheeks heated, no doubt turning my face a lovely shade of neon pink. I didn't have many friends because it was easier to avoid getting close to people than looking them in the eye and lying about my life. However, at five dollars a day, it looked like Camden and I were stuck together—lies and all.

"No!" He spun around so fast he tripped, stumbling over his own feet.

I barely jumped out of his way in time to keep from getting plowed over. "Jesus, Cam!"

He righted himself and stared at me with wild eyes. "You don't have to ask your dad. It's no big deal. I'll buy some next week."

Okay, seriously, Camden was weird.

I rolled my eyes. "My dad doesn't care. They've been sitting in our garage for, like, a year. Do you have any idea how useless C batteries are? They don't work for anything. Except apparently your radio."

"Okay," he said, but it wasn't a question or a statement. It was more like two syllables he'd left hanging in the air to fill the space between us.

"Ohh-kay," I replied, glancing around for any possible escape from the awkwardness. "Anyway. We could go for a swim. We're already soaked and there's a deep part down by the tree stump that—"

And that was all I got out before The Flash himself ran past me in a blur, calling over his shoulder, "Last one in is a rotten egg!"

Never one to turn down a challenge, I took off after him.

He beat me to the water, but he didn't brag or gloat. Which was probably the only reason I didn't dunk him the first chance I got.

We spent the rest of the afternoon splashing around and getting to know each other. I made good on my promise and didn't at yell him anymore. It wasn't too hard though, because once I gave him a chance, Freaking Camden Cole was actually super nice.

We talked about Alberton. He agreed it stunk, but we argued on whether it was more of a dead animal stench or dirty socks. He made the trek up to his bag not once, but twice to get me a butterscotch. I hadn't asked him either time. And I filled him in on the people in Clovert. Mainly, who to talk to and who to avoid.

He listened patiently and never took his eyes off me, which was a tad uncomfortable at times, but for the most part, we got along like cheese and apple pie—an odd combination, but somehow, it worked.

When the bright afternoon sun started its descent, Camden sprinted from the water just as quickly as he'd entered it. His grandparents were strict about dinner time, so he needed to get home ASAP to get his chores done first.

I'd spent a lot of time alone in my life, avoiding my dad, hiding from people who might be able to see through my façade. However, that day, as I watched Camden running through the tall grass, carrying his bucket and his backpack while water streamed from his cutoffs, I could honestly say I was really looking forward to having some company for a change.

Without any place to be, I took my time making my way back to our dirt beach. I walked straight to my bucket, and as a young girl who had been wronged by people she loved too many times, a part of me expected to find it empty. He could have easily taken them when I hadn't been looking and cashed them all in himself. In my experience, when things sounded too good to be true, they usually were.

But not with Camden.

Never with Camden.

Not only was my bucket filled with worms, but there was the ten-dollar bill, wrapped around the handle. Written in black marker across the top of the bill, it read: *This is yours. Fair and square.*

FOUR

Nora

"Hey," he said, lurching to his feet when I arrived at the creek.

I shrugged off my tattered backpack and dropped it at my feet. "You're here early."

"Yeah. I wasn't sure what time you came in the mornings, so I left straight after breakfast. I would have been here earlier, but the bait shop doesn't open until seven."

"Seven? Jeez, do your grandparents always make you get up that early?"

He shook his head. "They didn't make me get up. I just thought if you were here, I wanted to be here too."

My whole body locked up tight. It could be said that I wasn't the best at understanding or processing feelings, at least not the good ones. Outside of Ramsey and Thea, I didn't have a lot of experience with that kind of stuff. So I couldn't be completely sure what happened inside my body in that second. But whatever it was, it made a lump form in my throat.

"I usually get here about nine," I mumbled.

He nodded without saying anything else and I suddenly feared he knew about the lump in my throat too.

"Nice shorts," I blurted.

He looked at the blue shorts covered in what I thought were

supposed to be cartoon sharks, but the pattern on the fabric had been cut in all the wrong places, making it look like a shark massacre. "All right, all right. Don't give me crap about these. My grandma made 'em and I was already in the doghouse after… Well…" He cut his gaze over my shoulder. "I didn't tell them where I was going the other night. I've been picking up dog poop in the yard ever since, so no way was I risking more trouble by complaining about these."

I ignored the urge to ask him where he'd gone and chewed on my bottom lip to stifle a laugh. "You have a dog?"

"Grandma does. It's a mean little shit that bit me while I was sleeping once."

"Maybe you were snoring?"

"Maybe it was bred from the devil himself." He dove toward me, clinking his teeth like he was pretending to bite.

I jumped away laughing and not the kind of laugh I used when I needed to prove to Ramsey that I was okay or give adults a show so they didn't ask too many questions.

This was real. And genuine. And so incredibly terrifying that I abruptly stopped and just stared at him.

"What?" he said, glancing over his shoulder. "What's wrong?"

There was nothing wrong. In that second, at the creek, laughing with a kid who had shown up at the crack of dawn just to hang out with me, there was absolutely nothing wrong for the first time in quite possibly my entire life and it made the lump in my throat swell to the size of a watermelon.

The sweetest concern colored his face as he took a step toward me. "Nora, what's going on? You okay?"

I backed away and desperately tried to compose myself, but my voice came out as a croak as I replied, "It's just the shorts. They're really ugly."

He blew out a loud breath and then barked a laugh. "Jesus. You scared me. I thought you were having another heat stroke or something."

Nope. Not a stroke, but something was happening inside my body and the jury was still out on whether it was a good something or a bad something.

He bent over and grabbed his bag. "Well, if you can forget about my shorts long enough to hang out, I snagged you some bug spray. I'm not sure if it works on beetles, but it should keep the rest of the ear monsters away." He exaggerated a shiver and then shot me a smile.

Oh, God, he'd brought me bug spray.

The lump in my throat morphed into a ball of fire, stinging my eyes and my nose as I took the spray bottle from his hand. I'd never even thought to buy myself bug spray.

But Camden had.

"Thanks," I whispered, not trusting my voice.

He rocked onto his toes and then back down to his heels. "No prob."

I drew in a deep breath, holding it until my lungs ached, and tried to get myself together. This was ridiculous. It was just bug spray.

"You got the worms?" I asked.

"You know it. Hey, look what else I did." Grabbing my forearm, he dragged me after him, talking a mile a minute as if he'd been saving each and every one of those syllables for me since seven a.m. "So, last night, I was thinking if we always turn in exactly a hundred worms, Mr. Leonard might get suspicious. So, each day, we need to take him a few less and sometimes a few extras. Mix it up. It will equal the same each week but not the same every day. But we gotta have somewhere to keep them on the days we give him less or we'll be out the money." He stopped beside an old oak tree and swung his arms out to the side. "Tada!"

Twisting my lips, I glanced around, trying to figure out what was so amazing about this particular tree. It wasn't even one of the big ones, and if I was being honest, it was kind of crooked too. "It's a tree. I don't get it."

"Oh, right." He jumped into action. Bending over, he sank his fingers into the dirt and came up with the lid of a plastic container about the size of a shoe box. "Worm storage." Full of excitement, he bounced his gaze from me to the container he'd buried in the ground. "Pretty cool, huh? I talked to my dad on the phone last night and he said worms can live for weeks as long as you keep them somewhere dark and cool. So I tossed in some dirt, poked holes in the lid, and boom—Stewart and Cole Worm Farm is in business."

I openly gaped at him.

Holy smokes, this kid had thought of everything. I probably would have just tossed out a few worms every day. No, wait, I wouldn't even have thought about turning in the same number every day and would have gotten myself fired by the end of the week.

I'd been wrong. Camden Cole wasn't a genius.

He was the genius who taught the other geniuses.

He was next-level genius, and at the moment, he was my business partner. And it had not escaped me how he'd put my last name first in our company.

But most of all, I was starting to feel like he might be my friend.

Cue the lump in my throat again.

And the something-good-or-something-bad pain in my chest.

And this time, add all the flutters in my stomach.

I had no idea how to react to any of those things. For as little experience as I had in the feelings department, I had infinitely less in the boy department. With Camden's blue eyes and bright smile homed in on me, waiting for all the praise he rightly deserved, there was only one thing left to do.

I gave him a titty twister and took off like a Gold medalist, straight for the creek.

"Last one in!" I yelled, stripping my clothes off to reveal my purple tankini as I ran.

"Hey, that hurt, you cheater!" He laughed, hot on my heels, rubbing his pec.

As I was toeing my shoes off, he did a cannonball, beating me into the water once again.

But it was okay.

While he was underwater, I took a second to compartmentalize all the feelings screaming inside my mind. It was a trick I'd learned shortly after my mother left. Everything had a nice, neat drawer in my head, hidden out of my thoughts so I didn't have to deal with any them until I was ready. Sometimes, late at night, I'd plunder through those drawers—considering and contemplating. But for the most part, I'd sealed them shut, never to be visited again.

If the last two days were any indication, I was going to need a lot more drawers for Camden Cole.

We played in the water for several hours. Made bets on who could hold their breath the longest—him. And who could do the most flips underwater—me. We even played Slapjack, and surprisingly enough, he beat me twice. By the time we returned to our little slice of peace on the creek bank, our fingers and toes were prunes and the sun hung high in the midday sky.

"I'm starved. You hungry?" he asked, collapsing onto his towel.

I shook my head despite the emptiness of my stomach.

"Oh, come on." He started zipping and unzipping various compartments on his bag. "No use in us sitting out here wasting away." When he found what he'd been searching for, he lifted two plastic baggies in my direction. "I brought one peanut butter and jelly and one turkey and potato chip. Made 'em myself. Your pick."

Oh. My. God. This was worse than the bug spray.

So, so, so much worse.

Because it was so, so, so sweet.

I couldn't accept it though. Ramsey and I had made a deal years ago not to take handouts from strangers. It was easier to keep our secrets that way. If we weren't in need, nobody asked questions.

"Thanks, but I'm not hungry. I had a really big breakfast." Technically, the bowl had been really big, but the leftover cereal mixed with the dust from the bottom of the bag inside said bowl was a different story. Still, my body's built-in lie detector did not accept half-truths and my cheeks went up in flames.

He eyed me curiously. "You sure? You gotta be hungry by now."

"I'm positive."

That should have been the end of it. He could eat his lunch and then we'd be back to normal. Just two normal kids hanging out at a creek, running a racket on worms.

Only the speed in which his smile disappeared as he tucked not one, but both sandwiches back in his bag wasn't *normal* at all.

His whole body deflated as he mumbled, "Okay. Never mind."

I narrowed my eyes and stared at the side of his face. What exactly was happening?

Was he...*disappointed?* Judging by his Stegosaurus backbone, he could have benefited from eating both the sandwiches himself.

I grabbed my backpack and sat on it so my wet bathing suit didn't get muddy in the dirt. "You can eat, ya know?"

He kept his gaze trained on the ground. "Nah. It's okay. I'm good."

"Cam, you *literally* just said you were hungry. Eat."

"I'm fine," he snapped, and it was so unlike him that it was jarring.

Wow. He *was* disappointed. Like, actually pouting because I didn't want to eat the sandwich he'd brought.

No. The sandwich he'd *made*.

For me.

That he must have made at the crack of dawn because he was already at the creek, complete with bug spray, at an ungodly hour *waiting on me.*

Damn, why did all of that make me feel like I was a jerk for not taking the sandwich?

This was why I didn't have friends. I didn't understand my own feelings, much less anyone else's.

We sat there in total silence for what felt like an eternity.

Him staring at the dirt.

Me pretending to pick at my fingernails just so I had somewhere to look that wasn't at him.

All of it super awkward.

None of it worth ruining both of our days over.

Besides, Ramsey couldn't get mad. He took food from Thea all the time. Camden wasn't really a stranger anymore.

RECLAIM

And I was hungry.

And he was hungry.

And there were two perfectly good sandwiches sitting right there.

I sighed. "On second thought, maybe I am hungry."

His whole face lit as if it were Christmas morning. Moving fast, he retrieved them from his bag. "Which one? The peanut butter and jelly probably tastes better, but I'm awful at spreading the peanut butter, so I think I tore the bread a few times. The turkey is good too though, but I don't know if you like sour cream and onion chips. Especially not on your sandwich. I thought about just going for regular turkey, but we were out of mayonnaise, and it seemed too plain." Grinning from ear to ear, he thrust two baggies toward me. "Anyway, I'm not picky. So whichever one you want, I'm good with the other."

I bit my bottom lip. Deep down, I didn't want either of them and not because of anything to do with torn bread or sour cream and onion chips. It was because taking his sandwich felt a whole lot like charity.

I didn't know the situation with Camden's life. I'd gathered they didn't have a ton of money and his grandparents were hard on him. But I knew myself and if I was going to take a sandwich from him and not choke on every single bite, I had to feel like it was tit for tat.

"What's your favorite kind of sandwich, Cam?"

He shrugged. "Whatever. I'm easy."

"No. You gotta tell me. Or I'm not taking either one of those."

He slanted his head to the side with confusion that was so cute it made me even more uncomfortable. "Why not?"

"Because you've been doing a lot of nice things for me and it's freaking me out. Just answer a question for once, would ya?"

"I like doing nice things for you."

Dang, he was smooth.

"Not an answer," I said firmly.

"Okay, okay. Fine. I think my favorite would have to be chicken salad."

I curled my lip and finally looked back at him. "Ew."

He laughed. "Hey, you asked."

"Well, I'm no chef, so do you like anything else?"

"I guess ham with pickles and mustard would be my second favorite."

Now, that I could do.

I took the peanut butter and jelly from his hand, because let's be honest, turkey with potato chips sounded disgusting. "Tomorrow, I'm bringing lunch."

He opened his mouth to object, but nothing came out.

"And two Cokes." It would take almost all of my money for the day to afford it, but whatever. Ramsey and Thea would eat a ham sandwich with pickles and mustard too. They'd have to buy their own Cokes though.

"Nora, you don't have to do that."

I took a big bite of the sandwich and peanut butter covered my hands because he wasn't wrong. He had shredded the bread. I talked with my mouth full. "I know I don't. But you brought lunch today. I'm bringing it tomorrow."

I felt his eyes boring into the side of my face, but he didn't argue as he unwrapped and ate his sandwich.

Things went back to normal after that. I broke out the batteries for his radio and we listened to music on the other side of the creek for a change in scenery.

We laughed.

We talked.

RECLAIM

We played.

I beat him three times *in a row* at Slapjack, leaving the backs of his hands bright red.

Then, right as the sun started to fade, he took off with his bucket of worms, running home in time for dinner.

I smiled watching him go because I knew he was doing it with the ten-dollar bill I'd snuck into the front pocket of his backpack.

FIVE

Nora

THE NEXT FEW MONTHS WERE PRETTY UNEVENTFUL FOR Camden and me.

We fell into an easy routine together, arriving every morning at nine, alternating who brought lunch and the occasional Coke, and then we did absolutely nothing for the rest of the day.

Sometimes we'd lie in the sun, reading magazines Thea had snagged from the waiting room at her dad's barbershop. Other times, we'd play hide-and-seek, which was really just a nice way of saying I'd hide and then jump out to scare the crap out of him.

The one thing that always remained consistent though was the ten-dollar bill we'd secretly swap each day.

We were always together, so hiding it in each other's stuff could be hard.

The majority of the time, I put it in the front pocket of his bag, and his go-to spot in a crunch was to wrap it up in my wet clothes. But every now and again, we'd get creative. Once, Camden used fishing line to sew it into a hole in the lining of my backpack. I searched for days before I found that thing. In retaliation, I used a safety pin to attach it to the back of his shirt. He'd told me he was halfway through dinner before his grandpa pointed it out.

RECLAIM

I had very few things to look forward to about going home each afternoon, but giggling like a fool while trying to figure out where he'd stashed the money always made the nights brighter.

Afternoon rain showers in Georgia were as much of a guarantee as death and taxes. On those days, Camden and I would huddle up under the canopy of trees with our towels held over our heads and talk about meaningless crap. He'd let it slip a few times that he was dreading going back to Alberton. His dad worked at the papermill in town, and he was already expecting his only child to follow in his footsteps—an idea Camden wasn't sold on. But from what I could tell, his mom sounded okay. He might have just been hungry, but he spent an hour one afternoon telling me all about her famous banana pudding. His smile was so big when he promised to bring me some one day that I didn't have the heart to tell him I hated bananas.

Shortly after that conversation, while fat drops of rain soaked us to the bone, he asked about my mom. I shut the question down quicker than she'd peeled out of our driveway the day she'd left.

Camden and I were close, and I was relatively sure my secrets would have been safe with him. But having a mother who'd not only abandoned you, but had also never once looked back wasn't bragging material.

Thankfully, Camden never asked about my dad. Ramsey and Thea came up a lot though. They were the only family I had to be proud of, so I was all too happy to fill his ears with hilarious stories about the three of us.

That summer, Camden killed thirty-five bugs for me. Thirty. Five. Most of which had never even gotten close to my body.

It worked out well, because come to find out, Camden was terrified of frogs and I had to rescue him a few times too. The first time one crossed his path, I was down at the other end of the creek and he screamed so loudly that it sounded like someone was torturing a cat. Being the good friend that I was, I never let him live it down and would occasionally just shriek at the top of my lungs mid-conversation to remind him what it sounded like. He glared at me a lot, but when he'd look away, a huge smile would break across his face.

I wasn't sure why Camden enjoyed hanging out with me. But for me, it was the fact that I finally had something of my own.

A place I belonged.

A friend who was always waiting for me.

A boy I caught staring at me out of the corner of his eye more often than not.

Since we only "worked" Monday through Friday, the weekends were long without him. I did my best to keep busy and away from my dad by hanging out with my brother, but it wasn't the same.

Mondays quickly became my favorite day of the week.

I laughed more that summer than I ever knew possible. It was usually at Camden's expense, but he got his fair share of practical jokes in too. Like the time he pretended to be allergic to peanuts when I'd slipped a few in his Coke. I thought I'd killed him for sure until he couldn't hold back his giggles. A few weeks later, he pulled the exact same peanut prank with a Snickers I'd brought us for dessert. He collapsed all dramatic, clutching his heart. He played dead for so long he fell asleep, and then when he didn't give up the act after I pretended to leave, I panicked, questioning whether I really had killed him that time. He woke up when I poked him with a stick and then laughed about it for weeks. And because it was so ridiculous, watching him laugh made me laugh too.

RECLAIM

After all the ham, pickle, and mustard sandwiches, Cokes, and gum for Ramsey every few days, I'd managed to save up over a hundred dollars. But learning how to truly laugh again might have been my greatest accomplishment that summer.

Camden made it easy though.

I knew it would end. Much like our job pretending to collect worms, my relationship with Camden was temporary. By the middle of August, I was painfully aware of how September would bring more than just cooler temperatures.

A few more weeks and Camden would be gone, leaving me alone all over again. School would help. Who knew? Maybe this would be the year I allowed someone to get close enough to be my friend.

But they wouldn't know my favorite candy or come up with any genius money-making cons or even have his boisterous laugh and bright-blue eyes. Most of all, they simply wouldn't be him.

I told myself it was okay. We'd spent the most incredible summer of my entire life under the trees at that creek. I should have just accepted it and been grateful I'd met him at all.

My body didn't understand that though.

About two weeks before Camden was supposed to leave, I woke up with knot in my stomach. At first, I'd thought I was coming down with a stomach bug, but as the days passed, it wouldn't go away. The constant ache made it impossible for me to sleep or eat, and sometimes, it felt like I couldn't breathe. It went on for days, and without any way to get me to a doctor, it scared the hell out of Ramsey. Eventually, I couldn't take his nervous glances and constant checking up on me anymore, so I faked feeling better.

He bought it. At least I think he did, but around the same

time, Camden started to worry about me too. There were only so many excuses I could come up with every day for why I wasn't eating lunch.

Yes, they were both right to be concerned. Something was seriously wrong with me, and as the summer drew to a close, the knot in my stomach had become a boulder that was too heavy to carry.

I was always tired.

I was always irritable.

I was always just one comment away from tearing apart at the seams.

But I didn't know what else to do. So I started lying to Camden too. And you know what? When you're scared and alone and you need something to be true so badly that you start to believe it yourself, it's not hard to lie to other people anymore.

I felt like death when I woke up that particular morning. I cried in the shower, clutching my stomach for over an hour, but being that it was Camden's last day, I pulled myself together, got dressed, and headed to the creek.

I was fifteen minutes late, but he was nowhere to be found. I searched for a while, hoping he was hiding, waiting for his moment to even the score for all the times I'd scared him in the past. But when I'd checked the plastic container he'd dug into the ground, I found it filled with worms and a note tucked inside.

Nora,

My parents got here last night to pick me up. They planned a whole stupid barbecue with all my aunts and uncles and cousins for today. I should be back around five, but I might be late, so bring a flashlight.

Camden

RECLAIM

P.S. Get ready! My mom is making banana pudding!!!

P.S.S. Mr. Leonard was still asleep, so the worms are all yours today.

P.S.S.S. Am I doing this P.S. thing right? I got a C in English.

P.S.S.S.S. I'd rather be there with you.

God, I was going to miss him.

I spent the morning staring up at the sky. I chalked it up as a practice for my sad, lonely future after he left. Yeah, fine. I was being dramatic. But I was eleven and losing the only friend I'd ever had. I was allowed to be dramatic.

The walk home seemed longer that day.

Cars passed. People waved. And my stomach ached with such a heavy weight that I had to stop and catch my breath a few times.

My dad was home when I got there, which meant I couldn't stay unless I wanted Ramsey to have a heart attack, so I grabbed my flashlight from under my bed and headed out to find my brother and Thea.

I'd always loved their tree, standing tall in the middle of the Wynns' hayfield. It had plenty of shade, a cool breeze, and enough space to give the illusion of privacy.

Our creek was still better.

Thea and Ramsey weren't there when I arrived, but no matter where they were, they'd end up at that tree at some point. I peeled my backpack off, sat with my shoulders against the bark, and did my best to ignore the overwhelming dread of waiting to say goodbye to my best friend.

"Hey, what are you doing here? I thought you were working today?" Ramsey asked when he showed up about twenty minutes later. I didn't have a chance to reply before his face suddenly paled. "What's wrong? You feeling sick again? What hurts?"

I shook my head, crossing and uncrossing my legs at the ankles. "Relax. I'm fine. It was hot earlier, so I'm going back tonight when things cool off."

With a twitch of his head, he cleared his shaggy, brown hair from his eyes as he studied my face to see if I was telling the truth.

I wasn't, but I was getting pretty good at the whole lying thing, so I passed the test anyway.

"Want me to go with you?" he asked.

"We could both go," Thea added, suddenly appearing as only my brother's shadow knew how. She grinned and sank down next to me. Sir Hairy—canine royalty of mutts—wedged himself between us and began covering my face with sloppy kisses.

I gave his ears a good scratch and replied, "It's the last Friday night before school starts. Don't you two have anything better to do?"

They looked at each other and shrugged, replying in unison, "Not really."

"Well, find something better. I'm good for the night."

"Suit yourself," Ramsey said, backing up several steps, his gaze aimed at his favorite branch above our heads. I'd seen him make that climb enough to know what would follow next. A run, a grunt, some magical foot work, and finally a sigh as he pulled himself up to sit on top of a branch.

Thea stopped him in his tracks. "Hey, Ramsey, can you take Hairy to do his business out by the ditch?"

My brother curled his lip. "Why didn't you let him go on the way over?"

RECLAIM

"Well, I did. But I don't think he was *really* done yet." She lifted the leash in his direction and gave it a shake. "Please. For me?"

It was a decent hike back to the ditch, but Ramsey would have walked through lava on two bloody stumps to make Thea happy.

"Ugh, fine." He took the leash and gave it a tug, trotting off across the grassy field with Hairy in tow.

As soon as he was out of earshot, Thea pounced. "So, who is he?"

"Who's who?"

"The boy at the creek who you've been hanging out with and hiding from your brother?"

I suddenly froze.

So, yeah... I'd, um, kinda, sorta decided not to mention Camden to Ramsey. Part of that was because he was overprotective and no doubt would have shown up at the creek and given Camden the third degree. Trust me—it was for the best. I'd seen my brother in action and he could be a hell of a lot scarier than a frog.

The other part was because I liked having someone of my own.

Ramsey and Thea had been best friends for years, and I'd always been a tad jealous of what they had. I mean, I could have lived without all the kissy crap they'd been doing recently, but before that, they'd been a team who had each other's back no matter what.

Sure, Ramsey was on my team too, but he was my brother. He was born into that position and took his duties very seriously.

Camden was different. Every day, when he showed up at that creek with a giant grin on his face and sweat beading on his forehead all because he'd been so excited to get there that he'd run the entire way, Camden chose me.

I wasn't one of the popular kids.

I wasn't rich.

I wasn't even one of the pretty girls.

To everyone else, I was just Nora—Ramsey's little sister—Stewart.

But to Camden, I was just Nora—ham-pickle-and-mustard-sandwich-making, ten-dollar-bill-hiding, hero frog wrangler, free to be whoever the hell I wanted to be—Stewart.

And I would have done absolutely anything, including lying to my brother and Thea about him, to keep it that way.

"I don't know who you're talking about," I replied, praying my newfound ability to lie also worked on her.

"Oh, really? So, when I went by there yesterday and I saw you laughing your head off with a boy who has curly, light-brown hair and chicken legs, you're telling me it was just my eyes playing tricks on me?"

I clamped my mouth shut and swallowed hard. There would be no lying my way out of this one. Unexplained anger seemed like the next logical response. "Why the heck were you at the creek?"

"Uh...because Ramsey is currently doing what Ramsey does best and freaking the freak out because you're still sick and hiding it from him. So he made me promise to go check up on you. I would have said hey, but I didn't want to interrupt." She smiled and it reminded me so much of my brother, it was as if they were starting to meld into one person. "So spill it. I want to hear all about this new boyfriend of yours."

A wave of panic struck me so hard I shot to my feet, ready to bolt. "Camden is *not* my boyfriend!"

RECLAIM

A slow grin crept up her face. "Oh, his name is Camden, huh?"

"Just drop it." I stole a quick glance over my shoulder. Unless Ramsey had taken Hairy on a walk to Hawaii, he was entirely too close for this conversation. "Look, I need to go. Did you tell Ramsey about him?"

"Best friend law doesn't allow me to keep secrets from him, but no. I haven't mentioned it yet. I wanted to talk to you first."

"Good. Then don't. I'm allowed to have a life, you know. I don't need permission from my brother to have a friend."

"What are you talking about? We don't care if you have friends. Ramsey would probably throw this Camden kid a party if he knew there was someone you finally liked."

"I don't like him!" I yelled so loudly that it felt as though it ripped from my soul. And based on the sharp pain it left behind in my stomach, it was definitely torn from somewhere vital.

Thea stood up and took a step toward me, lowering her voice. "Then why are you acting so weird? I just asked who he was."

I had to go. There was still a little while before I expected Camden back at the creek, but sitting there alone had to have been better than this.

My stomach rolled again, and I grabbed my backpack and slung it over my shoulder. "He's nobody."

She planted her hands on her hips and arched an eyebrow. "You sure about that?"

I had no idea what deep, dark drawer in my head the words came from, but they flew from my mouth faster than if they'd been fired from a gun. "It doesn't matter who he is because he lives in Alberton, and he's never coming back!"

And there it was, the constant knot in my stomach, the

heavy weight in my chest, the sleeplessness, the inability to breathe—all of it verbalized for the universe to hear.

I'd known since the day I'd met him that the clock on our time together was ticking.

Camden leaving was going to suck no matter which way you cut it.

But the most excruciating part was: What if he didn't come back?

What if this was it?

What if this was all I got?

One freaking summer to be happy, and now he was leaving? And I had to stay in that stupid town with my stupid father and a brother who was being forced to take care of me because our stupid mother had taken off and didn't even care enough to take her own children with her.

My throat closed and I stumbled forward, propping myself up on the tree. Why couldn't I breathe? Where the hell was all the air?

Thea looked just as startled as I was, but her face got soft as she rested her hand on my back. "Jesus, Nora. What's going on?"

"People don't come back for me," I croaked, my throat raw as though the confession had been made of razor blades.

"Don't say that."

"It's true and you know it."

Hooking her arm around my shoulders, she bent over with me, careful to keep her voice low. "No, it's not. Your mom was a selfish bitch who didn't care about anyone but herself. That is *her* problem. Not yours."

I wasn't so sure about that. I was only seven when she'd left, and for the first few months, I'd spent hours every day staring out the front window, waiting for her to come back. I'd imagined over a dozen scenarios where she'd suddenly burst through the front door, her arms full of presents and boxes of candy. She'd drop them all on the floor and wrap us in a tight hug, repeating over and over again how much she'd missed us. Her stories would range from simple things like losing her cell phone to the farfetched in which she'd been away on a secret mission with the FBI.

But in those daydreams, she'd always promise to never leave again.

As the months turned into years, I'd struggled with the idea that maybe I'd done something wrong to make her leave. At night when I climbed into bed, I'd bargained with a God I wasn't sure existed to bring her back. All I needed was one chance and I could make her love me again.

Ramsey told me repeatedly how she was never coming back, but at that age, I still viewed mothers as faultless superheroes. I hadn't even known it was possible for a mom to leave her kids. Dads, sure. I knew at least three people on our street who didn't have a dad.

But everyone had a mom.

Everyone but me.

"But it is my problem!" I yelled, years of pent-up emotions sliding down my cheeks. "She left me here. And I waited for her every day. And now Camden's going to leave me here too. I can't do this again. I can't. I just can't."

"Stop," she breathed, wiping my hair out of my face. "He's not leaving you. He's a kid. This isn't his choice."

"But it would be his choice if he didn't come back. He has a whole life in Alberton. What if he wants that more than he wants me? He has a family and a mom. He probably even has a few friends. He won't choose me, Thea. Nobody ever chooses me."

I was going to lose him—my one and only escape from reality. It didn't matter how bad things got at home, I'd always been one sunrise and two sandwiches away from Camden and forgetting it all.

And, now, he was leaving, going back to a life where I didn't exist, and there was nothing I could do about it.

A tremble worked its way through my body like a shockwave, but Thea was right there, linking her arm through mine. "Okay. Okay. Let's both take a deep breath. You're wrong about this. Me and Ramsey would choose you every single time no matter what. But I get it. Boys are hard to read sometimes. Have you talked to him about this? Does he know about your mom?"

I shook my head. "I don't... I mean, me and Ramsey, we don't...talk about her to other people."

She blew out a loud sigh. "You Stewarts and your secrets. You know Ramsey didn't tell me at first, either. He just held it all in and then one day he blew up on me like a volcano."

Boy, did that sound familiar.

I offered her a tight smile.

"Right. Okay. Well, Camden hasn't left yet, has he?"

I shook my head. "Tomorrow."

"Good. Then you have time." She released me and looked at her watch. "You've got six hours, fourteen minutes, and thirty-five...no, thirty-four seconds left in today. I highly suggest you make the most of it. Is he the reason you're going to the creek tonight?"

She was a sage thirteen, so I nodded, desperate for any and all advice she could give me.

Resting her hands on my shoulders, she looked me straight in the eye. "Okay, here's what you're going to do. Talk to him. Give him a chance to choose you. He can't stay, Nora. And you can't expect him to. Leaving is out of both of your control. But maybe he's scared you won't want him to come back. A lot can change in a year. But he's going to Alberton, not Zimbabwe. Telephones exist. I know you guys don't have one because your dad is the literal worst human being in history, but I have a phone at my house that you can use sometimes. And there's letters. Maybe even a visit at Christmas. But you have to give him a chance. If for some stupid, idiotic reason he doesn't choose you, that's his loss. That is not on you though."

"What's not on her? Why are you crying?"

We both froze at the sound of my brother's voice.

"*Shit*," Thea mouthed.

I closed my eyes and dropped my chin to my chest.

It would only be a matter of time before Ramsey knew everything about not only Camden, but my little meltdown too. He and Thea shared everything from secrets to spit. Honestly, it was a miracle she hadn't told him about Camden through telepathy the minute she'd seen me with him at the creek.

Filling my lungs, I prepared myself to spill it all.

Thea got there first. "Nora got her period."

"What!" I shouted.

It was followed by my brother's, "What the hell! Why would you tell me that?" He used a hand to block us from his view as if we were the blinding sun.

I hooked my arm through Thea's and gave her a hard tug. "Yeah, Thea. *Why* would you tell him that?" I leveled her with a pointed glare and finished with a mumble only she could hear. "Especially since it's not true."

She kept her smile aimed at my brother but whispered to me out of the corner of her mouth, "Because you're my friend, and I will always choose you."

My throat got thick. Tears over Camden still streaked my cheeks, but a whole new set welled in my eyes.

"Is that why you've been sick?" Ramsey asked, devastating hope filling his voice.

"Yep," Thea replied, popping the P.

His whole body relaxed, his relief almost palpable. "Oh, thank God."

Yeah, it was safe to say my brother loved me something fierce. As much as I hated how he worried over me, his reaction filled my empty chest in unimaginable ways.

Patting over his heart, he tipped his chin at Thea. "You still can't die from that, right?"

"Nope." She winked. "Nothing to worry about. Nora and I were just having a girl chat about…things."

He nodded at least a dozen times. "Do we, like…need to go to the store for you or anything? I mean, is there, uh, anything we should do? Or—"

I faked a gag. "Ew, God. Ramsey, stop. I'm not talking about this with you."

He lifted his hands in surrender and backed up a few steps. "Yeah. No. Not talking about this totally works for me too. Forgotten. Done."

Thea laughed, and to my oblivious brother, I'm sure it sounded sweet enough. To me, it was an evil cackle. I decided right then and there it was for the best she and Ramsey didn't do secrets. He was not ready to play on that field with her.

Scrubbing my face with my hands to clear away any lingering emotion, I said, "I'm leaving. Thanks for making this awkward. I can always count on you guys."

"Anytime," Thea chirped.

Ramsey shook his head and handed her Hairy's leash. Then

he made quick work of scaling the tree and settling onto his branch.

"I'll be right back," Thea told him as she followed me toward the main road. There was a shortcut through Mr. Leonard's property about half a mile up that was quicker than going back through the woods next to our house.

The grass crunched beneath our feet as we walked.

"Thanks for doing that back there. I'm totally embarrassed, but thanks for covering for me with him."

She smiled. "I meant what I said, Nora. I know you think we're only friends because of Ramsey, but I'm always here for you if you need anything."

"Thanks," I whispered.

She stopped at the edge of the road and turned to face me. "Now, can I say one last thing before you leave?"

"I'm scared to say yes."

She chuckled. "I can't imagine losing Ramsey. If he lived in Alberton, I'd be a mess too. But if this Camden kid has even half a brain, he won't just choose to come back next summer. He'll spend his whole life trying to come back to you. Maybe just cut him some slack for a few years until he gets a driver's license, okay?"

I didn't know it then, but Thea had proven herself to be something of a fortune teller, because that night was only the first of over a decade of excruciating goodbyes for me and Camden.

SIX

Camden

"Come on, Mom. I gotta go." I impatiently bounced on my toes.

She continued to spoon banana pudding into a plastic container slow as molasses. "Honey, relax. The creek isn't going anywhere."

No. The creek wasn't, but I was. My time with Nora was dwindling by the second.

I'd been dreading the day all summer. Going back to Alberton was going to suck on epic levels. Middle school was a nightmare on its own. I couldn't imagine it would be any better now that all the kids in my class had spent the summer hanging out without me.

Don't get me wrong; I regretted nothing of my days spent with Nora. Honestly, those humid mornings chilling by the water were some of the best of my entire life.

Originally, I'd felt like I was taking care of her, doing everything I could to make her forget about her piece-of-crap dad at home. I stayed later than I should have each afternoon and had to wake up super early in the morning to get all my chores done before I was allowed to go back each day. But it was worth it.

As time passed, Nora started taking care of me too. She

RECLAIM

might not have had much, but she gave me more than anyone else ever had: real, honest friendship.

It wasn't about ham, pickle, and mustard sandwiches. Though I did appreciate those. It was about how she noticed I never ate the crust. She didn't ask me why or tell me I was dumb. She just showed up the next day with the crust cut off.

We'd spent nearly a week trying to get a rope tied to the branch hanging over the creek. When we were finally successful, I chickened out on the very first swing. She didn't call me a wimp or harass me into giving it another try. She just spent the day using it to do flips into the creek and arguing with me when I scored them below a perfect ten from my towel on the bank.

I'd spent so much of my life trying to fit into a mold of who others thought I should be that I'd lost sight of who I truly was.

But Nora didn't want me to be anyone. She just liked that I was there.

We didn't get along about everything. She picked on me relentlessly about the sci-fi books I'd read while she got lost in a magazine from two years ago. But in the next breath, she'd plop down beside me and ask me all about it, just to be sure it was something she wouldn't like.

With Nora, I was free to be whoever the hell I wanted without consideration or consequence, and losing that when I went back to Alberton terrified me.

But all good things come to an end, right? At least that was what Mom had said when I'd begged her on my hands and knees to let me stay at my grandparents' and go to school in Clovert. It was an argument I'd never fathomed having three months earlier.

Dad had chimed in with a booming, "Have you lost your mind, boy?" He didn't even bother to read the three-page report I'd stayed up until four in the morning writing, detailing all the reasons why it would be beneficial for me to stay. None of those reasons mentioned Nora. I didn't figure confessing that my first, only, and best friend was an eleven-year-old girl was going to win me any points with him.

Without any other way to convince them, I'd accepted defeat, asked my mom for a double serving of banana pudding, and then browbeat her into letting me stay out past curfew. She had a million questions about what I was doing and where I was going. I lied, telling her I needed to turn in the last of my worms and clean up all the stuff I'd left behind at the creek.

Based on her squinted glare, she didn't totally believe me, but as she wrapped two spoons in two napkins and set them on top of the plastic container filled to the brim with banana pudding, she gave me all the permission I needed.

"Thanks, Mom."

She smiled and shot me a wink. "Now, go on. Get out of here before your dad sees you leave."

She did not have to tell me twice. After taking the container and spoons, I darted past her to the door, slowing only long enough to sling on my backpack.

It sucked knowing this would be the last time I saw Nora for a while, but I had five hours and the excitement of finally seeing her face when she tasted my mom's banana pudding in my future before I had to deal with any of the hard stuff.

"Camden, where you running off to grinning like that?" Grandma called as I ran past her and my aunt, who were sipping coffee on the front porch.

"Wor—" That was all I got out before I went sailing through the air.

Now, I was well aware that I was not the most coordinated person in the world, but there was always a reason when I fell. A tree stump, a sidewalk, a dip in the grass. *Something*. As I landed face-first, the banana pudding smashed against my chest, pain exploding at my knees and hands, I had not one single clue how I'd gotten there.

Until I heard their laughter. I shouldn't have been surprised. Any time our families got together, the mocking laughter of my cousins was something of the soundtrack of my life.

"Come on, Johnny!" my aunt yelled from the porch. "He has enough trouble running without you tripping him. Help him up."

My cousin continued to laugh, but he extended a hand down to me, muttering, "Pussy."

Stunned, I sat up, spitting out grass, and looked at my hands. A mixture of crushed vanilla wafers and blood covered my palms, and acorns fell to the ground as they dislodged from my bloody knees.

And the banana pudding I'd promised to bring Nora lay in an inedible pile of mush on the grass.

It was all I could take. No, it was more than I could take.

It started as a burning ball of flame ricocheting in my chest, each strike searing me at the core, until I felt like I was on fire. My body began to vibrate like an angry hornet's nest, years of torment and frustration warring for a way out.

I was tired.

Tired of all the snide comments.

Tired of the never-ending judgment.

Exhausted of being the punchline to every joke my entire family had ever thought to tell.

And now this? This…*asshole* had tripped me and ruined not only my dessert, but Mom's famous banana pudding I'd promised Nora—*my* Nora. The girl I had to leave for a whole damn year, not knowing if she was eating or if her dad was putting his hands on her again. All because life wasn't fair and my parents thought it was better for me to go to a school that made me miserable instead of staying with her and having even one single drop of happiness.

"Jesus, Camden. Get the hell up and quit embarrassing me," Dad rumbled from somewhere nearby.

And that was it. A match thrown into a can of gasoline.

I exploded off the ground. "Fuck you!" I roared at Johnny, charging toward him. His eyes flashed wide just before my fist landed on his chin.

He fell like a tree in the forest. The thud of his body hitting the ground was the most satisfying sound I'd ever heard. I followed him down, swinging, cussing, and screaming incoherently.

Dad was on me in the next second, hooking me around the hips and lifting me off my cousin with ease, but it only made my blinding anger turn on him. I kicked and fought against his hold on me until he set me on my feet. My lungs burned and tears leaked from my eyes, but dear Lord, I'd never felt more alive. The adrenaline high made me invincible.

"Fuck you too! I don't give a shit if I embarrass you. Don't you get it? I fucking *hate* you. I hate *all* of you! I—"

The rest of my rant died on my tongue as my dad grabbed me by the back of the neck, squeezing painfully as he walked me like a rag doll to our family SUV.

"Let me go!" I cried as he yanked the door open and tossed me inside.

He leaned in after me, his red face only inches away from mine, and seethed through clenched teeth, "Shut your fucking mouth before I'm forced to shut it for you. We're going home, and after that stunt, I haven't decided if you'll still be breathing by the time we get there. Do not press your luck, son. Got it?"

RECLAIM

I clamped my mouth shut, and all at once, every drop of the summer's warmth drained from my body. Reality—vicious, cursed reality—washed over me like a thunderstorm of knives. "No, no, no, please, Dad. We can't go home yet. She's waiting for me at the creek."

His pupils were so big that it made his green eyes look black. "I don't care if our Lord and Savior is waiting for you at the creek. *You* are going home to your room for possibly the rest of your life." He slammed the door with a deafening crack.

"Dad!" I cried, scrambling after him. I didn't dare touch the door, but I pounded on the window. "Please, I didn't get to say goodbye. Just let me say goodbye!"

He said nothing else as he stormed away.

Not ten minutes later, Dad was behind the wheel, Mom beside him, and I sat in the back seat covered in banana pudding and dying from the agonizing hole in my chest.

SEVEN

Nora

I WAITED BESIDE THE CREEK ALL NIGHT.

For the first few hours, I assumed he was running late, so I practiced what I was going to say. Thea was right. I just needed to talk to him, tell him I was going to miss him, maybe see if he wanted to keep in contact through the school year. And—if I could gather the courage—ask him if he was ever coming back.

Around eight, it started to drizzle. Wrapped in my towel and huddled under the tree, I convinced myself that maybe he was waiting out the rain. He could be a real complainer about getting his clothes wet sometimes, and if they were having a big family thing, he was probably wearing those stupid loafers again.

When the rain cleared, I stared up at the twinkling stars, a dark dread forming inside me.

I'd spent so much of the last few weeks subconsciously stressing over whether he'd come back next summer that I'd completely forgotten to be worried about whether he'd abandon me during this one.

But still, I held on to hope.

It was Camden. He would show up. He'd never let me down before.

RECLAIM

When I was sure I'd counted every star in that sky twice, I got up and started pacing. He wouldn't do this to me. Stuff had come up with his grandparents or chores or church in the past, but he always got there eventually.

I could wait.

For Camden, I could always wait.

I pulled out the letter he'd left me that afternoon and traced my fingers over the words on the last line. *I'd rather be there with you.*

But if that were true, where was he?

I clicked my flashlight on and off for a while, but when I worried I'd run the batteries out, I closed my eyes and willed my ears to hear his footsteps running through the field. The crickets were louder than usual that night. Or maybe it just seemed that way without his laughter filling the air.

As though they were a part of my anatomy, I felt the agony of each and every one of my hopes dying when my watch hit midnight. Loud sobs tore from my throat, and I balled my towel up and covered my mouth to muffle my cries for fear I'd wake Mr. and Mrs. Leonard.

But no amount of tears, screams, or sobs offered me any relief.

He was gone.

And he hadn't chosen me.

I was no stranger to heartbreak.

Growing up, I'd fallen asleep every night to the lullaby of my father yelling at my mother or the song of her sobs as she cleaned the blood he'd left on her face.

I'd been beaten and told I was worthless.

I'd been cussed at, spit on, and all-around neglected.

It was safe to say my life was as far from rainbows and

unicorns as one could get. But the grief I felt that night from knowing that Camden was never coming back was some of the worst I'd experienced in my short eleven years.

Around one in the morning, a flashlight in the distance caught my attention. A tsunami of renewed hope crashed into me and I scrambled to turn my flashlight back on and frantically waved my arms in the air so he'd know I was still there.

My excitement morphed into devastation as soon as I heard his voice.

"There you are," Ramsey said, stomping my way with Thea holding his hand. "What the heck are you still doing here? When I got home and you weren't there, I was scared to death you'd been kidnapped or something."

I'd have rather been kidnapped or something.

I cleared my throat and got busy gathering my things so he couldn't see my tear-stained cheeks. "Yeah. I was just getting ready to come back now. I must have fallen asleep."

Thea walked over and pretended to help me shove my towel in the bag, whispering, "How'd it go?"

Awful. Terrible. Soul-crushing.

I had to swallow twice before I could answer. "Good. Everything's good now."

She smiled huge. "See? I told you it'd be okay." She slung an arm around my shoulders and pulled me in for a brief hug.

I was too numb for it to warm me.

"Holy hell, this place is amazing," Ramsey said, shining his flashlight around the creek. "I don't think I've ever been back this far on the Leonards' property before. Is it deep enough to swim down at the other end?"

Oh, no. No freaking way. I wasn't good enough for Camden Cole. Fine. That I should have expected. But as much as I wanted to light that place on fire and never look back, I was nowhere near ready to let Ramsey and Thea take over *our* spot.

"No," I lied. Memories of Camden cannonballing into the water flashed on the back of my lids, causing another nail to pierce through my heart. "It's terrible here. There's snakes and bugs. I'm pretty sure I saw some leeches in the water the other day."

"Gross," Thea said.

"Yeah. Stick with your tree." Slinging my bag over my shoulder, I marched away from them—and every single memory of Camden I'd never be able to forget.

When school started on Monday, I did my best to pack all things Camden into a neat, little drawer in my head and locked it. He'd hurt me. So what? I should have been used to it by then.

It was time to put on a happy face and get back to my most important job of all: hiding from the world.

I woke up every morning.

Went to school all day.

I smiled more that first week than I had in years.

All of them fake.

All of them painful.

And all of them to mask how I was secretly withering away.

Regardless, I smiled on cue. Laughed when I heard a joke. I even skipped home when I got off the bus to put the final stroke on my masterpiece of deception. I was so good at playing the part that not even Ramsey and Thea realized I was only one breath away from suffocating.

A few times I'd slip up and ask someone around town if they knew where the Coles' house was. No one did. Besides, what would I say if I went there? They probably didn't even know I was alive.

And for what it was worth, I wasn't.

It took two weeks and a chance run-in with Mr. Leonard before I returned to the creek. He'd cornered me at the grocery store and asked why I hadn't been delivering him any worms. Fishing season was coming to a close, but there were still a few days warm enough for him and his boys to hit the lake.

There was nothing between those rocky banks that didn't remind me of Camden, including the five dollars a day that was no longer in my pocket. I didn't even have our ten-dollar bill because I'd hidden it under the insert in his shoe the last day I'd seen him. I couldn't be sure if I was bitter enough to actually spend it or not, but I resented not having the choice.

Thea agreed to buy me the worms from Lewis Tractor Repair, Bait, and Booze each day so I didn't get caught, and by that weekend, I was gainfully employed again.

My first day back at the creek was rough. I kept waiting for him to pop up. Any time I'd hear a rustle of the leaves or a breeze blew through the grass, an unwelcome pang of hope would spike my pulse.

I did everything I could to erase Camden from the creek. I swept away the piles of stripped leaf stems he'd left scattered around, and I switched to a different bank on the other side, where the memories of him weren't as strong. I buried a new worm-holding area in the dirt using a metal box I'd found in the garage and threw away the bug spray he'd left hidden between two rocks. I would have rather had a beetle build a colony inside my ear than ever use anything of Camden Cole's again.

I wasn't always strong. A girl could only pretend that her heart wasn't breaking for so long. One afternoon, in a moment of weakness, I wrote him a note and included my address and Thea's phone number. I stuffed it into a Ziploc bag, tucking it

RECLAIM

into our old plastic worm-holding area where I knew he'd find it if he ever came back.

He never did though, but then again, hope had never been my friend.

By the end of October, Mr. Leonard had hung up his fishing rod for the year, but Ramsey and I had saved up enough money to get through the holidays.

Winter came with cold temperatures and even a few flurries of snow. I'd almost gotten to the point where I hardly thought about Camden at all. His drawer in my head was still there, and every now and then, it would slide open, bombarding me with an avalanche of conflicting emotions. Like a teacher calling roll call, all the familiar feelings were accounted for. Anger. *Present.* Resentment. *Present.* Betrayal. *Present.*

And I hated him that much more because he'd made it so easy to let my guard down that I'd ultimately failed myself.

As green leaves filled the trees and the azaleas began to bloom again, I turned twelve and my body started changing. With boobs came attention from boys. Camden didn't want me, but plenty of other boys did. Desperate for the high their attention gave me, I started sneaking out and going to the freshman and sophomore bonfires. Being Ramsey's little sister came in handy; nobody questioned why I was there, even when he wasn't.

Cue Josh Caskey—ninth-grade high school quarterback with all his straight, blonde hair and blue eyes. They weren't as nice as Camden's, but unlike somebody else, Josh had actually chosen me. That was all I really needed back then: to feel special and important.

As the mayor's son and one of the few rich kids in town, Josh could have had any girl he wanted.

But he wanted me and that filled my lonely soul in ways nothing else could.

We started hanging out after school, and because I was still in middle school, he made me swear not to tell Ramsey. My brother was so wrapped up in making out with Thea any chance he got, keeping a secret wasn't all that hard.

Besides, he knew Josh. They'd been in school together for years. It wasn't a big deal.

At first, my time with Josh was innocent enough. We'd meet up in the empty dugouts after his baseball practice and talk and get to know each other until it got dark.

He loved taking pictures of us together on his cell phone. I thought it was so cool that he had a cell phone—and that he wanted to fill it with pictures *of me*.

One Friday about two weeks before the end of school, he got brave and stole a kiss. Like most girls my age, I'd dreamed about my first kiss for years. Wondered what it would be like or how it would feel. My heart stopped when he roughly shoved me against the wall, a board from the dugout digging into my back, and jabbed his tongue into my mouth.

It should have been a red flag.

I should have told my brother.

I should have kicked him in the balls and run as far away from Josh Caskey as I could get.

Yet I went back the next day.

And the next.

And the next.

A few days before school let out, Mr. Leonard tracked me down and asked if I wanted my summer job back. His feud with Old Man Lewis was still running strong and he'd somehow managed to drag half the town into it. True to his threats, he'd set up a bait stand in his driveway complete with at least a dozen "Screw Dale Lewis" signs lining the main road and a scarecrow dressed in a clown costume wearing a Lewis Tractor Repair, Bait, and Booze T-shirt. It was a small-town elderly TKO at its finest.

It had been a while since I'd really sat down and thought about Camden Cole. In some ways, it seemed like it had been a million years since we'd played in that creek together, laughing for hours on end. But as the summer started and I once again found myself sitting at the edge of the water every day, it also felt like it had been just yesterday when he had been there, sipping a Coke and grinning over at me with those vibrant baby blues.

I was still hurt, but while time had not healed the jagged gash Camden had carved in my heart, it had at least allowed it to scab over so the ache was no longer devouring me.

Nevertheless, I was a ball of nerves when I arrived at the creek for the first time that summer. Just a year before, Camden had appeared with a wicked grin and a bucket of worms. He obviously didn't care about me, but money was money and selling worms to Mr. Leonard was as easy as it came. I didn't know what I'd say to him if he showed up again. *Fuck off* seemed appropriate, but I had a whole lot of pent-up *What the hell happened to you?* that I wouldn't have minded having answered, either.

It was all moot. He didn't show up that day, and the most confusing mixture of earth-shaking relief and heart-wrenching disappointment rocked me to my core.

I didn't care about Camden.

Fuck him. Fuck his stupid life in Alberton. Fuck every single thing about the boy who didn't even care enough about me to say goodbye.

I *hated* Freaking Camden Cole.

Or so I'd thought.

The very next day, while I sat with my toes in the water halfway through *Seventeen Magazine*'s "Does he really love you?" quiz, the deep rumble of three words changed my life forever.

"Catch anything good?"

EIGHT

Camden

I HAD BEEN IN TOWN FOR APPROXIMATELY TWO MINUTES and eighteen seconds—or however long it had taken me to jump out of the car before it was in park and sprint directly to the creek. I was sweating and panting and had nearly died stumbling over a pile of fire ants, but when I saw her long, brown ponytail hanging down her back, none of that mattered anymore.

Swallowing hard, I wedged a hand into my pocket only to nervously switch to the other hand for maximum coolness. She hadn't heard me walk up, so I had the element of surprise. I'd briefly considered scaring the crap out of her, but I'd spent nine long, excruciating months waiting to see her again. I wasn't chancing that she'd punch me in the first thirty seconds.

Quietly clearing my throat, I smoothed down the front of the collared shirt my dad had forced me to wear. Luckily, I'd well past grown out of the penny loafers from last year, but I didn't think she was going to like my boat shoes any better. Whatever. Changing clothes would have meant wasting time getting to her.

I sucked in a deep breath and then spoke through the perma-grin I'd been sporting since my parents had agreed to let me come back to Clovert for the summer. "Catch anything good?"

Holding my breath, I waited for her reaction. I was betting

on a scream, though there was a strong possibility I might even get a hug out of this reunion.

Grinning, I stared at her back, waiting for her to recognize my voice. It was a little different from the last time she'd heard it though—everything was different, actually. Eighth grade had been good to me. I'd been growing fast, topping out at a mountain of five six. Dad had told me I was even taller than he was at thirteen, so I had high hopes that I wouldn't be the runt of the family forever. Thanks to the seven-a.m. basketball drills Dad had forced me to do year-round—a small price to pay to avoid his precious football field—I was starting to fill out. Everyone in the school still hated me, so nothing had changed on that front, but Nora had never cared about that anyway.

When she didn't turn around, I moved closer and repeated, "Catch anything good?"

"I heard you the first time," she snapped. "What do you want?"

Well, I guessed my voice had changed more than I'd thought. She didn't recognize it at all. "Nora, hey, it's me. Camden."

"Oh, I know exactly who you are." All at once, she stood up and spun on me.

Or at least I thought it was her.

Gone was the freckle-faced little girl who wore glitter barrettes and tie-dyed shirts. She was taller, though nowhere near as tall as I was, and makeup rimmed her golden-brown eyes. A pair of silver hoops hung from her ears, and it struck me that I didn't even remember if she'd had her ears pierced the summer before. Her denim skirt was short, but nothing the girls at my school weren't wearing too.

But the icing on the holy-shit-who-is-this-girl cake was the red tank top hugging curves that I was absolutely one million percent positive had *not* been there before but still made my mouth dry.

Holy shit, Nora Stewart was gorgeous.

"Wow," I breathed like a total idiot. But that was all I had. "Wow" was the literal height of my intelligence in that moment.

Her cheeks pinked as she crossed her arms over her chest and glared. "Why are you here?"

"What do you mean why am I here? I came to see you, crazy."

She barked a laugh and stomped past me, her shoulder clipping mine when I didn't move out of her way. A wave of honeysuckle lingered behind her.

Damn, she smelled incredible. That was new too.

Roughly folding her towel, she avoided my gaze. "Look, I already have worms for today. I paid for 'em and I'm going to turn 'em in, but if you want to work tomorrow, that's fine. I'll stay gone."

"That's gonna make hanging out a little difficult, don't ya think?"

She scoffed. "Hanging out? Could I be so fucking lucky? Must be nice coming and going whenever you want without a care in the world." Folding her hands in prayer, she brought them to her lips. "Oh, yes. Please, Camden. Hang out with me. I'm so, so desperate." She rolled her eyes with a skepticism that had never been aimed at me before. "Ha! You wish."

Confusion slapped me across the face. "What the hell are you talking about? I'm not coming and going whenever I want. I just got back to Clovert, like, three minutes ago and came straight here. If anyone looks desperate, it's me." I paused. Given her current attitude, it wasn't the easiest thing to admit, but it was the absolute truth, so I said it anyway. "I've missed you."

Yanking and tugging, she fought with the zipper on her backpack. "Bullshit. Don't feed me that crap. You didn't even care enough to say goodbye last year and left me sitting here all damn night." Hoisting her bag onto her back, she started past me.

I stepped in front of her, blocking her path. "That's not what happened. I tried—"

"I don't care!" She craned her head back. "Get out of my way."

"Not until you listen to me."

"I don't want to listen to you, okay? It's not a big deal. Just because we tolerated each other last summer doesn't mean we have to do it again this year."

I flinched as her words slammed into me with the force of a sledgehammer. We *tolerated* each other? What the hell was that? She was my best friend. I'd been busting my ass day and night all year to make sure my parents would let me come back to Clovert. But apparently, she'd only been *tolerating* me.

I could barely speak with the knife hanging from my back. "Why are you acting like this?"

"Move, Cam. I don't give a damn if you do look seventeen now. All it'll take is one kick to the balls for me to drop you."

That kick would have hurt less, but I stepped out of her way.

"You can have tomorrow, but fifty worms only. Got it?" She stomped to the container I'd dug into the ground all those months ago and pulled out a plastic baggy with something inside.

My eyes narrowed on the shake of her hand as she struggled to get the baggie into her pocket. Every time she'd get part of it in, the air inside would redistribute and cause a bubble that forced it right back out. I could see some numbers written on the piece of paper that could have been a phone number, but why was it in the container we used for worms?

RECLAIM

"What is that?" I asked.

"Did you hear me? Fifty worms. The rest are mine. You may have hatched this plan, but I've been running it since you vanished without so much as a 'see you later.' So don't you dare think you're going to screw me over by turning in a week's worth all in one day." She pulled the baggie out and switched it to the other side as if that pocket might be bigger.

It wasn't, but all her frenzied twisting and tucking allowed me to see one word written on the paper in big, black letters.

Camden.

As if the universe had finally decided to stop torturing me and throw a little luck my way, she dropped the baggie in the next blink.

I dove after it, not one clue what was inside. But without anything left to lose, I snatched it up.

"Hey!" she shouted. "Give that back."

"Then tell me what it is."

"None of your business!" She jumped, trying to grab it, but it was a wasted effort. I had her in height by at least six inches.

"Then why does it have my name on it?"

She started tugging on my arm, her whole front becoming flush with my side in the scramble. "Damn it, Cam. Give it back."

The fact that she was freaking out only made me that much more curious.

The other facts that she was gorgeous and touching me didn't exactly hurt, either.

Careful to keep it out of her reach, I opened it and pulled out a folded-up sheet of notebook paper. Using me for leverage and channeling her inner Michael Jordan, she almost ripped it out of my hands twice, but I was able to read it before she finally snatched it away.

Camden,

I don't know what happened or what I did to make you leave without saying goodbye, but I'm sorry. Okay? If you'd just come back, I'll fix it. I swear. If you get this and I'm not here, call me at Thea's house or maybe just write a letter with your address so we can talk.

Nora

At the bottom was a phone number and a street address, both of which would have been really helpful over the last nine months. However, it was the pure desperation on that page that made my stomach sink.

"You didn't do anything to make me leave. You know that, right?"

"Ugh," she growled, tearing the note into a tiny pile of confetti at my feet.

"Nora," I breathed, inching forward until I was hovering over her. "Look at me."

She shook her head and continued shredding any proof that remained on the paper. "You shouldn't have read that."

"What the hell are you talking about? I should have read it nine months ago. And I swear to you, if I'd known you'd left it for me, I would have done just about anything to get it just so I'd have a way to contact you again."

Suddenly, her hands landed on my chest, giving me a hard shove and sending me stumbling back. "Then why didn't you?"

Through my confusion, I managed to stay on my feet. "What?"

She advanced on me, black makeup smeared beneath her eyes. "Why didn't you figure out a way to contact me? Huh? You said you missed me, but you never even tried to reach out to me."

RECLAIM

"I didn't know how."

"Hitchhike!" she yelled so loudly it echoed off the trees. "Ask your grandparents to find my address. Hell, mail a letter to Mr. Leonard. I don't know. Anything."

I blinked. Damn, why hadn't I thought about mailing Mr. Leonard a letter?

But she was wrong. I had tried.

After my family had gotten back to Alberton, I was grounded for a month. No phone. No TV. The only thing I was allowed to do was go to school, do my mile-long list of chores, and write a letter of apology to my cousin for cleaning his clock. I smiled through pretty much every word of that letter. However, when I finished the horseshit apology and my parents gave me a thumbs-up on draft four million and four, I put a little P.S. down at the bottom.

While I had no idea what Nora's address was, I knew how to get to her house. Past the grocery store, through the woods, last brown house on the left. All I needed was a pair of legs in Clovert to take the route for me and send back a street name and number.

My cousin, Johnny, wasn't exactly known for his community service, so I included my last twenty bucks in the envelope, hoping I could bribe him into following through.

Shocker, he didn't. But I spent every day for a month checking the mail and listening to the messages left on the answering machine, hoping he would.

When Christmas rolled around, I was sure we'd at least go to Clovert to exchange gifts. A fire at the papermill changed everything though. Dad was working overtime, and Mom didn't want to leave him alone for the holidays even long enough for a day trip to see our family. So there I was, once again stuck in

Alberton. On a phone call on Christmas Eve, I finally got the nerve to tell my grandma about Nora and asked if she could find the Stewarts' phone number for me.

She laughed and told me girls were the least of my worries right now, but if I kept up with the basketball drills, made the track team at school, and got honor roll for the second semester, she'd talk to my dad about letting me spend the summer in Clovert again.

Honor roll I could handle.

Even basketball drills each morning in the privacy of my own driveway were doable.

However, track—putting one foot in front of the other and not falling on my face in front of the whole school—was my own personal, custom-made nightmare.

But with a lot of practice, honing my skill, and fine-tuning my natural abilities, I managed to become Alberton Middle School's fifth-string long jumper and water boy. I did way more of the water boying than the long jumping, but hey, I'd kept up my end of the bargain with my grandma.

And just a few days ago, she'd made good on her end by convincing my parents that another summer of family bootcamp was exactly what I needed.

"I *did* try," I told Nora. "I swear I did. I called in favors from my archnemesis for God's sake, but I couldn't find you. And I'm sorry. But I've been working my ass off all year long just to be sure I could get back here. And you're standing here, telling me you tolerated me?"

Her eyes flashed wide, and her surprise fueled my fire.

"You know what? Why didn't *you* hitchhike to Alberton? Why didn't *you* find my grandparents and ask them where *I* was? Why didn't *you* give me the benefit of the doubt that maybe, just maybe, I wanted to be here that night to say goodbye but something happened? *To me.* Did you ever just stop to think maybe this isn't the Nora Stewart show?" Sucking in a deep breath, I shook my head and dug into my pocket. "You know what. Forget it. If I wanted to spend my summer in a place where I was *tolerated*, I'd have stayed at home."

I threw our ten-dollar bill, which I carried with me everywhere for no other reason than it reminded me of her at her feet, and turned to stomp off.

NINE

Nora

I WASN'T SURE IF MY HEART HAD TAKEN A SINGLE BEAT SINCE I'd laid eyes on him again.

My chest hurt and my lungs burned, but it was the nearly constant battle to keep my tears at bay that surprised me the most.

He'd missed me.

And he'd tried to come back.

And he'd wanted to say goodbye.

I wasn't sure if any of it was true. In my experience, lies were as easy to come by as sunrises.

Just hearing him say those words were a gasp of air to a drowning soul.

The ten. Oh, God. It was ours. I could still see his sloppy chicken scratches scrawled across the top. He'd kept it. Nine full months and he'd never spent it. Not on one of his coveted Cokes or a candy bar. Nothing.

If I was being honest with myself, he was right. I had been living in the Nora Stewart show. The night he hadn't shown up to say goodbye, I hadn't lain on the bank, staring up at the sky, worrying that something had happened to him. Let's be honest, this was Camden. It was equally as possible he'd fallen into a ditch and broken his leg, but my mind had gone straight to how I wasn't good enough.

RECLAIM

I wasn't worth his time.

I wasn't worth his attention.

I wasn't worth him staying.

So he'd moved on. Gone home. Never cared about me in the first place. And never looked back.

In my head, Camden had abandoned me just like my mother had because that was more believable. It didn't matter if he was a twelve-year-old boy who had spent a summer catching worms with me and she had been a grown woman who was supposed love and protect me until her dying day. Nope. None of that mattered.

The only thing I knew for certain was he hadn't chosen me.

But what if he had? What if Thea had been right and he was just a kid who didn't get to make choices?

Maybe he was selling me a dream of lies, but I needed to know what he'd done with the choices he could control.

"Camden, wait!"

He stopped only a few steps away and turned around, planting both hands on his hips. "What?"

God, he had changed so much. Not only was he a giant now, but he had a jawline and little muscles under his shirt. Yes, it was a button-down with the sleeves rolled up, and he was wearing boat shoes, but Freaking Camden Cole was pulling it off.

"Why did you keep that?" I squatted and picked up the money off the ground. "Why not spend it? There must have been something you wanted over the last year."

"There was a lot of stuff I wanted, Nora. Almost all of them involved being here with you though. That ten was as close as I could get. Maybe it was stupid, and I should have bought a dozen slushies or something. But I didn't because I thought we were friends."

"We *are* friends," I whispered.

He shook his head. "Doesn't feel like it right now. You know, I was so excited about getting here today. I was already sitting in the car when my dad's alarm went off this morning. I had it all mapped out. If we got on the road by six, I could beat you here and surprise you. But then he wanted coffee and breakfast and we had to run by the papermill, where I sat in the car for a million years. Then we had to run back past the house. And then it was lunchtime, so we had to stop for that." He shuffled his feet. "Anyway. You get the point. I got here as quick as I could."

Oh, God. That was sweet. Rambly. But sweet.

Then again, Camden had always been sweet—and, yeah, rambly too.

"What happened? That night when you didn't show?"

He scratched the back of his neck, a ghost of a smile pulling at his lips. "I got in a fight with my cousin. He was being a dick, so I punched him." His grin stretched so wide I feared for his lips. "Knocked him clean out."

"What?" I gasped, trying to wrap my mind around the idea of Camden knocking anyone out. Last year, he hadn't been what I would have considered a fighter in any capacity. Though he did look like he'd be able to take care of himself now.

"Yeah. I wasn't thinking about all the trouble I'd get into. My temper just got away from me. I never would have done it if I'd known I wouldn't be able to see you again. I spent all year doing chores, working out, making good grades—anything to get on my parents' good side just so they'd let me come back here. You've gotta believe me."

Trust. That wasn't my strong suit.

But if it meant being able to keep Camden, I'd risk it all to try.

RECLAIM

Talk to him, I heard Thea's voice say in my head. It would mean exposing myself and hoping he wouldn't run for the hills all over again, but if I didn't say something, I was going to lose him no matter what.

I swallowed hard and crossed my arms over my chest, faking an attitude to cover the tears welling in my eyes. "You can't do that to me again. Do you hear me? You can't just leave and expect me to assume it's because you got into a fight with your cousin or tripped and fell into a ditch. My brain doesn't work like that. I freak out and panic. And…I don't know. My mom left when I was seven. She met a guy and moved to Texas. If I can't get my own mom to come back, if I wasn't good enough to make her stay, what reason do I have to expect that you would, either?"

"Because I will," he promised. "It might not be right away and you might have to wait for a while, but I'll always come back."

"You say that now but—"

"But nothing. We're friends, Nora." He took a giant step toward me, completely in my space without actually touching me. His breath fluttered across my bare shoulder, and his words wrapped around me like a blanket in the middle of winter. "Friends stick around even when they live three hours away. Even when their parents ground them for a century. Even when their parents are idiots and take off. Even when all the worms in Georgia have been caught. Friends—*true friends*—always come back." He extended an outstretched pinky my way, and I'd done enough pinky swears with Ramsey to know what he was asking for. "Okay?"

I drew in a shaky breath and stared at his hand. "But what if—"

"No what-ifs. You don't have to trust me now. I'll prove it to you. As long as you can tolerate me, I'll always be around."

Guilt iced my veins, and my head snapped up, an apology poised on the tip of my tongue.

But he was smiling. His gorgeous, blue eyes danced in the sunlight. Camden Cole, in the flesh, tall and strong, was standing in front of me, telling me all the things I'd never even dared to dream.

I couldn't get my pinky hooked with his fast enough. "Friends. True friends."

Using our joined pinkies, he gave my hand a tug. "Thanks for telling me about your mom. I won't tell anyone. I promise."

I chewed on the inside of my lip. "Yeah. That'd be good. I don't talk about her much. It's kinda weird."

He shrugged and never let go of my hand. "No weirder than my dad asking me if I was gay on the drive here."

"What?" I half laughed, half shrieked.

"Yeah. Fun story. I told my grandma about you and how much I wanted to come back, thinking she'd be able to convince my parents. Well, she told my mom, and then by the time the story got back to my dad, there was a kid that I hunted worms with who she thought I had a crush on."

I dropped his pinky so fast you would have thought I'd been electrocuted. "Wh-why would they think that?"

"I don't know. But let's just say Dad was super relieved to hear you were a Nor*a* and not a Nor*man*."

Nervous laughter bubbled from my throat. "That's crazy." I tucked a piece of hair behind my ear, but since my hair was in a ponytail, it wasn't a real piece of hair and I just looked like a fool.

"Meh, whatever. He winked and told me I don't have to be home until nine tonight, so I'm not complaining. So, what are we going to do first today, *friend*?"

Oh, shit. Shit. Shit. Shit. Of all the days for Camden to come back.

RECLAIM

"Actually, I, um, have to go soon."

"What? Why? I just got here."

"I know, but I kinda sorta have a date."

He wasn't fast enough to hide his wince. "Oh."

"Yeah, I mean, it's nothing big. We've been talking for a little while. He's gonna make a picnic for us tonight."

"Oh," he repeated.

"Yeah. Probably just sandwiches and stuff. No big deal." I nodded so many times that I must have looked like a bobblehead.

He stared off into the distance over my head. "Maybe you'll get lucky and he'll bring you ham, pickle, and mustard."

My stomach knotted.

"Maybe," I replied, wishing the awkwardness would go ahead and swallow me already. Anything had to be better than this.

There was literally no reason for me to be uncomfortable talking about this with Camden. Friends could go on dates with other people. Especially when said friends had just come back after a year of me kinda-sorta-not-really hating him. Sure, he was more grown up and hot now. But that was neither here nor there.

"All right. Well, have fun, I guess. I'm gonna stay here until it's time to go back. That way, my grandpa can't put me to work until tomorrow. Hey, can I get the ten back before you go?"

My back shot straight, and a wave of panic stole my breath. "You're taking it back because I'm going on a date?"

He barked a laugh, deep and rich. "I'm not taking it back, crazy. I'm writing my address on it. And you have to do the same. That way, if I get into another Royal Rumble or you decide to take up that hitchhiking you bring up so much—seriously, what's that about? We'll always have a way to find each other."

I smiled, and for the first time in almost a year, it wasn't fake. And it was such an overwhelming rush that my hands shook as I passed it back to him.

"Heads or tails?" he asked, turning the bill in his hand.

"Heads," I whispered.

"Good choice," he murmured. Flattening the bill across my shoulder so he could bear down, he wrote his address and phone number in Alberton just above the image of the US Treasury. "There." He handed it back to me along with the pen and offered up his shoulder in return.

I blushed as he peered down at me while I wrote my address and Thea's phone number beside Alexander Hamilton's photo. It was unnerving to be that close to him, but it also felt so ridiculously comfortable, like it was the most natural thing in the world.

"Leaning Oak Drive, huh?" he asked, smiling down at me, his mouth only inches away from mine.

My breath caught, and unable to find coherent words with him that close, I nodded.

We stared at each other for a long beat, making no effort to move away, his hypnotizing blue eyes holding me captive.

His Adam's apple bobbed, and I licked my lips.

I didn't know what was running through his mind in that second. But I knew what was running through mine. And it had not one damn thing to do with me going on a date with Josh Caskey.

Camden cleared his throat and suddenly walked away, leaving me standing there, holding our ten-dollar bill in midair, the pen still poised over it.

"How long until you have to leave?" he asked, walking to the same big rock he'd spent at least half of last summer perched on top.

RECLAIM

"Like an hour."

He smiled. "All right. Well, fill me in on all things Nora Stewart before you go."

Now, that I could do.

Camden stripped leaves on the rock beside me while we caught up. I strategically left out all the pissed-off, bitter, and depressing parts of my year. It didn't leave a lot to be told. He filled me in on the happenings in Alberton. To hear him tell it, it still stunk literally and figuratively. He hadn't had much luck in the making-friends department, but he'd read a couple of really cool books. This digressed into long, animated stories of complex sci-fi plots I didn't care about in the least.

But I listened, rapt and with a smile on my face, for no other reason than it was Camden talking. He was so excited to tell me about aliens and distant planets he didn't even notice when I slipped the ten-dollar bill into his pocket.

I'd really missed that nerd.

Choices. Everyone makes them.

And my choice that day was to leave the best, truest friend I'd ever had to go out on a date with a boy I no longer cared about in any way, shape, or form.

And in a matter of hours, that choice would ruin us all.

TEN

Nora

"**W**HAT THE HELL ARE YOU DOING?" JOSH HISSED AS he opened his grand front door complete with two golden lion head knockers. I'd always thought they were hideous and kind of snobby, but so was the six-foot-tall iron fence that surrounded the mayor's mansion. In a world where you could buy anything, why get golden lion head knockers? Being rich must have been weird.

I smiled at my date. "I had to pass here to get to the baseball field. I figured we could walk together."

Josh slid outside and quietly shut the door behind him. "Have you lost your mind? People might see us."

"Excuse me?"

He nervously glanced around. "Ramsey can't find out about us. You're still in middle school. And if people see you over here, you know word *will* get back to him before you can sneak back home tonight."

"Why are you so worried about Ramsey? I bet if we just talked to him, he—"

"Nobody can know!" he whisper-yelled. "I already told you that, like, a million times."

"Okay, okay. Sorry. Relax."

He let out an irritated huff. "Just go wait for me in the

dugout. I need to grab my stuff. You didn't tell anyone where we were going, right?"

I rocked back on my heels, not at all impressed with his tone. "No."

"Good. Now, get out of here, and I'll meet you there."

I nodded, and as soon as I turned away, I rolled my eyes. Great. He was in a bad mood. Just what every girl dreamed of on their first real date. I should have just canceled and hung out with Camden or not shown up at all. I'd felt like a jerk leaving him at the creek on his first day back, and if I was being honest with myself, that's where I would have rather been anyway.

I'd spent months obsessing over Josh. Did he like me? Did he think I was pretty? Did he want to be my boyfriend? I liked that he was older and part of the cool crowd. He was super cute in a football uniform and soccer uniform and baseball uniform.

But he wasn't Camden, and at first, that had been his greatest quality.

Now that Cam was back though…

But Camden returning was temporary. In a few months, he'd be gone again and I'd be alone in Clovert *again*, for an entire school year without him. No, Josh wasn't currently ready for people to find out about our relationship/non-relationship. But he'd get there eventually. And when Camden inevitably left, life would be a lot easier if I still had a way to fit in. Josh was that ticket for me.

Though, if he was in a crap mood and we rushed through this picnic in time for me to get back to the creek before nine, I wouldn't be too upset.

I waited for at least fifteen minutes before Josh came sauntering into the dugout with a duffel bag thrown over his shoulder. His blond hair feathered out from beneath a Clovert High baseball cap and not surprisingly, he had on his summer uniform of a polo shirt and cargo shorts.

"Hey," he said, setting his bag down on the bench beside me.

"You know we can hang out somewhere other than the baseball field, right?"

"I thought you liked it here."

Yeah. A stinky, dirty dugout where during baseball games over a dozen sweaty boys sat trapped like caged animals. Every girl's dream.

I looked at my watch. It was only six. I still had about three hours before Camden had to be home. "No. It's fine. Soo…what'd you bring for our picnic?"

"Shit," he breathed, snatching his cap off. He ran a hand through the top of his hair before turning it around and replacing it on his head backward. "I forgot to pack food."

"Oh," was what I said. *Jesus Christ, seriously?* was what I thought.

"But hey, look what I did bring?" He dug through his bag and pulled out his phone. "I need a new picture of my girl for my wallet."

I usually swooned when he called me his girl. That night, I just rolled my eyes. Maybe I was the one in the bad mood and not him.

"Don't you already have one of those?" I asked.

He shrugged. "Yeah, you're probably right. But you know what I don't have?" He lifted a camcorder out of his bag.

My heart stopped immediately and the hairs on the back of my neck stood on end like some sort of sixth sense, but my brain wasn't nearly as quick. "Wh-what's that for?"

"You know how I like pictures of us and stuff." He opened the flip screen and angled it just right before setting the camcorder on top of the bat holder at the end of the dugout. "This is better than pictures. This way, when I can't see you, I can watch the real thing." He clicked a button and a tiny, red light illuminated at the corner. "Wave to the camera, sexy."

It could have been as innocent as he'd said. Just a kid wanting to record funny videos with a girl he liked. But even at a completely inexperienced, naïve twelve, I knew it wasn't. The alarm bells didn't just start ringing in my head; they screamed like blood-curdling sirens.

He prowled toward me, and the smile I'd only weeks ago thought was charming and cute suddenly appeared sinister and cruel.

I quickly stood up, backing toward the exit on the other end, my pulse thundering in my ears. "You know what? I just remembered I told Ramsey I'd be home by six."

"You can be late. I'm sure he's doing the same thing with Thea."

"If I'm not there, he'll come looking for me."

"Not here, he won't."

In a miscalculation that measured in mere inches but would alter the course of my entire life, instead of backing out of the dugout, my back hit the wall.

He was on me in the very next beat.

I'd spend years trying to forget that evening.

The feel of his fingers biting into my flesh.

The screams burning my throat.

My back on the cool bench, deep splinters driving into my skin.

His teeth mauling my neck and shoulders.

The overwhelming panic of being pinned down beneath him.

I kicked and hit and punched, but it was useless. I opened drawers in my head at lightning speed, shoving the blistering pain and devastating emotion inside them until I finally gave up. My body went slack as I mentally crawled into a drawer myself like it was a morgue, the absolute darkness my only reprieve.

I don't remember a lot about what happened in the minutes after he let me go.

I know he talked to me, though not everything was clear to my panic-stricken mind.

He told me how hot I was, how good it had been for him.

He asked if I'd liked it. I was too frightened to say no, so I nodded.

He told me not to tell anyone. He winked and said that if I did, he'd show everyone all the pictures and video he'd taken of us over the last few weeks. I wasn't sure what exactly the camcorder had caught, but I knew how filthy I felt, and I was mortified at the idea of someone else seeing it too.

Smiling and making chitchat, he was in no rush as he packed his bag up. I was wilting into nothingness, but it was just another take-whatever-you-want day for Josh Caskey.

Just before leaving, he stopped in front of me, and used one finger to tilt my head back, forcing my gaze to his. "Let me know if you want to hang out again." He winked and it was all I could do not to throw up on him.

My whole body shook—trembling all the way down to my soul—as he walked away. The second he disappeared, I took off out of the other side, sprinting as fast as I could in the opposite direction.

I ran and I ran and I ran, my lungs burning and my feet aching. My dad was lounging on the couch when I got home, but I raced past him.

RECLAIM

The man who should have been my hero would never help me.

I slammed the door to my room, and when I was positive I was alone, the way God had so clearly intended for me to spend my life, I put my back to it, sinking down so nobody could get inside.

Only then did I cry.

ELEVEN

Camden

SHE DIDN'T SHOW UP THE NEXT DAY AT THE CREEK.

We'd left things on good terms before her "date." That sneaky girl had even managed to slip the ten back into my pocket at some point before she took off.

I might not have known this new, older version of Nora Stewart, but I knew when she was lying or faking a smile, and when she'd left me at the creek, the one gracing her beautiful face was one hundred percent genuine.

The good news was I didn't think she was avoiding me.

The bad news was I still had no idea where she could be.

I wasn't jealous or anything, but her boyfriend was a total fucking idiot who would never deserve her. And no, I didn't need to know what he looked like or who he was to know that.

Maybe her stupid boyfriend had convinced her I was lying about the way I'd left last summer. Or maybe he just didn't want her hanging out with me in general. If she'd even told him about me at all.

He was a douchebag, so I wouldn't put anything past him.

Yeah, okay, maybe I was a teensy bit jealous.

I told myself not to flip out. After all, hadn't we just had a long conversation about giving each other the benefit of the doubt? She probably had something come up. I tried to

RECLAIM

preoccupy my swirling mind with scenarios where she'd caught a cold or had to help her family around the house.

Then I remembered her house.

And her dad.

I'd never prayed so hard in my life for someone to have a stuffy nose and a fever.

I bought worms and turned them in so she didn't miss out on a day of cash, but when she didn't show up the next day, either, money was the least of my worries.

We'd made a deal. If either of us disappeared again, we'd know how to find each other. And being in Clovert and not three hours away in Alberton, I could actually do something about it.

So, armed with nothing but a Coke, a Snickers, and an indelible memory of how to get to her house, I set out to find her.

Over a year had passed since I'd been there, but in the daylight, the house looked worse than I recalled. The grass was cut, but weeds had overrun the patches of dirt that I assumed had once been flowerbeds. The tan shutters hung crooked, each one leaning in a different direction, and the post beside the door was completely rotted out. Thankfully, her dad's truck wasn't in the driveway, but even if it had been, that wouldn't have stopped me from getting to her.

Rocking from one foot to the other, I knocked on the door and then cleared my throat. I was nervous, and she was probably going to yell at me for worrying, but the last two days without her had been miserable. I was more than willing to take my tongue lashing if it got her to come back.

The door cracked open with a deafening creak, a single brown eye appearing in the one-inch gap.

I leaned to the side so she could see me and waved because what the hell else was I going to do with my sweaty palms? "Hi!"

"Camden?" she breathed, pulling the door wide, a mixture of surprise and embarrassment heating her cheeks. "What are you doing here?"

I thrust the Coke in front of me, saving the candy bar in my back pocket in case I needed a backup bribe. "I brought you this."

Stepping outside, she attempted to shut the door behind her, but it jammed and she had to tug it three times to get it to close. I narrowed my eyes at her sweatpants and oversized hoodie. It had to have been a hundred degrees that day.

"Oh, thanks? That's…nice of you." She extended an arm to take the soda and the cuff on her wrist inched up a fraction from the movement. A huge black bruise peeked out from underneath.

"Holy hell," I whispered as my stomach sank. "What is that?"

"Nothing. Just fell off my bike the other day." She quickly covered her wrist and spun on a toe, ready to dart away. Luckily, the door didn't open any more easily than it shut.

"Nora, come on. Don't hide from me."

"I'm not hiding. I haven't been feeling great, but as soon as I get better, I'll be back at the creek. Thanks for stopping by." She finally got the door open, but if I let her escape, there was a good possibility I'd never get her back.

"Wait," I said, grabbing the back of her hoodie.

Her whole body winced, and a cry she couldn't muffle tore from her mouth.

Oh, God. How many other bruises was she hiding under that thing?

I immediately let her go and begged, "Please just talk to me."

She looked down, a curtain of brown hair covering her pink cheeks. It was a dead giveaway that she was about to lie. "There's nothing to talk about, Cam. Just drop it."

RECLAIM

"Did your dad do that to you? I know he puts his hands on you, Nora. You don't have to lie to me."

Tears hit her eyes, but then she laughed, loud and heartbreaking. "That's bullshit! I have to lie to everyone. About everything. My entire fucking life is a lie. I'm not even sure I know how to tell the truth anymore."

I stabbed a finger at my chest. "You don't lie to me."

She barked another sad laugh. "Are you sure about that?"

"Nora, you told me my shoes were stupid the first time we met, and once, you spent an entire afternoon talking about my ugly swim trunks. I'm pretty sure you don't pull punches where I'm concerned. And if you have lied to me, I don't care. We're true friends, remember? That means having each other's back no matter what. You can trust me."

"I can't trust anyone!" she screamed so loud her face vibrated, and the sheer act of that alone shifted her hoodie, revealing bruises on her neck, dark blue and purple with a hollow center as though she'd been bitten.

A wave of adrenaline flooded my veins. "Yes, you can!" I yelled right back. "I'm standing right here. I know about your dad. I saw him in action."

Her chest heaved with unshed emotion, but her fire momentarily quelled. "What?"

"I followed you home one day after we first met. He was screaming and cussing. He pushed you down before punching your brother. Then that piece of shit said it was your fault your mom left, and you know what, Nora, I never mentioned one single word of that to anyone, but only because you never showed up with bruises. And trust me, I didn't even like swimming in the creek that much, but there's not much you can hide in a bathing suit." I swung a finger at her wrist. "This is different." I pointed at her neck. "That sure as hell is different. If he did that to you, then—"

"Then what? What are you going to do about it, Cam?"

I clamped my mouth shut. Now, that I didn't have the answer to. But I couldn't turn a blind eye and ignore it like every other person in her life. "I don't know. But if you would just talk to me, I could at least try. I'll listen. You might not realize it, but there's not much I wouldn't do for you. And if that means sitting here on your porch and having a man-to-man with your dad myself, then so be it." Right smack in the middle of her front porch, I sat down. I turned and leaned against the brick, kicking my leg out in front of me, all the while hoping my parents wouldn't be casket shopping by the end of the night.

"Okay, he's due back any minute. Suit yourself."

I swallowed hard. "Thanks. I will."

"Fair warning, he and his girlfriend broke up, so he's probably drunk and looking for a fight."

Shit. "Fine by me."

"Did I ever tell you about the time he spent the night in jail for dislocating a man's arm during a bar fight?"

No. She had not. *Fuck.* "I'll take my chances."

She let out a groan. "Cam, stop being ridiculous and go home."

"I'm not leaving. He can't treat you like this and expect to get away with it. Your dad and I are going to have a conversation about those bruises. Honestly, we should have had it last year. So it's long overdue."

"Oh, good Lord," she huffed. "Fine, have it your way. Thanks for the Coke."

I reached into my back pocket and retrieved a slightly smooshed and melted Snickers. "I got you a candy bar too."

She plucked it from my fingers. "Thanks. See you at the funeral home."

"Bring a book. I'm not gonna be there for about eighty years."

She slammed the door behind her.

The odds were not in my favor if her dad did come home, but if I left, I would be just like everyone else in her life.

Last summer, Nora might have *wanted* a proper goodbye and promises that I'd always come back—and all the closure and security that came with them. I'd failed her in spectacular fashion all because I couldn't keep my temper in check.

But that day, sitting on her porch, I was the only person even quasi-brave enough to stand up to her dad. She *needed* that more than anything else I could ever give her.

TWELVE

Nora

"**W**HY ARE YOU STILL SITTING THERE?" I WHISPERED at the window. From my vantage point, hidden behind the piece of plywood Ramsey had used to secure the window, I couldn't see all of Camden, just his sneakers crossed at the ankle.

It had been an hour since he'd sat down declaring his intentions to have a "man-to-man" with Dad. Which, let's be honest, was laughable. My father didn't understand the concept of having a real conversation unless it involved shouting at the bartender for another drink.

Despite what I'd told Camden—luckily for all of us—my dad wouldn't be home anytime soon. Based on the shouting the night before, he had, in fact, broken up with his girlfriend, but it just meant he was on the prowl again. Last time this happened, he didn't come home for six days.

I'd considered telling Camden this information at the thirty-minute mark, but deep down, I was waiting on pins and needles to see how long he'd last before giving up and going home.

God knew I could use the support. The last few days had been a nightmare of emotions I couldn't wake up from.

I tried to pretend.

I tried to forget.

RECLAIM

I dissected what Josh had done to me, stripping it down to the most basic feelings and shoving them into all their disgusting drawers.

But nothing worked.

Physically, I ached head to toe. New bruises appeared every day, and the splinters I couldn't reach in my back had become red and swollen. All that I could take.

I was no stranger to pain. My body would eventually heal. In a few days, when the bruises faded, I could ask Thea for help, making up some excuse for how the splinters had gotten there. Then, not too long after that, a day would come when there wouldn't be a single trace of what Josh had done to me at all.

Nobody would ever know but me.

There was no magical remedy for the festering wound he'd left inside my soul though. The pieces he'd ruined inside me would never heal or even scab over. Guilt and filth devoured me every waking moment, but when I slept, the nightmares were worse. So the last two days had been spent in purgatory, staring off into space and crying.

And then there was Camden with his Coke and Snickers.

Sweet, innocent, oblivious Camden.

I'd wanted to throw up when he'd told me he'd followed me home last summer and seen my dad in all his drunken glory. My time at the creek with Camden was my safe space. He didn't know about the hell at home. The fact that Ramsey and I were practically raising ourselves. Or the constant struggle to keep our ugly lives a secret.

All he knew was what I'd told him. For the same reasons I hadn't shared Camden with the people in my life, I hadn't wanted to share my world with Camden, either.

But he knew. He had always known.

And still, he'd come back.

Another hour passed with him sitting on the porch. He'd gotten up at one point and walked away. The disappointment of watching him leave was almost as intense as the relief that he was finally gone. The warmth filling my hollow chest and the tears that stung my eyes when I realized he'd only gone to the hose on the side of the house for a drink of water were the most telling emotions of all.

When a thunderstorm rolled in at the four-hour mark, I was positive he'd finally leave. He didn't like to get his clothes wet at the creek and always wrapped himself up in his towel like a mummy. While thunder rattled the windows, the sky dumped buckets of rain, and the angry wind pelted him, he stayed.

It made me the worst friend in the world, but I sat inside, dry and warm, watching out the window in absolute awe that he cared enough to be sitting there. The broken and ugly parts of me were desperate to see how far he'd go—or, more accurately, what I was truly worth to Freaking Camden Cole.

Hour five, I paced, gnawing on my fingernails and getting frustrated. This was just ridiculous. What the hell was he doing? He was soaking wet, and despite it being a million degrees outside, every time the wind blew hard enough, he'd shiver. Why wasn't he giving up? He must have been bored and hungry. He'd been sitting there so long I bet his butt was asleep too.

He'd made his point. He cared. Okay, great. Caring didn't equal trust though.

Did it?

"You're gonna wear a hole in your floor if you keep pacing like that!" he shouted from the other side of the door.

I froze and squeezed my eyes shut. Of course he heard me. It wouldn't have been my life if he hadn't. "Go home, Camden!"

RECLAIM

"You still got those bruises? Then I'm not going anywhere. Because if you have those now, it's gonna get worse one day. And it might be during the school year when I'm not here to sit on your porch for the next eighty days if need be. I know you've got your brother, but it's never a bad thing to have a friend watching your back too."

I walked to the door and dropped my forehead against it. "Why are you doing this? You've only been back, like, three days."

"What's that got to do with anything? You might have hated me while I was gone, but you were always my best friend."

A shrill *You barely even know me!* hung on the tip of my tongue. I guessed that wasn't true anymore, was it? Camden Cole knew me in ways no one else ever had.

But he didn't know it all. He didn't know about our dirty house or how only one of the toilets worked but only half the time. He didn't know I had to hide food from my dad or how on more than one occasion he'd passed out with a cigarette in his mouth, so I slept with an expired fire extinguisher under my bed.

People made assumptions based on how we looked and where we lived, but nobody truly understood Ramsey and me.

Ramsey had chosen to let Thea into our hell. She knew all the secret little details of how we survived, but I'd always been of the mind that letting someone in would only run them off.

Maybe that was exactly what I needed to do to Camden—run him off before he had the chance to realize, friend or not, I wasn't worth staying for anyway.

Snatching the door open wide, I stood on the curled linoleum revealing the concrete slab of our entryway and let out an aggravated groan. "Just come in already."

"Well, when you say it all sweet like that..." He stood up with a grimace and shook out his legs. "Ah. Ah. Ah. Pins and needles. Pins and needles."

"That's what you get for sitting out there all day. After that storm, you'll be lucky if you don't catch pneumonia too." My anxious stomach knotted as he lumbered toward me. I'd never invited anyone into our house before. The point of this was to show Camden the real me and run him off, but I couldn't help but be embarrassed all the same.

"I don't catch pneumonia, Nora. Pneumonia catches me."

I scoffed and perched a hand on my hip in the rickety doorway. "Then you better get in here. I've played tag with you before. Trust me—you aren't that hard to catch."

"That was before I carried the Alberton Middle School track team to an eighth-place participation ribbon at the city meet. There were only eight teams and I carried the water more than anything to do with running, but you're talking to a track star now, Nora. Time to show some respect."

I would have laughed if I hadn't been holding my breath when he strutted inside. He stopped abruptly at the edge of the carpet. Frankly, it only resembled carpet in the sense that it had a few fibers left between the bald patches.

This was it. This was the moment when he looked around, realized the filth in my life wasn't limited to our house, and took off.

It was for the best, really.

He'll bolt any second now.

He didn't need a friend like me dragging him down.

Yep. Soon he'll be long gone.

"If you want to leave—"

He looked at me, those damn blue eyes boring into my soul.

RECLAIM

"Any chance I can borrow a towel? I'm gonna soak the floor if I walk on it in these wet clothes."

I stared at him for a beat, searching his face for any sign of disgust or sarcasm. I couldn't have blamed him; I cringed every time I walked through the door too. But Ramsey and I had long since given up on trying to be my father's maids. It didn't matter how many times we attempted to make things look presentable, we were always just one drunken night away from my dad ruining it.

Camden stared at me, waiting for a response, but all I wanted to do was cry.

There was no criticism. No pity. No repulsion.

Just a little confusion and a touch of impatience.

"Nora, seriously, pneumonia is catching up fast."

All at once, I became unstuck and jogged to my room, grabbing the towel from my creek bag before returning.

"Thanks," he said with a smile, patting himself dry and then toeing his shoes off.

I studied his gaze shifting around the living room as we walked to my bedroom together. The only thing his eyes lingered on was a baby picture of me and Ramsey that my mother had hung on the wall before she'd left.

My room was nothing fancy, but I was proud of it. The window was cloaked with hot-pink curtains I'd made myself, and a gray-and-white-striped comforter I'd found at a yard sale stretched across my double bed. A lot of my odds-and-ends arts and crafts decorated the walls, including an earring tree I'd made from an old picture frame and a piece of mesh.

As we stepped inside, he said, "Nice room." It wasn't a comparison to the rest of the house. Just a statement. Kind and sweet. Pure Camden Cole.

"Thanks." I pointed to the wooden chair that sat at a small vanity in the corner. "You can sit over there. Your wet clothes won't mess it up. You hungry?"

"I'm almost certain my stomach has eaten my backbone at this point. But yeah, I'm still starved."

I grabbed one of the sandwiches from the cooler I kept hidden in the back of my closet so my dad couldn't find our food. I'd made a bunch of ham and cheese in advance so I didn't have to leave my room and chance a run-in with my brother. He would have lost his mind if he found out about Josh. My stomach rolled at the very thought of him.

Unaware, Camden was still quick to the rescue. "You have a cooler in your closet? That's awesome. Why haven't I ever thought to do that?"

"Yeah." I laughed awkwardly and sat on the edge of my bed.

He scarfed down the sandwich in four bites, and I handed him what was left of the Coke he'd brought me. That was drained within a few seconds too.

I wiggled my way farther onto my mattress, crossed my legs, and searched the room for something—anything—to talk about to avoid the black-and-blue elephant in the room.

"I was offered a job babysitting this summer," I blurted.

"You were?"

Picking at the frayed hem of my sweatshirt sleeve, I shrugged, feeling a few of the splinters snag on the inside of my shirt. "It didn't pan out though. So I'll still be dealing worms, but maybe next year. I couldn't get my certificate."

His blue eyes were intently on me, paying close attention as I spoke.

"I didn't have the money or a way to get to Thomaston to take the Red Cross test."

RECLAIM

I almost laughed at the confusion on his face.

"The mom and the dad are both nurses. I guess that's why they're so big on their babysitter being certified."

"I didn't even know that was a thing." He looked down at his feet and then scratched the back of his neck. "I hate that you didn't get a better job this summer, but truthfully, the creek wouldn't be the same without you."

Boy, did I know all about that. Nothing had been the same without Camden over the school year.

"Oh, well. I probably wouldn't be any good at it anyway."

"Watch how you talk about my friend. I bet kids would love hanging out with you. You're patient. I'm no fool—you couldn't care less about the books I read, but you listen. You're reliable. I never had to worry about you not showing up. You're funny when you want to be." He wadded up the plastic wrap I'd had the sandwich in and tossed it at my wastepaper basket and missed. "You make a killer ham and cheese too."

It wasn't often people said nice things to me, let alone *about* me. So I was kind of speechless.

"Heck, when you grow up, you'd probably make a pretty great teacher."

Wasn't that a fairytale? Kids like me didn't make it to college, but I didn't want to say anything negative back since he was being so nice.

Kindness was in short supply in Clovert.

"Yeah, maybe I will."

His face split into a winning smile, and after that, we just talked. For a few hours, everything was almost easy. Well, until the sleeve on my hoodie rode up, revealing yet another bruise.

His jaw got hard. "So, when's your dad supposed to be home again?"

I closed my eyes and sighed. "It wasn't my dad, Cam. At least not this time."

He inched to the edge of his chair. "Then who was it?"

I couldn't tell him. He wasn't from Clovert, but it was a small town. I couldn't risk that word would get out and Josh would share those pictures or, God, the video. But if Camden was still sitting there, wearing his hero cape, thinking he could fix even one of my problems, he had to know that it was an impossible pursuit.

And the sooner he realized it, the better off he'd be.

"My, um, date didn't go so well." Staring at the floor, I grabbed the bottom of my hoodie and pulled it over my head, revealing a black tank top that almost blended in among the watercolor of my bruises.

"Nora," he breathed, walking over to me, stopping only inches away. "What the hell happened?"

"I don't want to talk about it."

"No. No. No. You can't show me these and leave it at that. You look like you were in a car wreck." He prowled around me in a circle, not touching me. But his gaze became tangible, raking over me like the softest feather.

"It doesn't matter."

"Oh, God," he whispered, cupping both hands over his mouth. "Is that a splinter in your shoulder?"

I fought back a gag, and I didn't even realize tears had started to drip down my cheeks. After everything Josh had done to me, I still felt more exposed standing in front of Camden, looking like I did.

"Yeah," I croaked, my voice feeling like it had traveled over a mile of gravel before escaping my throat. "They're all over my back."

RECLAIM

Then I waited, bracing for the explosion.

Camden was a good kid, so I was fairly confident he wouldn't just leave because he'd seen them. I had an overprotective brother, which meant I was familiar with how some male brains worked. Camden would get mad first. He'd lecture me on why I needed to tell somebody. He'd rant and rave about how he was going to kill whoever had done it to me.

Yet the universe loved to prove me wrong.

Maybe one day, I'd learn to stop underestimating Camden Cole.

He stood in front of me, bent at the knees to bring us eye to eye. With soft and gentle hands, he wrapped them around my forearms. "Are you okay?"

Short of playing Slapjack and me giving him the occasional titty twister, Camden and I didn't touch often. We were kids; that kind of intimacy was still a foreign concept. But with one simple gesture, a connection from such a thoughtful and caring human being, who when faced with some of the most embarrassing and disgusting things life had to offer, all he wanted to know was if I was okay. And for a girl like me, it didn't just open the flood gates. It tore them off the hinges.

"No," I cried, crashing into his chest.

He released my arms but only so he could wrap me in a hug. It hurt like hell, but I shuffled close, our bodies becoming flush head to toe. A chill rocked down my spine—not because of the temperature in the room, but because Camden was so warm and safe that any part of me that wasn't connected to him felt as though it were at risk of freezing.

"Oh, God, Cam, it was so bad," I confessed through sobs. "I didn't want him to touch me like that... He, he, he... He just pushed up my skirt... And he taped it. And, now, I don't know what to do. He says he's going to tell everyone. Oh, God. I didn't even want to be there. I just wanted to go back to the creek and be with you."

"I know. It's okay. I'm here now."

Pinned against his chest, I could hear his heart pounding at a marathon pace, but he kept his cool, murmuring gentle words I couldn't make out. They soothed my soul if for no other reason than they were coming from his mouth.

Standing there in the middle of the room in damp clothes, he held me until every last tear had drained from my body. When I had nothing left to give, I sagged in his arms, broken and spent.

And still, he didn't leave.

"Have you told anyone else about this?" he asked.

"No."

He sighed. "Is there anything I could do to convince you to turn this kid in? We could call the cops or my mom. She could be down here in a matter of hours."

For a brief second, the drawer in my head slipped open, snapshots of bone-chilling memories assaulting me from all angles.

Josh's smile.

My screams.

The weight of him as I pleaded for mercy.

I slammed the drawer shut so fast it made me jerk. "I don't want to talk about this."

He rumbled a muted groan but hugged me tighter. "Can you do me a favor, then?"

I nodded against his chest.

"I'm not much of a nurse, but I'm clumsy enough to have gotten my fair share of splinters. How about you grab me some tweezers and let me get those things out of your back before they get infected?"

RECLAIM

Great. I was sure that was exactly how he wanted to spend his day.

"You don't have to—"

"Nora. Please. Just let me take care of you. I know you don't want to talk about it, and I'll respect that, but there is no possible way my legs are going to be able to carry me away from you today. So, please. Let me do this."

In that moment, there wasn't much I wouldn't have given Camden.

When I finally stepped out of his arms, the loss was huge, but he smiled, making the warmth linger.

I started to walk away, but he suddenly stopped me.

"Hey, Nora."

"Yeah?" I whispered.

"It's gonna be okay. It probably doesn't feel like it right now, and I'm not even going to pretend to know how you feel. But I promise I'll make it okay."

He couldn't possibly promise that, but I was so desperate for any sort of relief that I allowed myself to believe him anyway.

After slipping on a dry pair of Ramsey's basketball shorts, Camden sat on my bed and picked every single splinter from my back with the patience of a saint. When day shifted to night, I expected him to race home for dinner the way he always had when we were at the creek. Instead, he reclined on the bed beside me, kicked up his legs, and asked for another sandwich.

We talked for a long time about nothing but somehow also everything.

He even got a few smiles out of me.

Eventually, we started laughing and it was the euphoric reprieve I never thought I'd feel again.

Nothing was fixed. Nothing was better. Nothing was even remotely close to being okay.

But with Camden beside me, I wasn't alone.

I fell asleep that night listening to him talk about why he believed aliens would one day inhabit the Earth—that is, if they weren't here already. I woke up a while later and he was asleep too, but his arm was under my head and I was snuggled into his side.

I should have woken him up. With my luck, he'd get shipped back off to Alberton again for staying out all night. But when the bitter chill of reality is all you've ever known, you learn to hold on with both hands to whatever warmth you can find.

So I went back to sleep—safe with my one true friend.

Or so I'd thought.

THIRTEEN

Camden

Just after midnight, I snuck out from under Nora. She was sound asleep, her lips parted in peaceful slumber. I hated to go, but if I wanted to see the light of day again, I needed to get home and do some serious lying about falling asleep at the creek.

I found a colored pencil on her nightstand and a tore a scrap of paper out of a sketch pad on her vanity.

Nora,

I have to get home before my grandparents send out a search team. I'm sure I'll have to do a million extra chores in the morning, so I'll probably be late getting to the creek. Here's a fun thought... You should meet me at my grandparents' house and do them with me. You like picking up dog poop, right? You could finally meet Satan's Chihuahua. Tempting, I know.

2560 S. Turner Hill

I liked hanging out with you last night. You snore like a Grizzly bear and there was a puddle of drool on my shoulder when I woke up, but you didn't kick, so that's all that really matters.

Thanks for trusting me. You won't regret it.

Your true friend,

Cam

P.S. My parents have forbidden me from going by Cam because "If they had wanted me to go by Cam, they wouldn't have named me Camden." I've always liked the way you say it though. I wish I could always feel like Cam.
    P.S.S. I'll make lunch tomorrow. Fair's fair.
    P.S.S.S. I got an A in English this year and still have no idea if I'm doing the P.S. thing right.
    P.S.S.S.S. I'd rather be there with you.

She didn't budge as I left the note and our ten-dollar bill sitting on the nightstand. Thankful she didn't have a screen, I snuck out of her window. How she slept at all after what had happened to her, I had no idea.

I'd tried to play it cool and not pressure her into talking about it, but as I'd picked those splinters from her back, I'd plotted the death of a kid I'd never even met a dozen times over.

My Nora was feisty and filled to the brim with attitude and giggles, so to feel her crumbling in my arms was a rusty knife to the gut. I had not one damn clue what I was going to do about the things she'd revealed to me. Her house was falling apart around her, the stench of smoke and mold worrying me the most. Her room was nice though, and I'd double checked that the lock on her door worked, so it eased my mind to know she at least had a safe and comfortable space to sleep at night. Though, if she didn't do something about the fucking asshole who had forced himself on her in the process of leaving those marks on her, there was no guarantee she'd stay safe.

As to be expected, my grandpa was sitting on the porch when I got home just after midnight. I braced as I walked up the driveway, mentally preparing myself to witness my own murder.

But whatever hell he was about to rain down over me, Nora was worth it.

Being there for her. Holding her. Making sure she knew I'd always have her back. Totally worth it. The fact that she'd actually trusted me enough to let me into her life proved it had been the right thing—the only thing—I could have done.

Grandpa had a cigar between his fingers and a glass of lemonade at his side, his gray beard casting a shadow on his belly in the porch light. If he was smoking, it was a guarantee that Grandma was already asleep, and I couldn't decide if it was a good sign or not.

Squaring my shoulders, I stopped at the first step, rested my hand on the wooden railing, and peered up at him. "Sorry, I'm—"

"How's Nora?" he asked with a wicked grin.

Outstanding. Grandma had been running her mouth again. Now, not only was I in trouble for staying out late, but I was in trouble for staying out all night *with a girl*. Awesome.

Ignoring his question, I rambled on with a carefully crafted lie so mediocre that it had me wishing the lemonade was a beer instead. "I was at the creek and got tired from work. Then I fell asleep under the—"

"Save it, Camden. We're all just relieved a girl actually wants to spend time with you. Give me a heads-up next time you plan on knocking boots all night. Your grandma was worried sick."

I blinked up at him,stunned into silence.

On one hand, I was thoroughly insulted by the way they were all *relieved*. I mean, what the hell was that? I was thirteen, and they kept me busy with chores and stupid sports I hated with a passion. When exactly did they think I had time to find a girlfriend? Or even run a girl off trying to become her boyfriend?

But on the other hand… "Does this mean I'm not in trouble?"

"Now I didn't say all that. Your grandma doesn't like to worry. But you aren't in trouble with me."

Grandma I could handle. In addition to the dog poop, she'd make me dry dishes after dinner and play crossword puzzles with her on Sunday, but at least it wasn't manual labor.

I grinned, and he smiled right back.

"Now, when you gonna bring this Nora girl around? You've been hiding her like she's fat and ugly or something."

He continued to smile, but mine fell and not because Nora was fat or ugly. Rather, it was because this was the first time in my entire life that I realized my grandpa wasn't just stern, trying to raise his grandsons to become men. He was a total dick in general.

"Um, yeah," I muttered. "She might come by tomorrow. She's not really my girlfriend though."

"Maybe not yet, but if you're anything like your grandpa here, she'll be begging for more first thing in the morning." He clucked and shot me a wink, and then he took a huge toke off his precious stogie.

Yeah. Huge fucking dick.

Keeping the thought to myself, I bit the inside of my cheek and nodded.

He snickered and then jerked his chin at the house. "Go on, boy. Get up to bed so you can be up bright and early to help your grandma with breakfast."

I stared at him for a beat, but when I was absolutely positive this hadn't been some kind of trick before banging the gavel and grounding me for life, I raced past him, through the house, and straight to my bedroom.

RECLAIM

Grandma was indeed pissed when I woke up. I spent the morning whisking eggs—my only talent in the kitchen—and then washing dishes as she prepared a massive family breakfast that seemed overboard for just the three of us. But it made more sense when my aunt pulled into the driveway with my two asshole cousins in tow. I managed to avoid them for a solid hour by pretending to do my chores. Though the majority of the time I just hid behind the shed, thinking and worrying about Nora.

I had no idea what I was going to do to help her yet. Until I figured it out, all I wanted was to be there for her.

Yeah, okay, fine. That was a little selfish too.

Being with Nora was my favorite thing to do. It didn't matter if we were laughing and talking or just sitting in silence. Wherever she was, that was exactly where I wanted to be.

When the clock hit nine, I grabbed the weed-eater and moved to the front yard, hoping like hell she'd take me up on my offer to hang out at my grandparents' before we went to the creek together. I nearly cut my ankle off twice, squinting down the hill and hoping to catch a glimpse of her in the distance.

A huge smile split my face when she appeared, her long, brown hair catching in the breeze as she marched up the sidewalk, my note held out in front of her as she scanned the houses for the right address.

I immediately turned the weed-eater off and jogged out to wave her down. Her eyes flared wide when she saw me, pure confusion wrinkling her forehead.

"Hey, you," I said when she stopped in front of me.

Anger pooled in my gut as I took in her black turtleneck.

The weatherman had predicted triple digits for the high. She was going to melt in that thing. After last night, I knew she wasn't hiding from me, so I felt pretty confident that I could convince her to swim with me at the creek.

"You... Um, your grandparents live here?" She swallowed hard as her eyes locked on the front porch over my shoulder.

Normally, I never would have invited anyone out there to see the place. The six-bedroom mansion with its two levels of wraparound porches surrounded by acres upon acres of plush pastures was over the top. Hell, just the twenty-stall barn filled with Grandpa's precious racehorses at the edge of town was ridiculous on its own. Most people didn't realize this, but nothing—not even being the clumsy, unathletic nerd who was obsessed with books—made a kid more of a target than being labeled as the rich kid. Especially when said kid lived in a town like Clovert or Alberton where struggling to survive was the norm.

But this was Nora. We were friends. If there was ever a person in my life who wouldn't judge me, it was her. And damn if that didn't do something in my chest.

Smiling, I scratched the back of my neck. "Yeah. But don't hold it against me. This place has been in the family for—"

That was all I got out of my mouth before the front door flew open and my cousin came flying down the steps.

"What the fuck are you doing here?" he hissed.

"I live here, asshole," I snapped back. God, it was always some bullshit with him.

He ignored me completely and stopped in front of Nora, leaning into her face as he seethed, "Why are you here?"

All the blood drained from her face as she stumbled back, tripping over her own feet before falling.

RECLAIM

I lurched forward but didn't get there in time to stop her from hitting the sidewalk.

"What the hell, Josh?" I snarled, bending over to offer Nora a hand.

She didn't take it. On all fours, she scrambled away, her eyes locked on Josh, pure terror showing on her beautiful face.

"You know what will happen if you make a big deal out of this," he whispered. "You tell one single soul and I'll—"

Realization hit me. It wasn't like a light bulb going off over my head at all. It was more like being strapped into an electric chair and somebody throwing the switch.

My vision faded to black in the corners, all of my focus honing in on my cousin and one single scratch on the side of his neck.

Vile puzzle pieces began clicking together until the final image of Josh on top of Nora—*my Nora*—as splinters embedded in her back was all I could see.

I exploded, shoving him as hard as I could and swinging a fist into the side of his face. He was bigger than I was, no disputing that, but I was more evenly matched with him than I was his older brother, Jonathan. However, this would be the first time I beat the ever-living shit out of him—for no other reason than he was going to have to kill me before I would be willing to give up after what he'd done to her.

I threw punch after punch, nothing making me feel better. Not even the pain when he landed a few of his own. It wasn't until I heard her feet pounding the sidewalk as she sprinted away that I took a moment to breathe. I could have punched him until my hands fell off and it still wouldn't have helped *her*.

In that moment, Nora didn't need vengeance; she needed a friend.

When I was sure Josh wasn't getting back up, I took off after her. I could barely see her as she weaved through backyards and out to the main road. I'd never run so hard or so fast in my entire life, and as she cut through the woods just past the grocery store, I finally caught up.

"Nora, wait," I panted.

She didn't stop.

She didn't slow down.

She didn't even look back at me.

I followed her all the way up to her front porch, catching her arm just before she had the chance to go inside.

"Nora, please stop."

"Let me go!" she seethed, yanking her hand away. Tears streaked her cheeks, but make no mistake about it, she was a lion ready to strike. "You're a Caskey!" It wasn't a question. It was an accusation in every sense of the word.

I planted my hands on my hips and spoke with heaving exhales. "Not really… My… Mom was… But my dad—"

"Then you're a Caskey!" Like a shield, she crossed her arms over her chest and rounded her shoulders forward. "Oh my God. Oh my God. This isn't happening. I told a Caskey. I told a fucking Caskey."

"Stop saying I'm a Caskey. I'm not anything like them."

"But you are!" she yelled with wild eyes. "You're rich, aren't you?"

I must have looked like a fish standing there opening and closing my mouth, not a single word coming out. I wanted to say no. I wanted to yell at her that she had no idea what she was talking about and that I was nothing like either one of my stupid, psychopath cousins.

But she wasn't wrong. My family did have money, and technically yes, I did have Caskey blood running through my veins. It wasn't the same though. My mom… She was different than they were. The good kind of different.

Nora took a step toward me. "That's it, isn't it? Back in Alberton, that's why everyone hates you. All that bullshit about God giving you ten dollars after church and then showing up with dirty cut-offs and holes in your socks was all just an act." She shook her head, and while she had all the false bravado in the world showing on the outside, her voice broke as she said, "I trusted you, and just like everyone else in my life, you lied."

"You can still trust me."

"How? How, Camden?" She stabbed a finger at my chest. "We spent a whole summer together and you never once thought to tell me your uncle was the mayor?" Another stab. "Or that your grandparents were bazillionaires who owned a farm of racehorses?" Another stab. "Or…or…or…maybe that your cousins were Jonathan and Josh fucking Caskey! You knew he was the same age as Ramsey. You knew your family name would have meant something to me, so you just never mentioned it?" She pushed up onto her toes and yelled into my face, "Why?"

"Because I didn't want you to know!" The words flew from my mouth before I realized a coherent thought had been formed.

I hadn't lied to her. Not exactly. But I hadn't told her the truth, either. It had never been a conscious decision to keep the truth about my family from her. But after years of being the only rich kid in a small town, you learned to guard your secrets or risk having no one to tell them to.

Yeah, I wore my crappy clothes to the creek. My parents would have killed me if I ruined the nice stuff they'd bought me, but mainly it was because I wanted *her* to like *me*.

Nora had made it clear during her rantings the first night when I'd followed her home from the store that she didn't like rich kids. And honestly, after getting a taste of her life over the last few days, I couldn't blame her.

Money solved all problems, right?

In my experience, it made them worse.

I wasn't a normal snobby rich kid. My dad wasn't anything like Josh and Jonathan's dad. Camden Donald Cole had grown up in Alberton, sweeping the floors in the papermill. He'd worked his ass off to get a football scholarship so he could afford to go to college. He worked even harder to get his degree and then continued working his ass off until he saved up enough to buy the very same papermill. He believed in never giving up and always earning the things you wanted in life, and he was hell-bent on raising his only child with the same thought process. My parents bought me school clothes every year, but it was my responsibly to buy my own play clothes, socks, underwear, and shoes. Let me just tell you none of those things were high on my list of the ways I wanted to spend my measly allowance. But I did it to keep Dad off my back.

My parents' bank account had nothing to do with who I was, but okay, fine, I'd purposely never mentioned who my grandparents were—and thus the rest of my family.

I liked Nora. I couldn't take the chance that she wouldn't like me after she found out the truth. When she never point-blank asked who they were or where they lived, I said nothing at all. It was safer that way.

After last night, I'd thought things had changed though. She'd shown me her secrets, so I'd been dumb enough to think that maybe I could do the same.

I'd been wrong.

So. Damn. Wrong.

And that burned like the hottest knife.

"It wasn't an act," I whispered, all the fight and adrenaline ebbing from my system. "But yeah, I never told you because I wanted you to be my friend. I just wanted one person to like me for me and not judge me based on who my parents are."

"You mean, kinda like what you did to me?"

My head snapped back. "I never judged you."

"Oh, so when you started bringing me lunch and splitting the worm money with me, it had absolutely nothing to do with the time you saw my dad fighting with me and Ramsey in the front yard? Come on, Camden. You told me yesterday that you checked me for bruises when we went swimming. That's not judging me?"

"That was me being concerned." I waved a hand over her turtleneck. "Which, based on those bruises, I clearly had the right to be."

It was the wrong thing to say. I knew it the moment the words left my lips.

I just had no idea that it would cost me everything.

"You did this to me!" she roared.

I tried to dodge her words, but they hit me square in the chest, stealing my breath.

She tore the turtleneck over her head. She was already wearing her bathing suit—proof that she did, in fact, trust me enough to go swimming in the creek later, bruises and all.

Or at least she *had* trusted me when she'd gotten dressed that morning.

Now, she was a tornado spiraling out of control, and I was certain I'd never survive her wrath.

She stretched her arms out to the sides and spun in a circle. "If I had known Josh was your cousin, I never would have had anything to do with him. Because while you were gone last year, living in the Alberton mansion, I was still here. Alone. Missing you. Hating you. Desperate for even a tiny bit of the way you used to make me feel. You know, if I stop to think about it. It makes sense that I found him. He had your blue eyes and the same easy smile that made me feel safe. And I was so fucking broken I took whatever scraps of you I could get."

"Nora, I didn't leave you."

"But you did! Everyone leaves me. And everyone lies to me. And everyone *hurts* me. I can't take it anymore. Do you understand? I can't do this! I never want to see you again. *Never!*"

I was gutted—nothing but a corpse standing in front of her. Hollow and empty without the first way to fix it.

But I loved her, even if I didn't understand it yet. So I stood there, ready to fight an impossible battle. "You don't mean that. Please. Come on. Let's go to the creek and figure this out."

She drew in a shaky breath and stared me right in the eye, twin rivers streaming off her chin. "You think I'll ever be able to look at you again without thinking about what he did to me?"

I frantically shook my head. "I'm not like him. You know that."

She slanted her head, and with an eerie calm, she moved in close and dealt her final blow. "You both lied to me and used me until you got what you wanted. You're more of a Caskey than you know."

I felt her push something into my front pocket, but I was too panicked to figure out what.

"Nora, please," I begged as she spun on a toe. I didn't have much time. The door would stick, but she'd get it open. And then she'd be gone. "Jesus, stop. Please just listen to me. I would never knowingly hurt you."

She stopped at the door and looked at me over her shoulder. "Prove it."

RECLAIM

A surge of relief flooded my system. "Anything. I'll do anything."

"Then go home and leave me alone. Don't make this hurt any worse than it already does. I don't have anything left to give you, Cam."

Cam.

My stomach knotted.

All I wanted was to be her Cam. But at what cost?

My cousin had raped her. That much was clear. Did I really want her to relive that every time she saw me? She was my friend, and I cared about her on levels I couldn't yet process. It would kill me to walk away, but that was my pain. Not hers.

I was only thirteen and already sure I would bear that cross for Nora Stewart every day if I had to. I couldn't change my DNA or what Josh had done to her, but I could leave.

For her, I would do anything.

I fisted my hands at my sides to keep myself from stopping her as she opened the door. The overwhelming desire to pull her into a hug and tell her it was all going to be okay was almost more than I could take.

It hadn't even been twenty-four hours since she'd trusted me enough to sleep at my side. I could still feel her in my arms, and now, I was letting her go for what I feared would be forever.

When the door closed behind her, I reached into my pocket and found our ten-dollar bill she'd tucked inside.

Yeah. That was it.

The arrow through the heart.

Nora was done. She didn't need my address in Alberton anymore. She had no intention of ever coming back to me.

As I walked away that day, lost and heartbroken, I was clueless if I'd made the right decision by not pounding her door down. I prayed to every God in the universe that she was just mad and would eventually come around.

I waited at the creek for a week. Day and night. My heart in my throat. Staring at the road and waiting for her to appear.

She never did.

Not for two long years.

FOURTEEN

Nora

THE BEST PART ABOUT EXPECTING THE ENTIRE WORLD TO fail you is that, when it finally happens, you at least have the peace of mind from knowing you were right.

Life didn't stop because Camden Cole was gone.

Nor did it stop because Josh Caskey was free without a care in the world.

My bruises eventually faded—at least the ones on the outside.

Inside, I was shattered, rotting, and severed from my only lifeline: Camden.

I woke up every morning and performed the herculean task of putting one foot in front of the other, and every afternoon, I'd collapse into bed, exhausted, and with aching cheeks from faking happiness I never truly felt.

Everything was a show, from the smiles and laughs to being social and hanging out with Ramsey and Thea. I was stuck in the darkness as the world spun beneath my feet, desperately wishing for a way out, all the while knowing I'd never find one. I never went back to the creek, but sometimes, I'd lie in bed late at night, the window open, crickets chirping and fireflies flashing, and pretend.

Camden was always there in those daydreams. His arms around me. Holding me like he had our last night together in my bedroom. A torturous flashback of the first and only time I'd felt truly safe.

I blew out candles on my thirteenth birthday and opened the few Christmas presents Ramsey and I exchanged every year. Thea and I became closer. She asked the most questions when things seemed off, but as long as she wasn't suspicious, neither was my brother.

Time passed, but the nearly constant ache inside me never did.

I ran into Josh around town. Most of the time, he ignored me, but on occasion, he'd try to talk to me. Even if it was only to lean in close and whisper how many times he'd watched the video of us together—essentially prying my ribs open and ripping my heart out all over again.

I wanted to disappear, and to be honest, I thought about it more times than I would ever admit. At night, when I wasn't pretending to be with Camden at the creek again, I'd imagine the blissful hollowness of death. The quiet. The absence of feelings. The constant stress vibrating in my veins finally stilling and my mind falling into nothingness.

I always woke up the next morning.

Same hollow chest.

Same fake smile.

Same despair.

My fourteenth birthday came and went, as did my first day of high school. Passing Josh in the hallway was something I had to get used to. By that point, I was so numb that I didn't have much left for him to hurt anymore. He still tried though and slipped a picture of us kissing with his hand on my breast into my locker. I spent the rest of the afternoon, throwing up and contemplating how long Ramsey would blame himself if I finally found the courage to end it all.

RECLAIM

In the end, I chickened out, but I would spend years regretting my decision not to do it when I had the chance.

One choice and I destroyed the lives of the three people I loved most in the world.

And one monster.

I startled awake at the groan of my window as it suddenly opened. Still foggy with sleep, I struggled to focus on the dark figure outside. My pulse spiked, and just before a scream tore from my throat, I made out my brother's broad shoulders as he climbed through.

Clutching my chest, I sat up in bed and hissed, "What are you doing?"

"My window was locked," he replied.

It was his birthday, and minus a brawl with my dad, he and Thea had been out at their tree all night. But as he stomped through my room to his across the hall, a shit-ton of pissed-off energy filling his wake, the hairs on my neck stood on end.

Throwing the covers back, I climbed out of bed and followed after him. "Are you okay?"

"Not even close," he muttered, swiping his car keys off his dresser.

Ramsey had grown up a lot in the last few years. He was over six feet tall and, at seventeen, had filled out into a man. He'd gotten a job and bought a clunker, where he and Thea spent the majority of their time making out in the back seat. He was still my brother though, so whenever I needed to go somewhere, I always had a ride.

"What happened?" I asked. "Are you still pissed at Dad?"

"Fuck Dad," he snarled out, marching right back through my room to the window.

I caught his arm, pulling him to an abrupt stop. "What is going on with you? Where's Thea?"

His face turned a shade of white that almost glowed in the darkness, but he didn't answer me before ripping his arm away.

Shit. Shit. Shit. This was bad. Ramsey was a live wire most of the time. He'd react to almost everything, but it was rare that he'd ignite into a wildfire. Though, as I watched him climb out my window, that was exactly what I feared would happen. He was my brother and he watched my back; it was only fair I returned the favor.

"Ramsey," I hissed, following him out.

He flung his car door open and folded inside without another word spoken, so I sprinted around the hood and slid into the passenger seat.

"Get out," he barked, stabbing his key at the ignition.

"No. There's something going on, and if you're not going to tell me what, I'm going with you."

The engine sputtered, not catching, so he gave it another try. "You cannot come with me tonight, Nora."

"Too bad. Looks like I already am." I grinned, buckling my seat belt.

"Suit yourself," he mumbled, jerking the car into reverse once it had finally rumbled to life.

I stared at the side of my brother's face as he backed out of the driveway. His jaw was hard, but there was pain I couldn't figure out crinkling the corners of his eyes.

He'd tell me eventually though. I just needed to give him time to process it himself.

We hadn't made it more than a few miles when he rumbled, "Where are the parties at tonight?"

"Uh," I drawled. "Since when are you up for partying?" My eyes nearly bulged from their sockets when the only excuse I could conjure up for his weird mood popped into my head. "Oh my God, did Thea break up with you?"

RECLAIM

"No." He winced and white-knuckled the steering wheel. "Just tell me where the hell everyone is hanging out tonight."

I motioned a hand over my basketball shorts and oversized T-shirt. "I'm hardly dressed for a party."

"Nora!" he boomed, making me jump. "Tell me where."

"Jesus, cranky much?" I mumbled. "Fine. Avery Johnson invited all the seniors over for a field party, but I heard a lot of the juniors were planning to crash."

He slowed at the stop sign and hung a hard right onto the long dirt road that led to the Johnsons' farm.

"You gonna tell me what's going on now, or should I start guessing?" I smarted.

He shook his head and stepped on the accelerator. His car sounded like it was going to fall apart each time we hit a bump.

I braced one hand on the dash and the other on the handle above my head. "Right. Yeah. This totally seems like nothing. We're just out for a late-night drive, huh?"

"Shut up," he clipped.

Cars lined both sides of the dirt road, and Ramsey slowed, squinting and searching each one. He flipped on the brights, but they were useless against the thick cloud of dust.

What the hell was he doing?

"Watch out!" I screamed when, out of nowhere, a shadowy figure appeared in the middle of the road.

Ramsey skidded to a stop inches away from him. I should have been relieved, but the pair of blue eyes that haunted my nightmares appeared in the headlights on the other side of the windshield.

Bile burned a path up my throat, and I peered at my brother, finding a sinister smile pulling at his lips.

"Stay in the car," he ordered.

Panic hit me so hard my head swirled. "Oh, God, why? What are you doing?"

He got out without replying.

Shit. He knew. He'd found out about what Josh had done to me. He was going to kill him. That was the look on his face. Pain. Rage. Disgust. All the things that lived and breathed inside me daily.

I scrambled into the driver's seat and frantically rolled the window down. "Ramsey!"

He never looked back.

Using his hand to block the headlights, Josh swayed on his feet and slurred, "What the hell, dude? You almost hit me."

Ramsey gave him no warning as he wrapped his hand in the front of his shirt and then buried his fist in Josh's face.

"You motherfucker!" Ramsey thundered, hitting him again. "You think it's okay to fucking touch a girl?"

Oh, God.

Oh, God.

Oh, God.

He landed a crushing punch to his eye and Josh stumbled back, but Ramsey yanked him forward again before roaring in his face, "My girl!"

Josh shoved at his shoulders. "Get the fuck off me. I didn't do shit to Thea that she didn't want."

My heart stopped.

Thea?

No. Oh, no. He'd done it to Thea. This wasn't about me.

Suddenly, the memories of Josh's hands on my body weren't the deepest gash in my soul anymore.

Thea—my sister.

Thea—the only friend.

RECLAIM

Thea—the love of my brother's life.

And by not telling anyone about Josh, I'd all but held her down and let him do it.

Holding him by the throat, Ramsey continued to hit him, and I felt each and every pulverizing blow as if they had landed in my gut instead.

"Stay the fuck away from her," Ramsey finally said, throwing him to the ground and landing a swift kick to his midsection.

Josh rolled to the side, coughing and spitting out blood, and let out a laugh. "If it's any consolation, she wasn't nearly as good as your sister."

All rational thought abandoned me. A guttural scream tore from my throat, so loud it felt like razor blades exiting my body. Years of anger and frustration all tied up in one ear-piercing note. I slapped my hands over my mouth, one stacked over the other as if it could somehow silence the cry, but it just kept coming.

All the drawers in my head blasted open at once, a war of emotions battling to be the first to escape.

Choices. Everyone makes them.

And when my brother stumbled back, shock contorting his face, I made mine.

Throwing the car into drive, I slammed on the accelerator and ended Josh Caskey's reign of abuse once and for all.

FIFTEEN

Nora

RAMSEY NEVER CAME HOME THAT NIGHT.

I waited until the sun broke the horizon before waking my dad up. He'd never helped me before, but if Ramsey had been arrested, surely he'd do something. I didn't get the chance to tell him any of the details before he mumbled some variation of, "Ramsey deserves whatever he gets," before passing back out.

The only other person I could think of was Thea, but when I looked out the window, two police cars were parked in her driveway.

Peeking through the blinds while my heart raced a million miles a minute, I waited for them to leave. When they finally came out, Thea was wrapped in a blanket, tears rolling down her face as they escorted her to her dad's car. Together, they all drove away, leaving me more terrified and alone than ever.

I had no idea what to do. Ramsey had assured me that it would be okay, but nothing felt okay.

Josh was dead.

It was my fault.

And my brother was in police custody.

I spent the afternoon alternating between pacing and dry-heaving, like I was in a gas chamber, suffocating on poison and waiting to die.

RECLAIM

My worst fear was confirmed that afternoon when the channel six news broke the story of Josh's death, airing it alongside Ramsey's mug shot with a headline reading *Murderer Confessed*.

Utterly dumbfounded, I stared at my brother's picture. He'd confessed? To what? He hadn't done anything except beat Josh up. However, since the cops hadn't stormed our house and arrested me yet, I had a sudden stomach-churning fear that Ramsey's confession wasn't going to match mine at all.

The reporter was still talking when I sprinted from the house.

My brother was my hero.

He had kissed every skinned knee I'd ever gotten.

He'd held me every night after our mom left.

And he went out of his way to protect me from our father's rage.

In all the ways that mattered, I was alive because of Ramsey.

Letting him take the fall for a crime I'd committed wasn't going to be the way I repaid him.

Arms swinging, legs pumping, pulse thundering in my ears, I sprinted to the police station. I couldn't breathe when I got there, but in my desperation, air was inconsequential.

"I did it!" I confessed, physically dropping to my knees in front of a young, uniformed officer. I wasn't begging; I just no longer had the ability to stand. "My brother didn't do it. It was me. I did it. I killed Josh Caskey."

The cop stared at me with a bored glare. "Girl, get up off your knees. He already signed the confession."

I folded my hands in prayer. "Arrest me. Arrest me please. I'm begging you. Just don't take him from me."

Grabbing my arm, the slender officer helped me to my feet.

"Okay, okay. Relax. You want to make a statement about what you *think* happened to Josh?"

I wanted to make *every* statement about what I *knew* happened to Josh as long as it led to Ramsey being released. "Yes. I just need someone to listen. It's not what it looks like."

Clovert was small, the police force even smaller, but there was another officer nearby who sauntered over. The small silver tag on his uniform read Perry. "Nelson," he said to the young officer, "we don't need a damn statement. We've got a motive, a confession, and charges filed. Don't you dare put more paperwork on my desk about this."

Panic built. "You have the wrong person. Ramsey didn't do this!"

Officer Perry, with his yellow stained teeth and gray hair, cocked his head. "And you expect me to believe *you* did? I was the first officer on the scene. We had a dead body and your brother's car covered in blood. Where the hell were you?"

"I ran home. I…" My stomach rolled at the memory. "I…" Oh, God, where were the words? I couldn't tell them Ramsey told me to leave. It would make him an accessory or something. No. If I was going to get him out of there, this had to be all about me even when it seemed irrational. "I did it. I swear. You have to believe me."

He shook his head and rolled his eyes. "Get outta here, girl. Go home. Your brother's getting locked up for a long time. Don't tie yourself to a sinking ship."

"He's all I have left! You don't understand. Josh did things to me. And to Thea. And… And…" My breathing stammered.

There was a long silence while I tried to catch my breath, and the two men exchanged pointed glances. Officer Perry shook his head while Officer Nelson looked down at his shoes and scratched the back of his neck.

RECLAIM

Officer Perry spoke first. "All right now. That's enough of that." He rested a hand on the backstrap of the gun on his hip. "If you quiet down and stop all this nonsense, I *might* be able to let you see him for a few minutes before transport gets here to take him over to the county jail."

My back shot straight, and my lungs filled with what felt like my first ever breath of air.

He was still there. Ramsey was still there.

He'd know what to do.

He *always* knew what to do.

"Okay. Okay. I can do that." Frantic, I started wiping away my tears and willed the shaking in my hands to still. I smoothed my T-shirt down and tried to hide the evidence of how I was tearing apart at the seams.

The men exchanged mumbles I couldn't quite make out, and then young Officer Nelson led me down an empty hall, florescent lights humming above us.

"You got about five minutes, so make it quick," he said, swinging a door open.

He might have said something else, but my eyes, mind, and heart homed in on my brother sitting on a metal chair, both of his hands cuffed to the table.

"Nora," he breathed, shooting to his feet, his red-rimmed eyes obliterating the tiny fraction of what was left of me.

"Oh, Ramsey!" I cried, racing over to him and throwing my arms around his shoulders. The second his warmth hit me, I dissolved into a puddle of hysterics. "What's going on?"

When he was unable to return my embrace, he tilted his head to rest on top of mine. "Shhhh, it's okay. I'm good. Everything's fine. Just breathe."

"Please tell me you didn't really confess."

His whole body turned to stone. "Nora, look at me."

Never releasing him, I tilted my head back.

Tears welled in his eyes, but it was Ramsey, so he smiled through the pain. "I did because I'm guilty."

"No, you aren't," I hissed.

"I *am*. That's the way it has to be from now on. I killed Josh. End of story."

I took a step away and stared at him incredulously. "What the hell are you talking about?"

"I love you. You know that, right? I don't say it enough, but I have loved you since the day you were born. And I know you're fourteen now and think you're all grown up, but you'll always be my baby sister. It's my job to protect you. I get it, I failed, and I will live with it for the rest of my life. But I can fix it."

"You going to jail for something you didn't do is not going to fix anything. That's creating a whole new set of problems. I was the one behind the wheel of that car. I hit the gas pedal. I made the choice. This is my problem. Not yours."

He sighed. "It'll always be my problem because I wasn't there when he did those things to you." His voice cracked, but he cleared it and kept going. "I wasn't there for Thea, either. But I can be here now. The Caskeys are powerful people. They will never rest until one or both of us are behind bars. So let it be me." His long lashes fluttered closed with a mixture of regret and agony. "I saw Thea tonight. What he did to her. The marks he left." He let out a low growl, shaking his head as if he could somehow erase the memory. "And now, knowing he did that to you too… Jesus, Nora. You've been through enough."

He was right. I'd been through hell, but it didn't mean I was going to allow him to take my place in the flames.

"I won't let you do this."

RECLAIM

"I'm not asking for permission. It's already done, but you have to keep your mouth shut."

"I don't have to do anything!" I yelled.

With his hands chained to the table, he couldn't stand at his full height, but his large body swelled until it felt as though he were filling the room. "I won't survive, Nora. If you push this and we both end up in prison and something happens to you, I will not survive it. I promise you that. I just need to know you're okay. We can visit and write letters. Thea's going to need you too."

"Oh, God, Thea," I croaked, crossing my arms over my chest to ward off the sudden chill. She would never be whole without Ramsey. "She's going to hate me for this."

"Which is why you can never tell her."

"What?"

His voice became sharp with urgency. "You can't tell anyone. Do you hear me? Not the cops. Not Dad. Not Thea. *No one.* Thea will look after you," he choked and cut his eyes over my shoulder before he was able to finish. "And I know you'll take good care of her for me too."

"But—"

His gaze collided with mine. "For me, Nora. I can take care of the rest, but I need you to do this for me."

"They're going to put you in jail though. Do you understand?"

"I know. What is it you always say about choices? Everyone makes them? Well, this is my choice. And if comes down to choosing between you and freedom, I'll choose you every single time."

How did those words feel good and hurt so fucking much at the same time?

My head spun as though I were trapped in a maze that kept changing. "I can't."

"You can and you will."

The door suddenly swung open. Officer Perry and his tobacco-yellowed teeth appeared on the other side. "Time's up."

"No," I breathed, the mere thought of leaving him there igniting me into a frenzy. "No. No. No. Just a little longer."

"Sorry, kid." He grabbed my arm and gave me a tug toward the door.

My fight-or-flight response exploded—and it was all fight. "Get your fucking hands off me!"

His lips thinned and his jaw muscles flexed, making his features nearly murderous. "You seem like a sweet kid, so I put my ass on the line and did you a solid by letting you talk to him. Now, I'm not playing games anymore. You've got two seconds to get your ass out of here before you end up in a cell beside him."

"Screw you," I spat as if this were his fault and not my own.

"Nora," Ramsey seethed, catching my attention. "You have to go, but promise me first."

The cop grabbed me again, dragging me toward the door, and I dug my heels in, desperate to stay with my brother even if it meant living inside that tiny room for the rest of my life. "Please don't make me do this. Please, Ramsey! This isn't your fault."

"Promise me," he ordered, emotion pooling in his eyes. "I need to hear it. I need to know you two will be okay." Tears rolled down his cheeks and they branded my soul in ways time would never heal.

I'd spend every single day he was behind bars rotting away, miserable, the seed of guilt growing and winding until its vines eventually choked the life out of me, but if my promise was what he needed, no matter how much I hated it, I would have given it to him a million times over.

"Okay. I promise!" I choked out between sobs.

RECLAIM

"Swear?" he asked, opening his hand flat on the table and lifting his pinky in the air.

Looking back on that day, it would seem stupid. Lives had been lost, taken, and altered forever and he was asking for a pinky promise. But we were kids who had relied on each other for everything. A pinky promise was the most solemn, unbreakable swear we had.

I dove forward, breaking the officer's hold on me, and hooked my pinky with his. The second our fingers touched, Ramsey's entire body sagged with relief so palpable it stabbed me in the heart.

The cop caught my arm again, cussing and making threats as he yanked me away, but through it all, I held my brother's stare, making silent promises I had no idea if I could keep.

"I love you!" he called out. "It's going to be okay."

It wasn't.

I was confused and beyond devastated, but I knew to the marrow of my bones it was never going to be okay again.

"I love you too."

And then he smiled because he was Ramsey—facing life in prison for a crime he didn't commit and smiling because he knew his girls would hopefully be okay.

I had no idea what I was going to do with my life without him. Ramsey leaving, even if it wasn't necessarily his choice, had never even crossed my mind.

Not long after that day, the blistering grief only raged hotter when he signed a plea deal downgrading his charges to manslaughter, however sentencing him to sixteen years in prison.

SIXTEEN

Camden

I'd never forget the wails of my aunt and uncle as Josh was lowered into the ground. It wasn't because they affected me with such a profound sadness that the emotion would forever be ingrained into my subconscious.

Rather, I'd never be able to forget because it was the first time I realized how sweet vengeance could feel.

The day I realized Nora wasn't coming back to the creek, I called my parents and asked them to come pick me up. They refused, but I was belligerent enough on the phone for them to at least drive the three hours so they could ground me.

When they arrived, I pulled them both into my room and carefully tiptoed around what Josh had done without specifically naming Nora. She'd trusted me with her secrets, and I'd never betray her. But somebody had to know. Josh couldn't get away with what he'd done while my Nora suffered in silence.

Not surprisingly, my tiptoeing wasn't nearly good enough, because Nora's name came up almost immediately. She was, after all, the only girl I knew.

My mom hugged me and said it was okay to be jealous of my cousin.

My dad lectured me on beating up a family member over a girl—then winked.

RECLAIM

I did enough yelling for my grandparents to get involved.

My grandpa said something about boys being boys.

And my grandma asked me who else I'd told.

My aunt and uncle showed up about an hour later, and after a hushed conversation, they berated me for making up such a heinous story about their sweet little angel.

While Dad loaded up my bags in the car that night, my mom assured me they would take care of everything.

And for some asinine reason, I thought it included Josh. I should have known better. The Caskeys were infamous in Clovert. One black sheep and the entire name would be tarnished.

They never made it more clear than when Josh was killed.

They knew about Thea Hull. They saw the pictures from the hospital. They heard what she'd told the investigators. For fuck's sake, they had actual DNA evidence of what the piece of shit had done to her. And instead of admitting any possible culpability on Josh's behalf, they asked their attorney to rush through a plea deal for Ramsey so they could avoid the truth coming out during a trial.

You know, priorities and all.

So, no. After I'd warned them about how Josh was a monster and they did not do one fucking thing about it, short of sweeping it under the rug, the only remorse I felt as I stood at Josh's funeral, listening to my family's cries, was that I hadn't put him in a grave two years earlier when I'd found out what he'd done to Nora.

After the funeral, as over half the town congregated at my aunt and uncle's house, I couldn't stand being in the same room with those people for a minute longer. So I took off for the only place I'd find any peace. I'd spent entire days out at the Leonards' creek in the week I'd been back to Clovert. I'd long since given up on seeing Nora there, but I hadn't gathered the courage to go to her house, either. If being a Caskey had hurt her a few years earlier, it would have slayed her now.

Selfishly, I wanted to see her, to check on her, to help her, but not if it meant breaking her again.

I trudged through the thick grass on my way back to the creek. My church shoes were getting muddy, but I didn't give one shit what either of my parents would think about it.

I'd just hit the dirt beach when I caught sight of her long, brown hair. My heart stopped and both lungs seized. I couldn't see her face, but her slumped shoulders and the soft sound of her cries didn't give me hope for how she was holding up. She was there though, and that alone made it the most beautiful sight in the world.

Sucking in a deep breath, I shoved my hands into my pockets and walked over to her.

She jumped when I sat beside her on the rock. Nerves rolled in my stomach, but I stuck with the familiar.

"Catch anything good?"

"Shit," she croaked. Turning her head away, she hurriedly wiped her cheeks, but there was no hiding her puffy eyes. "What are you doing here? I thought you'd be at the funeral."

I bumped her with my shoulder. "Is it wrong if I'm just happy you were thinking about me at all?"

"Considering my brother is in jail for killing your cousin, I'd say so." She stood up and dusted off the back of her jeans, ready to bolt.

"Nora, come on. Don't go. Just talk to me."

"About what?" She turned around and faced me, crossing her arms over her chest.

Holy shit, I'd thought Nora was all grown up the last time I'd seen her, but now... Jesus, she had to have been a half a foot taller and looked more like a full-fledged woman than the little girl I'd once known. Luckily, I'd done a little growing of my own, so when I stood up and walked over to her, I still had her by a head and shoulders.

"You can talk about anything with me."

"Mmm," she hummed, bringing a finger up to tap her bottom lip. "Okay, let's see, where to start? Ramsey's gone. Thea is so devastated she hasn't left her room. I haven't slept in a week. My house had been egged, the few windows we had left were broken out with firecrackers or bricks, and just last night, our grass was set on fire."

"What the hell?" I breathed.

"Oh, it gets better. I sometimes turn on the TV. You know, to try to drown out the sound of people driving past our house and screaming that we should all be in jail only to stop in front of Thea's house and scream what a fucking whore she is. But when I turn on the TV, all I see is some member of *your family* crying and holding up a picture of a kid who raped me while they preach about what an amazing person he was."

"Fuck," I mumbled, reaching out and resting a hand on her hip in a lame attempt to pull her into a hug, as if it could possibly help.

She immediately backed away but kept talking. "And the worst part is, this shit isn't even limited to *your* family. Just yesterday, my own father gave an interview to the news detailing all of Ramsey's *violent tendencies* and how he'd been expecting him to do something like this for years." She finished on a boom. "His own son!" She shook her head and drew in a shaky inhale. "So, sure, let's talk. Which part would you like to discuss first?"

I once again moved in close, stopping only an inch away. "Whatever part I can help with."

"Help?" She laughed without humor. "You should hate me, Camden."

"What in the world do I have to hate you for? Because my cousin was a psychopath? Because my family is delusional? Because your dad is a piece of shit who never deserved to be called Dad in the first place? What part of that has anything to do with *you*?"

"All of it!" she yelled.

"None of it!" I shouted right back. I hated raising my voice at her, but nothing else was getting through. "God, Nora. This isn't your fault. And I am so damn sorry people are taking this out on you, but they are clueless idiots who have nothing better to do. You have to remember *you* weren't the one who killed Josh. You didn't—"

I had a whole speech prepared in my head that may or may not have ended with me shaking sense into her if need be, but it died on my tongue when she jerked so hard it was as if she'd been shot. All the color drained from her face as she stared through me.

A sick sense of unease took root in my stomach, and I glared back at her. She blinked too many times for it to have been natural. She looked like a robot attempting to fit into society. Blink. Sway. Breathe. But the Nora I knew was lost in her memories.

I was suddenly terrified of what memories those might be.

"Nora," I prompted, catching her hand. I gave her a tug and she stumbled into me.

Her face collided with my chest, and while her arms hung at her sides, she pressed her body close. "I can't talk about this."

Oh, fuck.

Fuck, fuck, fuck, there was a *this* for her to talk about? I waffled for a minute, simultaneously wanting to know everything and nothing at all because denial was easier.

But it was Nora. She lived a life of secrets, but there was no way she could keep something like this inside without it festering into an infection that would eventually devour her.

Hooking one arm around her hips, I held her tight and glided my other hand into the back of her hair, tucking her face against my chest. "You can talk to me. You can tell me anything."

"Not this," she croaked.

"What if I tell you a secret first? Tit for tat?"

She shook her head, her tears soaking my shirt. Every single one of them felt like acid.

"All right, well, I'm gonna try anyway. So, if you feel like talking when I'm done, that'd be cool." I dipped low, put my lips to her ear, and whispered, "And there's no making fun of me for this. Got it?"

She didn't reply, but she shifted deeper into my hold and I took what felt like the risk of a lifetime.

"I met this girl a few summers back. Oh my God, Nora. She was incredible. She had these big, brown eyes and the cutest freckles across her nose. She would scream if a cricket so much as looked in her direction, but I'll tell you what. That girl was the bravest person I've ever met. And I would know, she saved me from quite a few rabid frogs that summer."

She half laughed, half cried, so I assumed I was doing something right and kept going.

"It sucked because I'm pretty sure she hated me at first, but I grew on her after a while. I knew she had it rough at home, but whenever she saw me, she'd get this huge smile that didn't just make me feel like I existed in the world. It made me feel like I existed for her."

Snaking her arms around my hips, she finally returned my embrace. "Oh, Cam."

Cam. God, I'd missed her calling me that. It was the obvious abbreviation for my name, but there was something magical about those three letters rolling from her tongue.

I closed my eyes, allowing the sense of belonging I only felt with Nora to envelop me.

Clearing my throat, I kept going. "But then I was a dumbass who got in trouble and had to leave. She hated me when I got back, but she had no idea how I'd spent the whole year loving her."

Her fingernails dug into my back as she clung to me. "Don't say that."

"What do you want me to say then? You want lies? Fine, I haven't thought about you every day over the last few years. Every time I've been in town, I haven't stood in the woods by your house, waiting for you to come outside just so I could see you. I haven't been carrying a ten-dollar bill in my wallet for two years now, hoping like hell you memorized my address. And I absolutely did not sit on my front porch every Saturday, waiting for the girl in the tie-dyed tank tops to show up and tell me she loved me too."

"Stop," she pleaded, but the words had been set free. There was no calling them back now.

"I'm a Caskey, and I wasn't honest about that from the start, and I know you can't look at me without thinking—"

That was all I got out because her head popped up and her lips collided with mine almost painfully. The tears from her cheeks spread to my face as she opened her mouth, her tongue finding mine, wild and consuming.

It was too many years in the making.

RECLAIM

Too much time apart.

Too much heartache and desperation all poured into one frenzied kiss.

I palmed the back of her head and took it deeper, searing need trumping any kind of nerves or insecurity that could have accompanied our first kiss.

She moaned into my mouth and moved her arms up to encircle my neck, holding me so close I almost convinced myself she'd never let go.

But that wouldn't have been my Nora. It seemed her superpower was the ability to slip through my fingers.

All at once, she released me and backed away. Panting and breathless, I watched a mask slip over her beautiful face. She stood up straight and squared her shoulders, but the trembling of her bruised lips gave her away.

"I did it. I was the one who killed Josh."

My heart stopped; maybe time did too. I had known that something was off, but there was no preparing for a bomb like that. A dozen questions hung on my tongue, confusion swirled, and my mind struggled to keep up.

And then there was Nora, standing only a few feet away, staring at me—defiant yet still vulnerable—waiting for my reaction.

On the inside, I was devastated. Not because I was mad or angry, but rather, after everything she'd been through now, she had to live with this on her conscience too.

On the outside, I showed her nothing. "Okay."

"I don't feel bad about it, Camden." She lifted her hand to cover her heart. "I can barely breathe knowing that Ramsey's in prison, but that is the only regret I have. So, yeah. That's me. Still love me now?"

It required exactly no thought for me to answer. "Yeah. I do."

She winced, and a cry bubbled from her throat. "Well, you shouldn't." Holding my gaze, she backed away. "I love you too, Cam. I love you enough to know you should love somebody better than me." She touched her lips, but it was the only goodbye I got from Nora Stewart.

"Nora!" I yelled as she took off running—and not into my arms where she should have always been. Deflated and lost, I watched her go.

I could have chased her to the ends of the Earth, but it would have done me no good.

She wasn't mine to catch.

Yet.

Before heading back to my grandparents', I swung past her house. Her dad's truck was out front, so I crawled in through her bedroom window and left the ten-dollar bill on her nightstand. At least I could sleep at night knowing she could always find her way back to me.

Just before I climbed back out, my gaze froze on a framed picture of her with Thea and Ramsey. Thea was on one side, laughing, and her brother was in the middle, his shaggy, brown hair hanging over his forehead, a huge grin splitting his mouth. It was Nora on the other side of him that stole my breath though. She didn't look much different than she did now, so it must have been taken in the last year or so. Which meant it was after Josh had…

But she was smiling—a real, genuine Nora Stewart masterpiece. The world had beaten her down, but I found immeasurable comfort knowing she was still able to smile—at least she could with the right people.

And with that, I added one last stop to my trip before I went home.

Luckily for me, it was only two doors down.

SEVENTEEN

Nora

One of my last memories of my mother was when she took Ramsey and me out on a pond in a tiny boat she'd found on the side of the road. It was my sixth birthday, and we were flat broke, but she wanted to do something special. The only problem was, when we got out into the middle of the pond, we realized the boat was only being kept afloat by a piece of failing duct tape across the bottom.

When water started rushing in and panic overtook us all, my mom and Ramsey frantically tried to plug the hole, while I sat there watching in horror.

It was the craziest thing. We all knew how to swim—Ramsey better than me, but I could doggy paddle back to solid ground without issue.

But we were in a boat.

And it was sinking.

So we stayed, desperately trying to fix the impossible.

After Ramsey went to prison, that was how I lived my life—in a sinking boat of guilt, panic, and overwhelming grief. I could easily escape it if I just told the truth, but I sat there, going through the motions of bailing myself out, all the while praying the rising water would eventually overtake me.

And it wasn't just me going down in that sinking ship anymore.

Ramsey had been right; Thea did take care of me. Within a matter of weeks of my brother's arrest and subsequent sentencing, Thea and her dad, Joe Hull, officially moved me in with them. Joe was amazing, kind, and soft spoken—nothing like the man I'd grown up with. My dad took off shortly after, and for once in my life, I had a safe and stable home.

One where I was forced to listen to my best friend cry herself to sleep every night because my brother was in prison—for something I'd done.

The three of us had family dinner together every night. We did homework together, laughed, and cried. Each week, Joe drove us to multiple therapy appointments, waiting outside in the car when he wasn't in a session himself. I couldn't tell a shrink the whole truth, so I did a lot of avoiding, pretending, and drowning. The lies were worse than not talking about it at all.

One breath at a time, I kept going.

Each year on the anniversary of Josh's death, his brother, Jonathan, would host a stupid fundraiser for his anti-bullying charity. For a week, the whole town would wear green—a nod to Josh's St. Patrick's Day birthday—and the local newspaper would write a completely biased, utterly trash article about the Caskeys' devastating loss.

Thea was a beast with how she handled herself and her healing process. During the celebration of Josh's life, she always found ways to keep it real. Once, she took out an entire billboard and covered it in pictures of the bruises Josh had left on her. It read in three-foot-tall letters: *The Real Josh Caskey*.

I, on the other hand, had never been brave enough to talk about what Josh had done to me.

Well, at least not with anyone other than Camden.

RECLAIM

Camden knew all my truths. He became the safe drawer in my head where I could go to feel free of the secrets and lies.

I'd lie in bed at night, tracing his address in Alberton on the back of our ten-dollar bill, playing out hundreds of scenarios where I got to see him again.

His family wanted to burn me at the stake because I was related to Ramsey, but Camden was such a good guy he probably would have greeted me with a smile and a hug.

That would have been all about me though. The comfort *I* needed. The sense of belonging *I* felt when we were together. The warmth only he could provide *me*.

I was a shell of a girl who had absolutely nothing to offer *him*—short of maybe shame and heartbreak.

So I stayed away—even when, deep down, I needed him the most.

As the years passed, I wasn't delusional enough to imagine he was thinking about me. In a way, it made me smile, the idea that he'd moved on and hopefully found a girlfriend who could be who he deserved. After all, we were kids when he'd told me he loved me. Even if I still held on to that moment at the creek like a life raft when I was too exhausted to swim.

Every chance I got, I went to visit Ramsey in prison. He was withering away in that place, and it didn't help that he'd decided the only way to keep Thea from wasting her life on him was to let her go too. It was insane. She loved him. He loved her. And they couldn't be together.

It felt like the Stewart curse.

Growing up was hard no matter the circumstances.

But for a girl like me, who had lived through hell and still carried the flames scorching me with every breath I took, the idea of a future bearing the never-ending agony was infinitely harder.

Not long after I graduated high school, the weight of my guilt became more than I could handle.

It took four years of self-loathing, but I finally convinced myself the world would be a better place without me.

Joe would no longer have to spend his time and money on a kid who never should have been his responsibility to begin with.

If I were dead, maybe Ramsey could tell the truth and have his sentence overturned.

Thea could get her soul mate back and start the life they were always meant to have before I'd stolen it from them.

And Camden, well… If there were even the tiniest part of him that still cared about me, I could free him too.

Honestly, swallowing that bottle of pills was an act of mercy.

Choices. Everyone makes them.

Luckily for me, they weren't always black and white.

Truth or lie.

Live or die.

Consequences come in all colors.

And this one came in a life-altering shade of Camden Cole blue.

The bright lights nearly blinded me as my lids fluttered open. Disoriented, I struggled to pinpoint where I was and why it felt like I'd been hit by a train.

"Hey, hey, relax. I'm right here," Joe whispered, his hand slipping into mine.

Everything came back in a rush of snapshots. Joe busting down the bathroom door. The paramedics showing up. Doctors and nurses surrounding me and barking out orders. Boulder after boulder landed on my shoulders and crushed me into the bed.

"Oh, God," I croaked, rolling to the side.

I'd survived. How? I had no idea. Thea was traveling—her favorite distraction—and Joe had been at work.

But the all-too-familiar agony in my chest didn't lie.

Joe leaned over my hospital bed and hugged me, his voice husky and filled with emotion as he rumbled, "Jesus, Nora, you scared the hell out of me."

Another boulder I wasn't strong enough to carry crashed down on top of me. "I'm sorry."

"Don't apologize." He brought our joined hands to his mouth. "Just promise me you'll never do that again."

I couldn't make that promise, but I was already standing on a mountain of lies. One more couldn't hurt. "I promise."

He never let go of my hand as I stared up at the ceiling, trying to harness the power to disappear, while nurses came into the room to poke and prod me, no doubt passing judgment too.

I was Nora Stewart. Judgment was nothing new.

When the room got quiet again, Joe gave my hand a squeeze and offered me a weak smile. "I'm going to run and grab a coffee and let you two talk for a while."

My brows furrowed. "You *two?*"

He jerked his chin to the foot of my bed, and I sat up a fraction to follow his gaze.

And there he was, like a fever dream: Camden Cole sitting in a chair with his elbows on his knees, his fingers steepled in front of his mouth, his piercing, blue eyes locked on mine with a burning intensity that seared me to the core.

However, it was the red rim of his eyes that shattered what little was left of me.

"Wh-what are you doing here?" I stammered.

"Currently?" he asked from behind his hands. "Losing my Goddamn mind with worry."

"You good?" Joe asked me.

I never tore my eyes off Camden as I nodded.

The door quietly clicked behind him as he left us alone.

Camden used his hands to scrub his chin, and if I'd been capable of it, I would have laughed because that scrawny nerd from the creek now had a five-o'clock shadow and muscles that showed beneath his gray, two-tone Henley.

He let out a groan and suddenly stood up, like *all the way up*. Jesus, did he ever stop growing?

He walked to the side of my bed and peered down at me, a storm raging in his eyes. "Scoot."

I blinked. "Um, where? This bed is tiny."

"Nora, I just spent eighteen hours jumping from standby flight to standby flight all the way from New York, terrified you might die. I don't care if we have to share a postage stamp. I need you to scoot over so I can lie down with you."

There were approximately a dozen things in his statement that I had questions about, but nineteen-year-old Camden Cole did not look like he was playing around, so I made scooting over a priority.

After toeing his shoes off and surprising me with clean, white, non-holey socks, he wedged his large body beside me. On his side, he draped one arm across my middle, curling his other under his head.

I watched him out of the corner of my eye, completely unsure if I was supposed to cuddle into him or what the hell we were doing after four years of not seeing each other.

"This okay?" he asked. "You comfortable?"

I was a lot of things. Confused. Lost. Overwhelmed by guilt.

But because it was Camden, comfortable was one of those things too.

As an answer, I rolled toward him and buried my face in his broad chest.

His whole body sagged as he began stroking the back of my hair. "Nora. Nora. Nora."

In a way, Camden and I were strangers, but as his heart played in my ear, I felt two puzzle pieces clicking into place. A calm washed over me. The dark cloud of my betrayals still existed outside of Camden's embrace; it just didn't seem so ominous anymore. He knew all the dirty and broken parts of me and still came back, holding me as though he could keep me together.

Sliding an arm around his back, I curled in close, shifting to tangle my legs with his. "I'm tired, Cam."

"I know," he whispered, hugging me tight.

"No, you don't. Nobody understands. I'm a disease who infects everyone who gets close to me." My breathing shuddered. "It hurts. Everything hurts."

"Do you remember our first summer together when a grasshopper got into the container where we held the extra worms? You screamed so loud when you opened that thing and it came flying out like a bat out of hell. It got on your shirt and then hung on for dear life. With all the racket you were making, the damn thing had to have been terrified, but he never jumped off. I had to peel it off your shirt, one leg at a time."

I gagged at the memory. "Thanks for reminding me of that. Awesome timing."

He chuckled and pressed his lips to the top of my head. "I'm the grasshopper clinging to your shirt, Nora."

Now, if that wasn't some good old classic Camden Cole rambling, I had no idea what was.

I tilted my head back, resting my chin on his pec, and peered up at him. "You do realize I have no idea what you're talking about, right?"

My cold, hollow chest filled with a warmth I hadn't felt in years when he grinned down at me.

"When I left the ten-dollar bill on your nightstand, I genuinely thought you'd find your way back to me. A phone call. A visit. Anything. But as time passed and I got older, I realized I fell in love with a girl who had no idea how to be loved."

My stomach wrenched, and emotion made my vision swim. "Camden, I—"

"No, just let me talk. Hear me out." He tucked a stray hair behind my ear and let his thumb linger at my cheek, sweeping back and forth. "I know you love me, Nora. It's flashed in your eyes every time you've seen me since we were kids. It's like every light in the house suddenly comes on, but it terrifies you, so you spend the whole time we're together running around, turning them all off, convincing yourself that you don't deserve for people to love you back. But we still do it. Joe loves you. Thea loves you. Ramsey loves you."

He paused and sucked in a deep breath. "I'll *always* love you. But it can't be me. I know it now more than ever." He caught a tear as it slipped from my eye. "I told you I would always come back, and I will keep that promise until the day I die, but what you need is someone who can be here for you. Someone who can *stay*. I can't be the only one who knows about this, babe. These secrets are eating you away from the inside out. You gotta let it out. You gotta tell Joe the truth."

My eyes flared, and I shook my head so fast it vibrated the bed. "I can't do it. I promised Ramsey—"

"To live," he interrupted, his tone so sharp it cut through my anxiety. "Jesus, Nora. I don't know Ramsey, but I guarantee you

RECLAIM

he has not spent the last four years in a cell just for you to end up in a grave." He inched down the bed so we were eye to eye and rested his forehead against mine. "All the pain. All the devastation. All the heartache. Something good *has* to come from this." He took my hand and intertwined our fingers. After bringing my knuckles to his mouth, he kissed each one. "Let it be you, Nora. Be the good."

"How?" I croaked through ugly sobs. "Just tell me how. After everything I've done."

"You have to forgive yourself and let people in. You can't change anything that happened. Some choices you don't get to make. Some are just made for you. But I swear to you, with my whole heart, not me, not Ramsey, not Thea, not Joe, regardless of what happened in the past, none of us would ever choose a world where you don't exist."

I wasn't sure if I believed him. Eighteen years' worth of drawers in my head disagreed with his logic. But if there was ever a moment I needed to hope, this was it.

I was at absolute rock bottom. What was there left to lose? Oh, right…

"What if he hates me? What if he hears the truth and never wants to speak to me again? I'd be all alone."

He sighed. "Then I guess our only choice is to sneak you into my suitcase and fly you back to New York with me. Fair warning, my roommate is a total douchebag. He plays bass in a band called Streets of Eyeless Brutality, hosts concerts for all six of his fans in our apartment every Saturday night, and has never once been to the grocery store but always manages to have food in his mouth, but other than that, Mooney's decent. He'll like you."

The slightest smile tipped my lips. How did he do that? How did Camden Cole always know what to say to put my turbulent mind to rest? Anchoring myself to him and his new life in New York wasn't an option, but Camden made it feel like anything was possible.

Even telling Joe. Something I so desperately wanted to do but was terror-stricken no less.

"How long are you in town?"

The side of his mouth hitched. "I guess it all depends on how long you need me to stay."

Forever hung on the tip of my tongue, but that wouldn't have been fair. He might have thought he loved me, but he had a whole life that didn't revolve around a girl who couldn't decide if she wanted to live or die.

"Do you have classes or work or whatever to get back to in New York?"

He smiled, bright and beautiful. "Yeah. I go to Columbia."

"Wow," I breathed.

"Don't be too impressed. I'd have gone to University of Antarctica if it had gotten me farther from my parents." He winked.

It was wrong to ask him to stay.

It was wrong to ask him for *anything*.

But I really wasn't ready to let him go. "Can you stay the night? And be here when I tell Joe. Whatever that entails."

Pride beamed in his eyes. "Of course." He released my hand but only so he could drag me into a hug. "Oh God, of course!" He shoved his face in my neck and laughed, and only then did I realize Camden had been living with the infection of my secrets too.

He deserved a break.

We all deserved a break.

He clung to me until Joe returned, and then, true to his word, Camden sat at my side, holding my hand while I confessed the depths of my soul. The truth poured out of me in a waterfall of confessions. Everything from how bad it had been with my dad, to Josh, to the night my choice ended his life. Ramsey at the police station. The guilt that had been ricocheting inside me ever since I'd promised my brother not to say anything. All of it, every single bit, right down to the moment I'd swallowed the bottle of pills.

As to be expected, Joe was shocked.

He cried.

I cried.

Camden held me tight.

When it was all said and done, nothing was better and everyone was still caught in my web of lies, but the weight of the world had been lifted from my shoulders.

The only time Camden left my side was when Joe pulled me into his arms, apologizing for things he had no control over. With a proud smile on his face, Camden winked at me before he stepped outside under the pretense of making a phone call. Joe immediately filled the gaping hole he'd left behind and perched on the edge of my bed, his hand wrapped around mine.

"We're going to get this sorted," he said, looking far older than his forty-five years. The room fell silent and Joe stared off into space, thought crinkling his forehead.

"How'd you know to call him? How did you have his number?" I asked.

"Who? Camden?"

I twisted my lips and leveled him with a glare. "No, the mouse in your pocket."

He grinned. "You aren't the only one who can keep a secret."

"Good, then you owe me a confession too. Spill."

He chuckled. "He showed up on my doorstep a few years

back. Right after Ramsey went to jail. I opened the door and Camden barely introduced himself before falling into a long, drawn-out dissertation about how I needed to let you move in with us."

My brows shot up. "What?"

"The boy didn't let me get a single word in for five solid minutes."

Yeah, that sounded like Camden, but he'd gone to Joe? About letting me move in? "Why would he do that?"

Joe shrugged. "He didn't think it'd be safe for you at your dad's without Ramsey around, so he all but dropped to his knees, begging me to let you move in and be close to Thea. I thought about it for a few days, but he was right."

I slapped a hand over my mouth. Of course it had been Camden looking out for me even when he was fifteen years old and I'd told him to love someone better. He had no idea how many nights I'd wanted to end it all, and the ten with his chicken scratches across the back was the only thing that had kept me alive. The very thought of Camden was a flicker of peace to my tumultuous soul.

"He calls every so often to check on you, I thought you might need your friend."

"I don't deserve him," I choked out around the lump in my throat. "It's been years since we saw each other, and he dropped everything to fly across the country just to be here. Who does that?"

Joe gave my hand a squeeze. "Someone who loves you. Someone who was scared out of their mind by the idea of losing you. Someone who sees all the incredible things about you even if you can't see them yourself. Nora, you are a beautiful, smart, funny woman with a heart so big it swallows you sometimes.

Camden is exactly the kind of man you deserve. But he and I can both tell you that until we're blue in the face and it won't matter until you can look in the mirror and feel like *you* deserve him too."

God, what I wouldn't have given to be that woman—the one who was good enough for a man like Camden. A woman who was more than just his *true* friend. But the very idea of her was so far in the future that she was barely visible on the horizon.

Different day, same negative Nora.

That stopped here. In this hospital bed. Camden was right. I had to be the good in all of this mess.

Hell, at least the woman I aspired to become was on the horizon now. Barely was still progress, and even if I had to crawl on my hands and knees to get there, I wouldn't stop until I did.

Closing my eyes, I rested my head on Joe's shoulder. "Help me. Please."

He put his chin to my forehead and sighed. "That's all you ever have to say, sweet girl."

As if he'd been summoned, that gorgeous man came strutting back into the room, holding three bottles of Coke and a fist full of candy bars.

His grin was so infectious my mouth had no other option but to follow suit.

"I brought us a snack," he announced. "You still a Snickers girl, or have we moved on to Twix?"

Fuck the candy. I was a Camden Cole girl, any and every way he came.

Or at least I wanted to be.

Camden stayed with me that night, wedged in the bed beside me, holding me close and prattling on about anything and everything that had happened to him over the last few years. He missed his prom because of his appendix, which was an awful story but got me a great shot of his abs when he showed me the scar. He laughed through the entire story of how he used Stewart and Cole Worm Farm as the basis for his accounting class project. Camden was valedictorian of his senior class and had been granted so many scholarships that his full first year at college was practically paid for. I smiled more in that time than I had in all the years he'd been gone combined.

Joe worked his magic and found a two-week inpatient program for me that was going to cost him a small fortune, but he'd just smiled and told me it was a small price to pay to get his second *daughter* happy and healthy.

Have I mentioned that Joe Hull was the absolute best? I didn't deserve him, either.

But I was hell-bent on getting there.

When it came time for Camden to leave the next day, it felt like I was losing an integral part of myself. He made me swear to call if I ever needed anything, but with renewed hope and a second chance at life, I prayed I wouldn't have to. I wanted to be able to call him when I wasn't a burden.

It was the first time we'd ever been together and didn't exchange the ten-dollar bill, but if I was going to get through the next few months and years, I needed as many reminders of what I was fighting for as I could get.

I couldn't expect, nor would I ever ask, Camden to wait on me. We'd shared one kiss and immeasurable love in the seven years we'd known each other; however, he had a life to live too. I wanted the world for Camden Cole even if I wasn't the one who could give it to him.

I needed to find the real Nora Stewart again, and while leaning on him for support would have been easy to do, it wouldn't

RECLAIM

have been fair or healthy for either one of us. We agreed that if he ever passed through Clovert, he was bound by pinky promise law to find me immediately. And if I ever found myself in New York—yeah, right—I was required to do the same.

Letting him go was bittersweet but necessary. And it only made it that much more satisfying when, three years later, I finally got the chance to repay him for being there on the day that ultimately saved my life.

EIGHTEEN

Camden

"Thank you for coming," I said, hugging a random old lady for the billionth time that day. My mom stood beside me, looking every bit the part of the devastated widow despite the fact that my parents hadn't shared a bedroom in almost five years.

"He was such a good man," old lady number twelve hundred and seventy-eight said, giving my hand a squeeze.

I nodded and forced a tight smile.

A few days earlier, my dad had dropped dead of a heart attack in my parents' driveway while climbing in his truck to go to work. It was truly shocking. I hadn't known that my dad had a heart until that day.

It was weird thinking how I'd never be the butt of one of his jokes again—a relief but still weird.

Old lady number twelve hundred and seventy-nine stepped up. "He'd be so proud of you."

Yeah, right. When I was a kid, I'd always assumed when I got older and bigger—maybe more coordinated—he'd be proud of me. In my twenty-two years, that day never came.

My cousin Jonathan scoffed. "He probably died to avoid being embarrassed anymore."

Now, it should be noted that Jonathan wasn't a prepubescent

kid who had spent the last decade trapped in time. In fact, he'd grown up quite a bit. Jonathan Caskey was a twenty-six-year-old police officer in Clovert now. In a true show of how fucked up that side of my family was, he'd carried a framed picture of Josh with him the day he'd graduated from the police academy. At least that was what I had been told.

There was no fucking chance I attended that shit show.

Yet there he sat, at my father's funeral, insulting me from the second pew. I scratched the side of my head with my middle finger, hopefully hiding it from old lady twelve hundred and eighty as the line of condolences continued.

The end was near on this circus. Since my father had been cremated, there was no graveside service to attend. Before I headed back to New York, Mom and I were planning to scatter his ashes near the overlook behind his precious papermill.

Nothing like dying and going right back to work, I guess.

The church was almost empty. Even our family had started to thin out, no doubt heading back to our house to eat the mountain of food people had delivered. Seemingly bored with my lack of a reaction, Jonathan got up and walked out too.

Right.

Past.

Her.

My back shot straight, and a smile I had no business wearing at a funeral spread across my lips.

Black dress. Black heels. Scarf wrapped around her head and huge shades covering half her face. It didn't matter if I hadn't seen her in three years—it could have been decades. I recognized her immediately. Part of that had to do with the hum in my bones which had always accompanied her presence, as if my body was a flesh-and-blood Nora Stewart detector.

"Would you excuse me for a moment?" I mumbled to little old lady twelve hundred and eighty-one before quickly ducking out the side door.

I jogged around the church, coming back in the front door, most likely looking like a fool to anyone who passed. I didn't give two shits though.

Nora was there.

She was scanning the room when I tiptoed up behind her and fought the huge to grab her by the hips and startle her like old times. She would have screamed though, and my shit-eating grin was already out of place enough for the both of us.

Leaning forward, I whispered into her ear, "Well, you look ridiculous."

She jumped, but a squeak was all that escaped as she spun to face me. "Oh my God," she gasped, covering her heart with her hand. "Damn it. You scared the hell out of me."

I shot her a teasing side-eye. "That mouth. In a church of all places."

She moved her hand to her mouth. "Shit, sorry."

My smile stretched so wide it was almost painful, and my pulse raced from having her there. In Alberton. She'd come to Alberton. *For me.*

"Damn," she whispered before shaking her head. "You know what? Maybe we should just get out of the church. That's probably easier for my mouth." Grabbing my arm, she dragged me out of the sanctuary, not stopping until we were outside, alone, on the far side of the building. She glanced around one last time before lowering her scarf and pushing her sunglasses up to the top of her head.

My whole body sagged as I drank her in. She looked good, not just the beautiful she'd always been. Nora looked healthy, rested, and... Alive.

RECLAIM

I put my hands in my pockets to keep them to myself. "Hello, stranger," I greeted with a grin and aching cheeks once we were eye to eye.

She threw her arms around my neck, pulling me in for a hug. "How are you? You holding up okay? I came as soon as I heard."

I was fine. It was no secret my dad and I didn't have much of a relationship. I'd spent years avoiding him and only coming home when I had to. In turn, he'd spent years pretending not to notice I was avoiding him. I'd been in New York for four years, and even though my mom had come to visit numerous times, Dad never had.

He was my father though. I was supposed to be devastated, and at some point, the finality of it all would probably sneak up on me, but I wasn't quite there yet. To be honest, I wasn't sure if I ever would be.

However, it did some serious things inside my chest to know she'd heard my dad died, hopped in her car, and drove three hours to Alberton to check on me.

"I'm okay," I said, returning her embrace with a bear hug of my own, complete with lifting her off her feet. "How the hell are you?"

Setting her back down, I released her to get another long look at her face. Nora was one hell of an actress, so whatever she was about to say, I wanted to get a good read on her to make sure it was the truth.

She rested her hands on my chest and toyed with my red tie as she beamed up at me. "I'm…I'm a lot better, Cam."

Cam.

God, I'd never get sick of hearing it. I corrected people who shortened my name on a damn-near daily basis. It just wasn't the same when anyone else said it.

"You look good. Really, really good," I said, not feeling the least bit awkward about it.

It apparently did not have the same effect on her. She cut her gaze to her shoes, her long hair curtaining off her face. "Compared to the last time you saw me? I would hope so. Hospital chic isn't really a look I'd like to repeat. God, that was awful."

I could never explain to her how watching her choose to live again had been the most beautiful thing I'd ever seen. Though, if she was smiling and wanted to keep things light, I was more than happy to follow her lead.

"Oh, whatever. I think you pulled it off pretty nicely. And look at the bright side: At least we were close to medical help when you broke my heart by telling me you only drink Diet Coke. My recovery has been touch and go, but I've managed to carry on."

As I'd hoped, she chuckled and lifted her head, making a show of it as she craned it all the way back. "Do you take, like, growth hormones or something? I swear Ramsey stopped growing at, like, eighteen and you're bigger every time I see you. This is getting a tad ridiculous, Cam."

Another Cam. Was it my birthday already?

I laughed. "I'm six-three. Thank you very much for noticing." I ran a hand over her head, to where she hit against my shoulder. "I'm assuming the other Oompa Loompas have voted you out of the factory by now?"

Her hand snaked out so fast that I didn't see it coming before she twisted my nipple.

"Ow, ow, ow. What the hell?"

She fluttered those dark-painted lashes as she peered up at me. "Oh, I'm sorry. Did that hurt?"

It did. But, fuck, I had missed her.

"I can't believe you're actually here."

She shrugged. "You're always there for me. I figured it was time to return the favor."

I gave her shoulder a teasing shove. "So, how long are you here for?"

"Depends. How long do you need me to stay?"

I grinned at the familiar words. "In the name of honesty, I must tell you I'm doing okay with all of this. So, technically, I don't *need* you to stay."

Her smile fell almost immediately, and it made me a dick, but damn, it felt good that she wanted to be there too.

Resting my hands on her hips, I playfully swayed her from side to side. "But I'd really fucking love if you did."

Her whole face lit like I'd mercilessly sacrificed a cricket in her honor. "Are there any hotels in this one-horse town? I could stay the night."

"Yep. Casa de Cole has a vacancy. Just don't read the Yelp reviews."

Like someone had flipped the switch, the light in her eyes went dark. "I can't stay at your parents'. The whole Caskey family is in town. I was careful not to let anyone see me here today, but I have a sneaking suspicion staying under the same roof might set off a few alarm bells."

"Fuck it. Let's set off the tornado sirens too."

"Camden," she hissed.

"Relax. Personally, I'm many years removed from giving a shit about what the Caskeys think anymore. But I'd never ask *you* to stay at my parents'. I don't even stay there anymore. Not since after a few years back, when my aunt and uncle showed up with Jonathan for an impromptu Christmas visit. Or maybe it was just impromptu for me. Anyway, I told everyone if they stayed, then I wasn't. So my parents gave me the keys to Dad's old hunting cabin and told me to kick rocks. Now, if you want my opinion, it was pretty fucked up how, in that situation, *I* was the one who got the boot out of the house, but I never gave the keys back. On the rare occasion when I come back to Alberton, I always have a place I can stay. And now, long story short, *you* have a place to stay too."

I was out of breath by the time I finished talking, but Nora was back to smiling, so I figured it was time well spent.

"It's good to see the growth hormones haven't affected your long-winded ramblings."

"I know. You're in for a treat with all the stories I have in store for you tonight."

"You know, on second thought, I think I left my stove on at home. I should go check on that."

She took a step away, but I hooked her around the waist, picking her up like a football under my arm. "Nope. Too late to run now. I haven't seen you in forever, and I'm not above kidnapping."

"Put me down. I'm in a dress." She laughed, slapping at my legs.

I tickled her with my free hand, and she squirmed so much I almost dropped her.

Suddenly, the side door swung open and my mom stepped out. "Camden, what in the world are you doing out here, making all that racket?"

I quickly righted Nora, and she turned into my chest to hide her face, something I hated but understood.

"Oh, hey, Mom. Sorry. Were we being too loud?"

"I'd say so. I was talking to the Worthingtons and heard you two all the way in the sanctuary." She raked her gaze down Nora's back. "Who's your friend?"

Nora went rigid, and I gave her hip a reassuring squeeze.

RECLAIM

Regardless of the consequences, I would have loved nothing more than to turn her around, throw my arm around her shoulders, and introduce Nora with pride. However, I only had her for one night, and standing there was wasting precious time.

I smiled at my mom, holding her gaze as I dipped low and put my mouth to Nora's ear. "Run." Then I took off like a madman, pulling her right along with me.

"Camden!" Mom yelled at my back, but I barely heard it over Nora's wild laughter.

Hand in hand, we raced to the parking lot.

When I broke left, she slowed down and pointed to the right. "My car is this way."

"Just leave it. We'll pick it up later."

"My bag is in there."

I tugged her hand. "I'll loan you some clothes." God, just the idea of her in one of my button-downs had my dick begging to be readjusted.

Her head fell to the side, and she argued, "I don't even have a toothbrush."

"Use mine."

"Ew!" she whined, and I couldn't help but laugh.

"Okay, okay, fine," I huffed. "Let me just introduce you to my mom and then we can grab your bag and get out of here."

Her eyes flashed comically wide, but it got her feet moving again—in my direction.

After digging the keys out of my pocket, I clicked the locks to my dad's old Jeep. I paused only to yank her door open before running around to the driver's side. We both dove in, panting and lost in hysterical laughter.

Drumming her hands on the dashboard, she shouted, "Go go go!"

Let's be real. It wasn't like my mom had chased us down or anything. The few people left in the parking lot hadn't even looked our way.

But I still threw my old Jeep into reverse and peeled out for no other reason than I was riding a high with Nora Stewart that I never wanted to come down from.

NINETEEN

Camden

"You're kidding, right?" Nora asked when I led her inside the cabin.

I hung my keys on the deer antler hooks next to the door and glanced back at her. "About what?"

"'This is not'"—she tossed me a pair of air quotes—"'an old hunting cabin.' You made it sound like we would be sleeping on squeaky floors and peeing in the woods." She pointed across the room. "There's a freaking pool table. I wouldn't call this roughing it."

I scanned the massive room, knowing exactly what she was talking about. Huge open layout. Leather sofa facing a fireplace. King-size bed facing another fireplace. Small kitchen with white-quartz countertops and stainless-steel appliances. Crown molding distressed to give it the illusion of being rustic, all while practically flashing dollar signs.

Not many years ago, I would have rather climbed into a hole and died than show her this place. But at the moment, I was almost a hundred thousand dollars in student loan debt, had three jobs I worked year-round, and lived in a shoebox apartment I shared with two other guys all because I'd refused to take a single cent from my parents for college. I had no idea what Nora's financial situation was, but chances were she was far better off than I was, even if I sometimes got to stay in a fancy cabin when I came home for holidays—and tragedies.

I shrugged and walked to the kitchen. "There's a hot tub out back too."

"Seriously?" She walked to the back door and slid the curtain open. "Jesus, Cam."

We were on the sixth Cam of the day, but it could have been number six hundred and I never would have been sick of hearing it.

Leaning against the counter, I explained, "I think my mom always hoped Dad would make this place their home away from home for weekend getaways. That's probably why she had her interior decorator come in and design it to her liking. In reality, Dad just bought the place for somewhere to get away from her."

She joined me in the kitchen and straddled one of the stools at the bar across from me. "I know you said you were okay…but do you maybe…want to talk about your dad dying?"

"I'd rather talk about you." I turned and opened the fridge, hooking my fingers around two longneck bottles before letting it swing shut behind me. "Beer?"

She nodded, and I popped the top off before sliding one her way. "Cheers."

We clinked bottles and then both took a sip, her pull noticeably longer than mine. A little liquid courage never hurt anyone.

"Okay, so, what do you want to know?"

I propped myself up on my elbows on the island. "Everything."

She blew out a long breath. "Hmm, let's go for the abridged version. Therapy. Therapy. Therapy. Anti-depressants. Anti-anxiety medication. Therapy. Therapy. Therapy. Joe got married. Thea started a travel agency. Thea and I moved to a little house about thirty minutes away from the old neighborhood. Oh, and as of last week, your uncle, good old former Mayor Caskey, managed to call in some favors and get Ramsey's request for parole denied. Ya know, same old, same old."

"Fuck," I clipped.

"Yeah, so, good times." She took another drink of beer. "Are you sure you wouldn't rather talk about your dad?"

I reached across the bar and caught her hand, and like it was the most natural thing in the world, she laced her fingers with mine. "Nora, I am so sorry. I—"

"Don't finish that. Not one more word."

I clamped my mouth shut and stared at her.

Never letting me go, she walked around the counter and moved in close. "This is going to come out wrong, but bear with me. Okay?" When I nodded, she announced, "I had fun at your dad's funeral. Let's not ruin it."

"Wow, okay. Not what I was expecting you to say."

She giggled, soft and sweet. "I just mean, when you snuck up behind me and told me I looked ridiculous. And then we made jokes and picked on each other outside. Even running from your mom. I swear, Cam, it's the most free I've felt in years. We don't get to spend a lot of time together and the last few times have been…well, a nightmare. So, what if we just pack away the heavy shit for tonight and have fun for a change? It'll be like old times again." She smiled up at me with those brown eyes that had owned so much of my childhood, and just like the good old days, I was wrapped around her little finger.

I could do that. Jesus Christ, I could do that.

I could give her the easy and carefree we both so desperately deserved and so rarely got. My week had been a never-ending drone of condolences and funeral preparations. I was more than happy to sit around and share a few beers with a bright, funny, gorgeous woman I hadn't seen in too damn long.

Fun with Nora was not a hardship.

So, when she pushed up onto her toes, adorably crinkled her nose, and asked, "What do you say?" I had but one answer.

"I'll need to get you a pair of my boxers and a T-shirt."

Her eyebrows sank together. "Why?"

I moved her hand to rest on my chest, mostly because I liked the way it had felt when she'd done it at the church *and* because I needed mine free to pluck her beer from her grip and set it on the counter. "Because your dress is about to get seriously wet."

All in one swift movement, I bent over, put my shoulder to her stomach, and lifted her off the floor.

"What are you doing?" she howled. "Mercy!"

"You wanted the good old days." I carried her out the back door and peeled back the top on the hot tub. "I don't have a creek, so this will have to do."

She screamed as I dumped her into the water, heels and all.

I almost busted my ass when she shot up out of the water and grabbed my tie, but I didn't make her work too hard at dragging me in with her.

Soaking wet, fully dressed, on a day that should have been one of the hardest of my entire life, being with Nora was the only part of the equation that mattered.

When she was done dunking me underwater, I stripped off my pants, tie, and button-down and Nora made me close my eyes while she peeled out of her dress, exchanging it for my wet undershirt instead.

We took turns getting out to retrieve beers. I tried not to stare at the way my white shirt clung to her mouth-watering curves. Barely scraping together enough self-control to keep my groans to myself.

Four beers in, when it was my turn to get us another drink, Nora no longer offered me the same courtesy—thank fuck.

"Holy shit, Camden Cole. Can we discuss where and how you got that six—er, eight pack?"

I passed her both the beers so I could slide back inside the warm water, the jets bubbling atop the glowing blue surface. "Finally, she notices. I almost pulled something and passed out flexing last time I got out."

She wagged her eyebrows. "That time, I was checking out your butt."

"Like I'm some piece of meat?" I clutched my chest. In reality, I loved every fucking minute of it. "Go on. And the first time?"

With a wolfish grin, she shook her head and settled deeper into her corner seat. "So, anyway. Are you still in school?"

I squinted to let her know I was onto her, but I gave her a pass with her less-than-smooth subject change. Under the water, I hooked my ankle around hers and she rubbed her foot against my leg.

Our chemistry would always be there. Nora and I had a dynamic most people couldn't possibly understand. Playful and physical. Cool and natural. The feel of her skin against mine was as familiar as my own. For most of our lives, we were each other's only source of attention and affection. So, even if it had started innocently in our youth, as we got older, our touches had become something else entirely.

Something more mature—an attraction and desire neither of us could deny.

But hey, if she could flirt and be coy, so could I.

Also, I was a little buzzed, so that seriously helped in the courage department.

"I'll tell you what. If you give me a kiss right here"—I tapped my cheek on the side she was closer to—"I'll answer whatever questions you have."

Her lips twisted to the side where she tried—and failed—to suppress a grin. "So that's how it's gonna be?"

"Is that another question?" I huffed and lifted my beer to my lips. "Keep 'em coming. I'll start a running tally. I'm fantastic at math, in case you've forgotten."

She sloshed over to me, slapping a big, wet, sloppy smooch right where she had been instructed. "There. Now, tell me about college."

"I'm going to be in school for the rest of my life at this rate." Holding my beer above water, I folded under the surface and grabbed her toe, pulling her foot back up with me. I rested her ankle on my thigh and began rubbing her foot with one hand.

"Mmm," she hummed, closing her eyes. She brought her other foot to rest on my lap as though it were waiting in line. "You've been holding out on me, Cam. How come you never did this back at the creek?"

"Because you would have punched me."

She laughed and set her beer aside. "Probably."

I put my drink aside too and readjusted so I could massage both of her feet at the same time. "Okay, my turn for a question."

"I do believe there's a price for that." She teased her slender index finger down her neck. "Fair is fair."

My mouth dried and my lips—among other places—twitched. "Just name the spot. I'm here for it. So fucking here for it."

The playfulness in her eyes transformed into a fire. Having

her look at me like that while sitting within arm's reach was better than any fantasy I'd had of her over the years. And believe me, there were plenty.

Her finger landed just below her earlobe on her neck. "Here."

I spread her legs and in one fluid motion gave her ankles a tug, dragging her into my lap so that she was straddling me. Water slapped the edges, and without hesitation, her arms wrapped around my neck. Cocking her head to the side, she invited me to press my lips to her wet skin.

Nora.

My Nora.

In the flesh. Happy. Smiling. Fucking stunning. And silently pleading for *me*.

I'd waited so long to have her like that. Most nights, I didn't even allow myself to dream that it would ever come to fruition. She'd always been a mirage I could never quite catch before it disappeared.

Brushing a few locks of her hair out of my way, I licked my lips and leaned in.

The moment my mouth brushed her skin, her breathing shuddered, giving me silent permission to lick and suck my way up to her ear.

"That feels so good. Don't stop," she moaned.

I could've died a happy man hearing those six words, but I prayed God would let me live through the night. If I had anything to say about it, neither of us would spend a moment of it sleeping.

I smiled against her neck and paused only long enough to warn, "If you think you're getting off the hook and not answering a question, you're sorely mistaken."

She rolled her head to the side and gave me more room to roam. "Then ask it and then do that tongue thing again."

I chuckled. "Nora, if my kissing you isn't a distraction, then I'm not doing a very good job."

She pulled away just enough to make eye contact. "I'm finishing up school to be a first-grade teacher. Multitasking is my city. Now, ask and get back to work."

Oh, a freebie. Not that I minded our method of payment at the moment.

So she was a teacher. Interesting. I liked that for her—and for more reasons than just the images of her bending over a desk.

"Yes, ma'am, Ms. Stewart." With my original inquiry out of the way, that left the door wide open to ask her something more personal.

But the woman was right, I had some necking to do too.

"Do you…" Kiss. "…ever think—"

"Mmmm," she hummed as my tongue teased at her earlobe.

"…about me…"

She shivered in my arms and moved closer until her core found my length straining against my boxers.

I hissed at the contact, barely able to finish my thought. "…at night?"

Her fingers latched onto my hair and she pulled my mouth to hers, hovering mere millimeters away. "You're the only man I've ever thought about." Her warm breath filled my every inhale. "Every night, Cam."

I kissed her hard and fast, sealing my mouth over hers as though oxygen were my enemy.

Fuck. Me.

The Cam tasted even better than it sounded.

A groan rumbled in my throat, her words sparking something primal within me. "I want to be inside you," I rumbled, palming her breast.

"Oh, God," she breathed, nipping at my neck while circling her hips over my cock.

"You can tell me to stop. I swear I won't do anything you don't—"

"Hey, Cam." She palmed either side of my face. "Shut up and take me inside."

I didn't turn off the jacuzzi.

I didn't even shut the back-fucking-door.

I didn't care whether my wet feet left spots on the hardwood floor, trailing to the bed where I carried her.

I didn't turn off a single light on the way.

And I didn't give a good Goddamn if the whole cabin came down around us.

For one night, I was going to say to hell with it all.

For one night, nothing in the world mattered.

Not the wet clothes we left on the floor after ripping them off each other. Not the fact that she'd be leaving the next day or that I was so far behind in my classes it would take a month to make up for the week I'd been gone, pretending to mourn a man I'd never really loved.

But everything vanished as I stared down at her naked, pink cheeks, all mine.

I put a knee to the bed and trailed a finger through her heat. Fuck me, she was wet and it had not one fucking thing to do with the hot tub. "I need a condom."

"Please, Cam." She rose from the pillow, pressing her lips to mine. "I'm on birth control. It's fine."

"I'm clean," I confessed. And because it was Nora, I didn't

even have it in me to be embarrassed when I admitted, "I haven't been with anyone."

Her eyes grew wide. "No one?"

"*No one.*"

A heart-stopping smile spread across her face. "Me either." She took a deep shaky breath and blew it out. "I sorta thought you'd know what to do."

Relief tore from my throat. I'd never dare ask her about other guys; I had no right. But learning that neither of us had been with anyone else, that we were going to have something that we would share forever, galvanized the lock she'd placed on my heart almost a decade earlier.

I'd always belong to Nora Stewart.

This first belonged to *us*.

A laugh slipped out. "Well, just because I haven't done it doesn't mean I don't know how."

"What if it's a train wreck?" She giggled through her unshed tears.

"What about us isn't a train wreck?"

"Good point."

Dropping to my elbows on either side of her head, I moved closer to her face and whispered, "Just talk to me, okay? I want it to be good for you."

Her hands gently slid up my back, and I settled between her legs.

"You know I love you, right?" she rushed out.

My chest got tight. "I know."

"No, Cam. I mean I really, *really* love you. I always have."

"I know that too, babe. And I love you too. Always."

"Then show me." Her mouth claimed mine. "Show me what love feels like."

Her hips rose off the bed, and in turn, I lowered mine to meet hers. Our mouths paused for a beat as we connected for the first time. I could wax poetic about how fireworks went off or how time stood still, but that wasn't us.

We were clumsy and inexperienced, but we learned together.

We were teeth clanking and a slip out here and there.

But eventually, we found *our* rhythm. Our stride. Our version of physical love.

With roaming hands and blissful moans, she was beautiful and sexy and passionate and wild. Somehow, ten years of Karma found me in that bed, because to my utter surprise and elation, I managed to find a spot that made her cry out.

"Just like that. *Yes.* Just like that. *Oh, Cam.*"

Unfortunately, Karma doesn't always have the best timing and my body chose that exact second to empty inside her. That moment was kind of like fireworks, but also kind of like blowing up your hand the second you lit the fuse.

Rolling to my side, I stared at her in horror. "Holy shit. I'm so sorry That was…"

Oh, God.

Following me over, she flipped on to my sweaty chest and kissed my pec. "Don't you dare be sorry."

"I just… I mean, it… It snuck up me. Christ, you felt good."

"I'll take that as a compliment."

"You can take it however you want as long as you don't leave this bed until I make it up to you."

She shrugged. "Okay, at that speed, you can make it up to me at least thirty more times before the sun even comes up."

I barked a laugh. "Always the smartass."

"You know it."

And that was how it had always been with Nora. She didn't

judge or make me feel embarrassed, even when I deserved it. There was a comfort and security between us that I'd never find with anyone else.

I lifted my head and pressed an all too brief kiss to her lips. "I'm so fucking glad you came. I could get seriously addicted to you, Nora Stewart."

And just when I'd thought nothing could be worse than premature ejaculation, her whole face turned white and she rolled off me. "I need to clean up."

I watched what was no doubt a spectacular show of her ass swaying as she padded to the bathroom, but I was too preoccupied trying to figure out where I'd gone wrong to truly enjoy it.

I sat up and snagged a pair of boxers from my suitcase, dragging them on while I carried a dry T-shirt to the bathroom door and rapped with two knuckles. "Hey, I brought you a shirt."

She opened the door a crack and extended her hand out, taking my offering. "Do you have any sweats I can borrow?"

Sweats? That seemed a bit much. What happened to talking about thirty more times?

"Um, yeah. Sure." I dug a pair from my suitcase and carried them back to her. There was another round of crack the door and take the clothes, but thankfully she didn't request a hoodie that time.

Assuming naked time was officially over thanks to my big fucking mouth, I got dressed and sat on the edge of the bed.

She smiled when she exited a few minutes later, but I knew Nora well enough to realize her grin was strictly for my benefit. And didn't that just fucking suck after the laughs we'd shared in the hot tub.

What did not suck was that she walked straight over to me, wrapped her arms around my neck, and climbed onto my lap.

Why hello mixed signals.

I folded her into a tight hug. "Did I say something wrong?"

She let out a sigh. "No."

"Then why are you wearing so much clothing?"

"I have to leave."

I swayed away so I could see her face. "Right now?"

She framed my face in her hands and stroked her thumb back and forth across my bottom lip. "No. But I will tomorrow. And, eventually, you will too. You have a whole big life in New York. And I'm finishing up my student teaching in Clovert. I don't know. Maybe we shouldn't have…ya know?"

I shook my head. "No. I can honestly say I don't know. Because there is nothing we did tonight that I don't think we should have done a long time ago and from now on a lot more frequently."

She looked away, but she wasn't quick enough to hide the quiver of her chin. "I'm really just sick of hurting you, Cam."

Leaning to the side, I forced my face into her line of sight. "Okay, now, I'm confused. What part of that do you think hurt me, exactly? Was it the noises? I promise you none of those were cries of pain, but if it bothered you, I can work on it. I'm always open to constructive feedback."

She laughed, but it was sad. "Me coming here was supposed to be about you. To support you through hard times like you've always done for me. But then I showed up and you were really hot."

I chuckled and hugged her tight. "Is it a bad thing?"

"Yeah, because now, I know how perfect you are. And you think you could get addicted to me, but I have to leave in the morning."

And there it was. The truth that always lingered between Nora and me.

Our story was a tangled tale of time and distance.

Choices and consequences.

Love and longing.

But, throughout, we were never on the same page at the same time.

When we were kids, it had been out of our control. She'd lived in Clovert and I'd lived in Alberton; a summer together was all we could have hoped for. We'd grown up, but the circumstances that surrounded us were more complex than ever. Did I wish that she'd asked me to stay when I'd left the hospital the last time I'd seen her? With my entire heart. Did I understand why she couldn't? With my entire being. I could never expect Nora to love me until she loved herself.

As a man who would have done anything to fix things for her, that was a hard fucking pill to swallow. I'd spent many nights raging at the unfairness of finding my soul mate in a shattered girl I could never quite hold on to. But those were the cards I'd been dealt, and I had to be realistic about my expectations of how things would play out.

The way I saw it, I had three options.

Walk away and close the door on Nora Stewart forever.

Show up on her doorstep, pulling her close and ultimately pushing her further away.

Or enjoy the moments when the universe saw fit to bring her into my life and hope like hell that, one of those times, I'd finally get to keep her.

I'd chose option three every single time because, in our story, it was the only plot line in which I got to keep her. Even just for a night.

Reclining on the bed, I dragged her down with me. With her knees on either side of my hips, she settled squarely on top of me, the right parts of her body aligned with all the right parts of mine. My cock stirred to life immediately; the greedy bastard was ready for more.

It would have to wait—preferably for when there wasn't an entire cotton field of sweatpants between us and she was back to smiling and laughing.

"I know how this works, Nora. I haven't spent half my life obsessing over you without learning a few things."

She buried her face in my neck. "Oh, God, don't say that. That just makes me feel worse."

"Hey, stop. It's not a bad thing."

"It feels bad. Knowing I can't be who you want me to be."

"Nora, you're here with me. After giving me what you just gave me, trusting me to be that man for you—you're *exactly* who I want you to be."

"Do you want to know why I've never had sex with anyone before?"

I chuckled. "Is it because you've spent your adult life hoping for two orgasm-*less* minutes in Heaven with me? Because…not to brag or anything, but I'm all about making dreams come true."

She giggled and lifted her head to kiss my jaw. "You know me too well." She was on top of me, gravity doing its thing, but when she sighed, she wiggled as though it could somehow bring us closer. "I don't trust anybody like I trust you, Cam. The minute I saw you today, sitting up front with your family, surrounded by the very same people who usually make my skin crawl, all the chaos in my head fell silent. The last few years, breathing has been a conscious effort. Every thought requires dissection, and every emotion needs to be processed and inventoried to make sure I'm moving in the right direction. But not when I'm with you. With you, I breathe and I laugh and…and I *feel*, Camden.

Good things. And I don't even have to try. It just happens when I'm with you."

With my heart in my throat, I rolled to the side and inched down so I could see her face.

Damp tracks streaked her cheeks, but there was a warm, content smile on her face.

I ran my palm over the top of her messy hair. "That's love, Nora. And just so you don't think I'm some magical genie, what you just described is exactly how I feel with you."

"I'm learning that."

I kissed her nose. "Good."

"I'm not quite there yet though. I'm working hard, Cam. Healing my soul and my heart. But I still think it's my head that needs it the most. I can't stop thinking that I'll never be enough for you. But I'm so selfish I can't convince myself to let you off the hook, either."

I squeezed her hip. "I like your hook, thank you very much. I will *never* ask you to let me off it. You sit there and talk about not being enough for me, but you have no idea how much I look up to you. To see everything you've risen above, and the fact that you're still fighting for yourself. Fuck, that's inspiring. It's safe to say I have my own mountains to climb. For fuck's sake, my dad is dead and I haven't shed a single tear. We have different depths of problems, but your well has been deeper than most. And like a badass beast, you're still clawing your way out. There is a solid possibility you're going to get out of there and see that *I'm* not enough for *you*."

"Cam," she whispered reverently.

"Please hear me when I say this. You were enough for me when you were eleven, barefoot and saving my life from frogs. You were enough for me at twelve, yelling at me for not choosing you, because whether you understand it or not, just knowing that someone cared if I chose them changed my entire outlook on life. You were enough for me at thirteen and fourteen and fifteen and sixteen, and fuck, Nora, you have been enough for me every single day of my life. Timing is everything and we're not there yet. But don't you ever fucking let me go. Do you hear me? Never."

Her shoulders shook with a cry. "I don't deserve you."

"I know. You deserve better. But you aren't the only selfish one in this bed."

She half laughed, half cried, and I hugged her tight, smoothing a hand up and down her back, hoping she knew I'd always be there for her even when I wasn't.

"So much for leaving the heavy stuff behind tonight, huh?" she said.

"Hey, the night isn't over yet. I still owe you thirty more almost orgasms."

Finally, she smiled bright and white, and I hooked a leg over her hips. "Then I highly suggest you get to work, Camden Cole. The clock's ticking."

And wasn't that the truth. The clock was always ticking with me and Nora. I just prayed that, after that night, it was finally counting down to a time when we could be together for more than just a night.

Between kisses and laughs, I stripped her out of her clothes while making proclamations about banning sweatpants for all of eternity. With brazen hands, I cataloged her every curve and dip, submitting them to memory as I explored her in ways that would make a porn star blush.

Or at least two virgins like us.

I found at least a handful of ways to show her my love with

my fingers and my mouth, and Nora whispered countless I-love-yous I'd spend years revisiting on cold and lonely nights without her.

We didn't make it to thirty that night, but when we both passed out, sweaty and sated, the pure erotic beauty of Nora Stewart mid-release had been ingrained in my brain three times over.

When I woke up the next morning, my perfect fantasy mirage had vanished. The loss was staggering, but I couldn't help but smile when I saw our ten-dollar bill on the nightstand, a handwritten note tucked beneath it.

Cam,

I couldn't bring myself to wake you up. You looked so peaceful and happy, like a weirdo smiling in your sleep. I'll take that memory with me instead of a long, drawn-out goodbye. I would have cried, and then you would have said all the right things, making it even harder for me to go. But know this: There aren't enough words to adequately express the gift you gave me last night. The hope. The unconditional love. The understanding that, while now is not our time, there might a future where one day the two of us find ourselves on the banks of our creek again, this time with free minds, whole hearts, and a lifetime to share.

Until then, wherever you go and whatever you do, I love you.

Always,
Nora

P.S. Alberton cabbies are brutal. They quoted me fifty bucks over the phone to get back to my car at the church.

RECLAIM

P.P.S. My dress was still wet, so I stole your sweats. I don't feel the slightest bit sorry. I'll put them to good use. I promise.

P.P.P.S. I may not go to fancy Columbia, but after several college English courses, I can definitively say this is the correct way to the do the P.S. thing. More P's and less S's.

P.P.P.P.S. I'd rather be there with you.

TWENTY

Nora

TRYING TO RECLAIM YOUR LIFE IS A LOT LIKE CLEANING A house. You can work your ass off sweeping down the cobwebs and taking out the trash, but there is always a closet to be organized or a baseboard to scrub. And just when you think you've finished everything, it's time to start all over again because, while you were distracted in one room, life happened in another.

But every day when I woke up and climbed out of bed, I told myself I was getting closer and closer to the woman I wanted to be. It helped a lot knowing that the people around me were thriving too.

Joe and his wife, Misty, were happier than ever, and because of Misty, I'd inherited a kinda-sorta stepsister, Tiffany. She was funny and always had the best fashion advice. Which, after years of forcing Thea into dresses and heels, was a nice change of pace.

Thea's online travel agency had taken off, bringing in more money for her to squirrel away for the future. I didn't have to read between the lines to know she wanted that future to be with Ramsey, even if they were virtually strangers now.

Ramsey was doing well-ish too. Or at least as well as possible when incarcerated. He had fallen in love with his career: working in the barbershop in prison. He and Joe had never been close before he'd been arrested, but it made me giggle that my brother had somehow managed to follow in his footsteps.

Work was amazing. Stressful and exhausting, but no less incredible. I adored being a teacher. Seeing their little faces light up every morning made me feel like I'd finally found my purpose in life. I hadn't had the best childhood, but I was bound and determined not to let any of those kids fall through the cracks the way Ramsey and I had.

So I did something about it.

First Step was an after-school program to keep kids engaged and surrounded by positive role models. It was a slow start, but after almost a year of paperwork and applications, I managed to secure county grants and funds to make it free for anyone who needed it.

My next major project for the school district was a brown bag lunch program. The majority of students in Clovert qualified for free lunches during the school year, but I knew all too well how long the summers could be with an empty fridge and a bare pantry. I developed a plan to set up brown bag lunch stations around town for students to pick up healthy, balanced meals over the months when school wasn't in session. However, it was an expensive endeavor, and I was denied city, county, and state aid at every turn. Eventually, with Thea's help, I started a fundraiser and took it to social media.

For as much evil that existed in our world, it was shocking how quickly we met our goal. And over the three years I'd been heading up the program, the money never stopped. I spent almost every Friday night during the summer in the school cafeteria surrounded by volunteers packing those bags until almost midnight, but seeing those kids' faces when they picked them up meant more to me than I ever could have imagined.

Camden's words from all those years earlier when I was lying in a hospital bed after having attempted to take my own life filled my thoughts on a daily basis. *"Something good has to come from this."* I'd never bought into his theory that I could be the something good.

But those kids. That was enough for me.

Camden and I had spoken exactly zero times over the last five years. I didn't have his number at school, but I knew that Joe did. He was the keeper of all secrets in our family. If he'd been able to find Camden when I had been in the hospital, I ventured to say he had probably kept in touch with him through the years too. But reaching out to him when I was still piecing my life back together wasn't fair. He'd told me not to let him off my hook, but constantly reeling him in just to toss him back out because I wasn't ready for more seemed cruel. If and when I reached out to Camden Cole again, I wanted to be the woman he deserved. Though, as time passed without so much as a peep from Camden, either, I started to wonder if maybe he'd let *himself* off the hook.

Around the three-year mark, I got tipsy with Thea one night and decided to look him up on Instagram. I found an account for him, complete with a profile picture of him in a suit, sexy as ever and smiling at the camera, but there were no photos uploaded to his grid. There were, however, a handful of photos other people had tagged him in.

One on a snowy mountaintop, his hair a tousled mess beneath a pair of ski goggles. There were six grinning men all huddled around him, and it made me smile to know that Camden had finally found his tribe of friends.

Someone else had tagged a picture of him at what appeared to be a restaurant, a cake with sparkling candles lit in front of him. It had been posted four months after his birthday, so I wasn't sure what he was celebrating, but I just liked knowing he had something to celebrate at all.

But the picture that hit me the hardest was an image of him standing beside a gorgeous blonde. They looked like Ken and Barbie. He was in chinos and a baby-blue button-down with the sleeves rolled up to his elbows—pure Camden Cole preppy. She was in a white silk blouse tucked into a high-waisted black pencil skirt and capped off with black stiletto pumps. She was taller than I was. Classier than I was. Prettier than I was. But most of all, she was standing in what should have been my spot at his side, and he was smiling ear to ear with his arm draped around her hips.

The caption read: *Nothing better than a night out with this guy.*

And she wasn't wrong.

I cried myself to sleep that night, simultaneously mourning the loss of a man who had never truly been mine and hoping he'd finally found someone who could make him happy.

Stalking Camden Cole quickly became my favorite guilty pleasure. He never added any pictures of his own, but every few months, one of his friends would tag him in something. As far as I could tell, Pencil Skirt Barbie hadn't lasted long, but as the years passed, it wasn't unusual for other girls to appear in photos with him.

What had I expected though? He was a gorgeous man in his twenties. Honestly, it was more surprising I hadn't run across engagement or wedding photos yet.

Deciding to follow Camden's lead, I allowed some of the teachers at school to set me up on a few dates. Most were dumpster fires, though a guy named Noah earned a second date. He was nice enough, funny enough, kind enough.

He just wasn't Cam.

So I threw myself back into work and swore men off for good. Well, all men except for my secret late-night rendezvous with whatever picture of @CamdenCole1019 had been recently added.

Between working on myself, working for the kids, and working toward keeping Thea from becoming a crazy cat lady sans the cats, time moved on.

Until one day, it stopped.

"You have a call from inmate—"

After twelve years, I didn't need to listen to the rest of the message. I pulled the phone from my ear and pressed the number one to accept the call. While I waited for the line to connect, I paused the "How to Make Creamy Tuscan Chicken" video on my iPad and dried my hands on my pink-and-white floral apron.

It had been a long day at school, complete with a first-grader sneezing in my face only to turn around and puke on the floor, but hey, at least it hadn't been the other way around. Thea was losing her mind, struggling with the latest update to her website, Travel For Me. I'd decided to cook her something yummy in my never-ending attempt to take her mind off things. I was a good roommate like that. Plus, I'd really wanted that Tuscan chicken since I'd stumbled across the recipe on my weekly Peeping Tom stroll through Instagram. Win. Win.

"Nora," Ramsey choked across the line.

I froze, my whole body going on alert. "What's wrong? What happened? Are you okay?"

There was some movement on his end, and I sucked in a deep breath, ready to face whatever hell the Department of Corrections had thrown his way this time.

"The parole board approved my release," he whispered as if speaking the words out loud might accidentally change them.

"What?" I gasped. "They approved it?"

This wasn't our first parole hearing. Ramsey had had one every twenty-four months since he'd become eligible after year six. The Caskeys did everything possible to keep Ramsey locked away. For a family who lived in denial about who their son had been, they sure held a lot of clout in the legal community. With Jonathan being a decorated cop, his dad the former mayor, and the entire Caskey name being something of a Clovert dynasty, they had entirely too many favors to call in.

After Ramsey's hearing at year ten, we'd had a good cry together during a visitation and decided not to put our hopes into an early release. He hated seeing me crushed each time he was denied, despite being a model inmate. And I hated knowing that, after everything he'd sacrificed, he was still trying to protect me.

We didn't talk about his parole hearing this time. I didn't spend months collecting, drafting, and rewriting letters to present to the board with the hopes they'd actually be read. And I didn't lose myself down a rabbit hole of hope only to end up in a black abyss of depression for days after the decision was made.

We didn't give up though. Ramsey still put in his paperwork and worked with his attorney. I still prayed to any and every God in existence, but we went into it with real expectations and restrained hope for the very first time.

And somehow, someway, it had finally happened.

"Holy shit, Ramsey. Is this real?"

He let out a loud laugh that cracked at the end. "God, I hope so. I could be out of here in a matter of weeks, Nora. Fuck."

Weeks.

Over twelve years in a cell and he could be home in a matter of *weeks*?

My nose stung, and tears burned my eyes. "Wait, is this a

done deal? When the Caskeys hear, Jonathan is going to lose his shit. Is there anything he could do to mess this up?"

"I...I don't think so. They brought me the paperwork and had me sit in on a call with this guy named Lee who's been assigned as my case agent. He's supposed to be calling you to check out the house and stuff." He blew out a ragged breath. "I think this might really be it." Emotion lodged in his throat, making his words jagged as he forced out, "Please let this be it."

I ignored the twist of the permanent knife in my heart when it came to Ramsey's time in prison. There was not a day that passed when I didn't feel a sense of guilt, but I was no longer drowning in it.

We'd both made choices that day. They were both right and wrong depending on whose eyes you were looking through. I wished every moment of every day that I could change the past, but I couldn't turn back time. It had taken a lot of years and soul searching for me to get to that place of peace. The pain was still there, but I no longer allowed it to dominate my life.

If this was real and Ramsey was finally coming home, there was a chance we could put this behind us once and for all.

"I have to tell Thea," I rushed out, the combination of excitement and adrenaline making my body hum like a hive of bees had taken up residence in my veins.

"No," Ramsey barked.

Jesus. Those two were going to be the end of me.

I'd spent twelve years being the middleman for Ramsey and Thea.

Ramsey desperately, and somewhat successfully, trying to force her to let him go.

Thea holding on to a ghost and the promises made by a seventeen-year-old boy.

RECLAIM

Both of them equally as stubborn.

Leaning around the bar dividing the kitchen from our living room, I peered down the hall. Thea's door was still shut, and if I knew her at all, she had her headphones on, watching travel videos while planning a top-of-the-line vacation she should have been taking herself. But just in case she wasn't, I kept my voice low as I laid into my brother.

"What the hell do you think is going to happen, Ramsey? You're going to get out and she's not going to find out? If nothing else, she deserves the chance to yell at you. You cut her out of your life completely."

He let out a groan. "I'm not having this conversation with you again."

"Fine, then just listen to me have it." I looked at her door again. "I love you and I respect you, so I've kept my promises. But when you get out of there, that word is no longer valid. You owe her a conversation. Hell, you owe *yourself* a conversation. You love her, dummy. Let her love you back."

"You have no idea what you're talking about."

"Oh, please. I'm the only one who knows what I'm talking about here. But I'm going to drop it for now because today is huge and I don't want to spend it fighting with you over the inevitable."

He cussed under his breath, but I smiled.

He was coming home.

Ramsey was finally coming home.

We talked for a few more minutes. I asked a million questions he didn't have the answers to. And we briefly talked about the logistics of his homecoming. He asked me to find a place for us to live without Thea. I lied and told him I would. If ever two people needed to be under the same roof, it was them. I'd tried to keep the drawers in my head as empty as possible over the last few years, but I was positive Cupid had told a few white lies in his time too.

After we'd exchanged I-love-yous, Ramsey and I hung up. I took the chicken on the counter and put it back in the fridge. Tuscany could wait for another time. Thea and I were officially going out to celebrate.

It was so close to being over.

Ramsey could be free.

Thea could be free.

Maybe then I could be free too.

TWENTY-ONE

Nora

"This isn't legal!" I yelled from the wrong side of the bars of a Clovert jail cell.

So, remember that "maybe then I could be free too" horseshit?

Yeah, things didn't exactly happen like that after Ramsey got out of prison.

What did happen was Officer Jonathan Caskey found new and unique ways to torture my entire family.

The day Thea and I had picked Ramsey up from prison was a dream come true. Sure, it had been hard for him to adapt to his new life of freedom—well, at least partial freedom since he was still on parole for the next three years. He and Thea… Well, that was a challenge to say the least. But, eventually, everyone got on the same page.

It only took a week before Jonathan Caskey showed up at our door, claiming he had information about Ramsey selling drugs out of the back of Thea's father's barbershop.

A fucking *week*. Of course, the cops found nothing, but that didn't mean Jonathan didn't get off on fucking with us.

We decided right then and there Ramsey would never be safe to finish his parole that close to the Caskey family. He requested a transfer from his parole officer and he and Thea moved upstate to Dahlonega. It sucked on epic levels. I'd just gotten my brother back, and thanks to the fucking Caskeys, I'd lost him again. But it was okay. He was happy and safe with the woman he loved. That was all I'd ever wanted for him.

Thea sold our place in Thomaston so she and Ramsey could buy a little cabin in the mountains. Living alone for the first time was a definite change, but I found a rental house closer to both work and Joe. Who needed a roommate when I had a class of thirty smiling six-year-olds to keep me busy?

My newfound loner status worried Joe. Emotionally, I was way past needing someone to check in on me, but he knew all too well how much I missed Thea. Misty was Joe's receptionist, but every Friday morning, he had her drive him past the barbershop to drop him off at my place. I thought it was sweet. To hear him tell it, he just liked chatting over coffee while I got ready, but I knew he was really just keeping an eye on me. It was fine. I liked the company. I'd drop him back off at the barbershop on my way to the school.

This was exactly how Joe and I ended up in the car together when Jonathan Caskey not only pulled us over at seven thirty in the morning, but also searched my vehicle and purse and then arrested me for the possession of marijuana that was absolutely not mine.

There. All caught up. Welcome to my hell.

"Hey!" I shouted at a uniformed officer as he approached my cell. I'd been cuffed behind my back all day, blisters rubbing on my wrists, my shoulders aching.

It was getting late and the drunks were starting to roll in. Slurring and stumbling, some of them flat-out belligerent, yet they were totally free inside that relic of a holding cell.

My head was pounding and I was pissed beyond all belief.

RECLAIM

It was a Friday, but shockingly, not a single judge had been available all damn day to set my bail. Cop after cop had told me it was out of their control, but the grin on Jonathan Caskey's face each time he went out of his fucking way to pass my cell said otherwise.

"I have the right to an attorney, you know. It's the law!"

Clovert's very own Barney Fife stopped at my door, and after a quick unlock routine, he slid it open. "If you would shut up for once, I'll take you to him."

My back shot straight and relief crashed over me. Finally, Joe must have been able to find me a lawyer in town willing step on some Caskey toes—and hopefully Caskey skulls too. Jonathan's minion roughly grabbed my arm and slammed the door shut behind me.

I winced. "Could you take it easy?"

He swung an icy gaze my way and lifted a bandaged hand in the air. "Did you take it easy on me when I was processing you?"

It was safe to say I had not. I'd bit this guy and kicked Jonathan in the shin. It was a real miss because I was aiming for his balls, but at least I'd made contact.

"You'll survive. I don't have rabies or anything."

"So you say." He hauled me down the short hall before stopping at an open doorway.

I'd had a lot of surprises in my life. Some rendered me speechless. Some broke my heart. Some changed the trajectory of my life as a whole.

But nothing, and I mean nothing, surprised me more than walking into that tiny room only big enough for a table and two folding chairs at the Clovert police station and finding Camden Cole standing inside.

This wasn't any version of Camden Cole I'd ever known, not even the sexy twenty-two-year-old I'd left naked and tangled in sheets five years earlier or the dozen pictures I'd obsessed over on Instagram.

No, this was Camden Cole all grown up.

Any other day, I would have flat-out drooled at the sight of this man. Gray three-piece suit. White shirt. Dark-gray tie. Thick muscles testing the skill of his tailor, because there was no way that suit had been anything other than custom made. He was roughly the same height, but his lanky frame now held the bulk of a man. His presence filled the room. Gone were the subtle curves of his jaw; now, he was all razor-sharp angles and he carried them with the resolute square of his shoulders.

Those blue eyes that had pierced my soul when I was only eleven years old were the same though. Well, they were the same if you didn't count the way they lit with a malevolent rage the minute they landed on me.

"How long has she been in those cuffs?" he snapped, his deep baritone demanding answers.

In that second, it didn't matter if we were standing in the middle of a police station and I probably looked like hell, as a chill rolled down my spine. It was all too similar to the one I usually felt in the shower, images of Camden on the backs of my lids, my fingers playing between my legs long after the water had run cold.

"Well," my badged escort drawled. "Caskey said—"

"All day," I jumped in, my voice breathier than I'd thought possible in my current predicament.

But come on. Camden Cole was fucking sexy.

"Caskey!" Camden boomed so loudly that the echo assaulted the entire room. His brown leather shoes—that were thankfully *not* his signature hideous penny loafers but rather seriously sexy in a way I was unaware men's shoes could be—pounded the tile floor as he stormed from the room.

He disappeared from my sight, but his voice could have been heard two counties over.

"Explain to me how keeping a woman in cuffs for over twelve hours while in a holding cell is either justified or reasonable!"

Jonathan Caskey's voice joined the conversation. "She was violent and resisting arrest. She bit one of my guys."

I noticed the coward left out the part where I'd punted him in the shin.

"And reasonable?" Camden snarled. "You're telling me there was no other *practical* way for you to restrain a one-hundred-and-twenty-pound woman other than cuffing her for twelve hours inside a holding cell, inside your police station. You have lost your fucking mind, and I swear to you, if she's not out of those cuffs in the next thirty seconds, you're going to lose your badge too."

Oh. My. God, I was going to orgasm right then and there. Camden Cole was gorgeous and powerful.

A smug grin pulled at my lips as Jonathan stomped into the room, Camden right behind him, barking all the way.

"Your gross ineptitude to follow procedure today is sickening. There were two judges taking bail hearings, yet my client sat in a cell? Cuffed no less."

My client.

My *client*.

My client?

Holy shit. Gorgeous, powerful Camden Cole was an attorney—*my* attorney?

My smile grew so big I feared it would swallow my face. His stormy gaze sliced to mine, and I actually blanched on impact.

"Ms. Stewart, is there a reason you're grinning while standing in a police station on potential resisting arrest, assaulting an officer, and possession of marijuana charges?"

Ms. Stewart? What the fuck was that? Shit. Gorgeous, powerful, attorney-at-law Camden Cole was also a bit of a cranky realist.

I licked my lips and looked at my shoes. "Uh, no."

"Right," he clipped.

My hands were freed, and my shoulders screamed as I stretched my arms out in front of me. And whether he was cranky or not, I moved to stand at my attorney's side.

"What the fuck are you even doing here?" Jonathan asked his cousin. "Don't you live in New York?"

Camden pulled a cell phone from his pocket and began stabbing his index finger at the screen. "Yes, but my client, who you have spent the majority of the day holding in unlawful restraints, depriving her of her physical rights and freedoms, lives here in Clovert. Rest assured, I am fully licensed to practice law in the state of Georgia, including, but not limited to, police misconduct cases." He lifted the phone to his ear and slapped Jonathan across the face with a challenging glare.

Jonathan's jaw locked up tight, ticking at the hinges. He took a long stride forward, getting all up in Camden's space. I backed away, but more for distance than any fear of Jonathan. If my attorney was pissed about the grin, he was going be livid at the giggle I was fighting to suppress when Jonathan was forced to tip his head back to peer up at him.

"Are you threatening me?" he seethed.

Camden returned his glare, somehow managing to look

more bored than pissed. "Just stating facts, Officer Caskey." He lifted a finger in the air. "Hello? Yes, your honor. He's right here." He tipped the phone toward Jonathan. "Judge Wallace would like to speak to you."

Jonathan's eyes flared and that was it; I lost the battle with my lungs.

A laugh slipped out and I slapped a hand over my mouth, but it was too late to stop it.

Luckily, gorgeous, powerful, cranky Camden was too busy doing his badass attorney thing to scold me.

He looked to the other officer and stated dryly, "Bail has been set and posted. Please prepare my client for immediate release."

For the next few minutes, Jonathan held the phone to his ear and said a whole lot of "Uh, huh" and "Yes, sir." Meanwhile, Camden did a whole lot of standing with his hand in his pocket, looking like a GQ model. This meant I did a whole lot of staring and willing my nipples to stop tingling.

Eventually, Jonathan lowered the phone, slapped it into Camden's hand, and then marched from the room.

Barney Fife stood there for a minute, nervously staring at a glowering Camden before finally thinking better of his life choices and racing out of the room.

Another laugh bubbled from my throat.

"Something funny?" Camden asked, turning his gaze on me in a way that both felt like a caress and a curse.

I hadn't been with a man in five years, so it was safe to say it was the verbal caress portion of that question that stole my voice. I shook my head.

"Good. Let's get you out of here, Cujo."

Cujo?

Holy shit, had cranky Camden just made a joke?

I didn't have time to ask for clarification before he swept an arm out for me to leave the room first. Ever the gentleman.

When we got to the front, Jonathan was swirling around behind the counter, slamming shit, and mumbling curses under his breath. It only took about ten minutes for him to practically hurl a stack of papers and a small plastic bag of the stuff I'd had in my pockets at Camden. "There. Now, get her the fuck out of my station."

"And the rest of her belongings?" He looked at me. "I was told by a witness at the scene you took her purse from the vehicle."

Joe. The only witness was Joe.

Jonathan grinned like a serpent in the garden of Eden. "You mean the evidence? Not happening. And go ahead. Call whatever the fuck judge you want, but you won't be getting that purse back until after a trial."

Camden held his icy stare. "Being the upstanding officer you are, I'm sure you'll see to it that you stay away from my client until we can resolve this matter. Given your history with her family and all."

Jonathan narrowed his eyes. "And what about my history with *your* family, Camden? You forget about that?"

"Of course not. Why else would I be here?" He grinned, rapped his knuckles on the counter, and nodded. "Have a good evening, Officer Caskey." With that, Camden turned, gently rested his hand on my back, and guided me out of the police station.

And because I was so mature, I didn't even flip off Jonathan as we left.

Just kidding. I totally did that.

"Nora!" Joe called when we got outside. He jogged over and drew me into a tight hug.

"Ow," I croaked.

"Easy, Joe," Camden rumbled. "She's spent all day in restraints."

Joe immediately set me away. "Jesus, honey, are you okay?"

"I'm not entirely sure yet." I glanced down at my wrinkled gray-and-pink-striped shirt I'd paired with black cropped skinny jeans and ballet flats that morning. "I need a shower, STAT."

Joe shook his head. "Come on. Let's get you home." He extended a hand toward Camden. "I really appreciate you making the trip down."

The two men shook hands.

"Anytime. I'm glad you called. But if you don't mind, I'd like to take Nora home myself. We can meet back up first thing in the morning and discuss our next step."

My stomach dipped. It had been five years since I'd seen him, and while I wasn't positive gorgeous, powerful, cranky, attorney, Camden Cole was still the same kid who'd sat at the edge of the creek playing Slapjack with me or even the man who'd made love to me for hours on end, I was just excited to be able to see my friend again—mercurial as he currently seemed.

"Works for me," I said. "I'm exhausted and would really like to be lucid for the castrate-Caskey plan."

Joe chuckled. "All right. Take her home. You sure I can't convince you to stay in my guest room tonight? Even braving Misty's turkey bacon pie for breakfast has to be better than the Clovert Inn."

I scoffed. "He's not staying in that dump."

Camden didn't even look at me as he replied, "Thanks, Joe. But I've already booked the room."

Curling my lip, I tilted my head back and semi-repeated, "You *aren't* staying at the Clovert Inn. Cam, I have plenty of space at my place."

His Adam's apple bobbed, but that was his only response. "Nice seeing you again, Joe."

After a quick round of hugs and handshakes, we all climbed in our respective cars. Well, I climbed into Camden's black SUV because my Honda was in impound.

"Nice car," I said, desperately trying to make conversation that didn't consist of a scold or stoic silence as I slid into the leather passenger seat.

He folded his tall body into the driver's side and pressed a button on the dash to start the engine, muttering, "It's a rental." Stone faced and unreadable, he stared at the backup camera as he maneuvered out of the parking spot.

I waited until we were on the main road before giving it another try. "I really appreciate—"

"Shh!"

My head snapped back. "I'm sorry. Did you just shush me?"

"Shhhh!" he repeated louder as though I'd misheard him.

"Um—"

Literally, that was all I got out before another, "Shhhhh!" headed my way.

Slack-jawed, I turned in my seat and glared at him. My day had been next-level fucked up, and while watching Jonathan Caskey get put in his place had possibly been the high point of my entire year, this eerily quiet and frankly rude guy who had shown up in my best friend's skin was seriously ruining it for me.

"Stop telling me to shh," I snapped.

"Then shh!" he clipped right back. His eyes remained on the road as he turned into an empty parking lot a few blocks down from the police station. The glowing sign of the Burger Max illuminated the side of his face.

What the hell are we doing here? hung on the tip my tongue, but I wasn't too eager to claw his eyes out if he shushed me again, so I gave him a second to dig deep and hopefully find a complete sentence.

"Four years of working my ass off to keep a four-point-oh in undergrad," he stated at the windshield, his long fingers opening and closing around the steering wheel. "Three grueling attempts at the LSAT. Three years of law school, where I became a glorified zombie who never slept. An internship where my mentor was banging his secretary and handing off the majority of his caseload to me before I'd even graduated law school. Then, when I did graduate and had to dive straight into studying for the MPRE and then the Bar—twice. Once for New York and again for Georgia. But oh. My. Fucking. God. Nora, I would do that shit seven times over just to finally watch that piece of shit cower." He pounded his hand on the steering wheel with a Grammy-worthy drumroll, and a loud laugh bubbled from his throat. "Fuck me, that was incredible!"

And there he was, my cute, sweet, and dorky Camden Cole, sitting in the driver's seat, laughing like he was a kid again. Though he was still in that suit, so the gorgeous and powerful things stuck around too.

I gave his shoulder a shove. "You scared the shit out of me. I thought you'd gone to law school and received a diploma in being a dick."

"It's more like a license to be a dick, and I reserve that specifically for Caskeys and courtrooms. Though you should have seen your face when I called you Ms. Stewart." He grinned wide, toothy, and bright. "How the hell are you, stranger?"

I dove across the center console and pulled him into a hug.

It hurt like hell, but he was too close to resist. When he wrapped me up tight, I melted into his strong, safe arms. "Well, today sucked, but suddenly, it's a lot better."

He released me, smiling and straightening his suit as he righted himself in his seat. "It seems you've picked up a Mary Jane habit since I last saw you."

I shot him a glare. "It wasn't mine. Your stupid cousin has it out for me. He started with Ramsey, but when they moved, Joe and I became his next targets. Do you have any idea how many times the city inspector has been to Joe's barbershop over the last three months?"

His smile fell. "We're going to figure it out."

I wanted to argue, but I really didn't have it in me. A shower, a change of clothes, and some catching up with Camden sounded far more appealing. "Why would you book a room at the Clovert Inn? You can always stay with me."

"And miss the complimentary shampoo?"

"I hear the bedbugs are complimentary too."

"You hear anything about frogs though?"

I barked a laugh and reached over to give his forearm a squeeze. "It's really good to see you. And not just because you saved my ass back there."

He rested his hand on top of mine and smiled, warm and content. "You too, Nora. You too."

"Come on. Let's go to my place and have a beer. I live off Springdale Road now."

"Um, actually, I really do need to get settled in and get some rest. I have a call with the prosecutor's office in the morning. He was out with his wife tonight, but I'd like to get a feel for where his head's at on all of this. Being a Saturday, I'm sure he'll want to keep it brief though."

I tipped my head to the side. "Why do you know the prosecutor in Clovert? And, for that matter, Judge Wallace too?"

He put the car into drive and got back on the road, answering, "Because I've made it my business to know them. It's the same reason I'm a member of the Bar in Georgia. Eventually, Jonathan was going to pull something, and I wanted to be the one to handle it when he did. Sets me on fire that he's decided to pull it on you, but I'm hoping to transfer that heat to him, and watching him burn might be more fun."

Awestruck, I sat there, staring at the side of his handsome face, a warmth filling my chest. Camden Cole still had my back no matter what.

My gut instinct was to feel guilty, to apologize for him having to take on so much of my issues to the point that he'd built a safety net for me into his own career.

I wanted to be embarrassed that I needed him and feel shame about how he was stuck with a friend like me.

But year after year, I'd been uninstalling the drawers in my head, so there was no longer a place to put those feelings other than out in the open.

"I hate that I've made so many of my problems your problems too."

He shot me a side-eye. "Are you kidding me? I'd have flown down here and planted weed in your purse years ago if I'd thought it would get me involved in a case with that prick."

"Okay, then at least let me pay for your plane ticket. I feel bad."

"It didn't seem like you felt bad while you were giggling back at the station."

"Well, no. You made Jonathan your bitch. That was fucking amazing. But I feel bad *now*." Reaching over, I slid my hand on top of his and intertwined our fingers. It was something so natural I didn't even question it. Yes, I would always be attracted to Camden. But this was not a *hey, I'd really enjoy ripping your clothes off again* type of physical gesture. It was more of the *thanks for always being there when I need you* variety.

The problem was, regardless of the variety, Camden immediately pulled his hand away. "There's no reason to feel bad. We're *friends*," he stated.

Remember that mixture of caress and curse he'd hit me with earlier? Yeah, this one was all curse.

I leaned back in my seat, an awkward sense of unease slithering across my skin. We were friends. There was no arguing that. But why had he said it with such a force it was as though he'd planted a shield in the ground at his feet.

It had been a seriously long day. There was a good chance I was just being sensitive and reading into things. "Right. Friends," I muttered.

He nodded and turned onto my street. "Which house is yours?"

"Corner on the right."

He slowed and I waited for him to turn into my driveway, but instead, he pulled up in front of my house and put it in park. The best part? He didn't even cut the engine.

"I'll be by to get you in the morning. Say about nine? We can grab your car from impound and then head over and talk to Joe. Hopefully, by then, we'll have more information from the prosecutor and know how to handle things. But you need to get some rest and I need to make a game plan."

He looked at me expectantly, but I just sat there staring at him with a curled lip.

"Are you seriously not staying with me?"

"I'll be up late working, and when I think, I do a lot of pacing and talking to myself."

"So…"

"So I'm going to stay at the hotel."

I stared at him, a knot growing in my stomach. Why did that hurt? We hadn't seen each other in so long; I wanted to drink up every single second of Camden Cole that I could.

And he wanted to stay at a hotel.

I sucked in a deep breath and willed my shoulders to relax. He had just flown all the way from New York to save my ass, and now, he was developing a "game plan" for how he was going to save it even further. Being a gorgeous, powerful, sometimes cranky attorney had to be exhausting. Maybe he just needed his own space to clear his mind and relax.

Yes. That was it. It had nothing to do with me or us or, well, us just being *friends*. It was a work thing. I color-coded crayons when I was stressed. I guessed it wasn't completely crazy if he wanted to pace and talk in a roach motel.

"Okay," I whispered.

He grinned. "Okay."

I forced a smile. "How long are you in town?"

The answer would no doubt be some variation of "How long do you need me to stay?" Historically, it was how Camden and I worked, and with as weird as things felt inside that SUV, I really needed the reminder of something normal.

He swayed his head from side to side. "Assuming the prosecutor has half a brain, it shouldn't take more than a week. I shifted some of my cases at home and can work on the rest remotely, but I'll need to get back sooner rather than later."

A sinkhole could have opened up and swallowed the car and I would have been less surprised than hearing Camden Cole say, "Sooner rather than later."

I mean, I got it. He had a job and a career. I felt guilty that he was there for me. But damn, it still stung.

"Totally understand," I muttered, grabbing the door handle and swinging it open before he had the chance to see the hurt in my eyes. "I'll see you in the morning."

I sprinted across my yard, right through the flowerbed I'd spent months planting and pruning. But who cared about gardenias when you were running away from the only man you'd ever loved?

"Goodnight, Nora!" he yelled out the passenger-side window.

I had no clue where my keys had ended up that day, so I dug my hide-a-key out from the flowerpot next to my door. With my heart in my throat, I opted for a wave over my shoulder before going inside.

I beelined straight to my shower, ready to wash away not only the filth from the cell, but the entire day, hopefully to cleanse away the awkwardness I'd never felt with Camden Cole before too. Being a trained professional who had put entirely too many tubes of chapstick into the washing machine over the years, I checked all of my pockets before throwing my pants into the hamper.

They should have been empty. Everything I'd had on me when I'd been arrested was in a plastic baggy now.

But in my front right pocket, there was a folded up ten-dollar bill.

A wave of emotions crashed into me. I had no idea how or when he'd snuck it in there without me feeling it. It was definitely our ten though, complete with the faded words *This is yours. Fair and square.* scrawled across the back.

And just like that, something felt normal again.

TWENTY-TWO

Camden

Calling the Clovert Inn a hotel was generous at best. I couldn't be sure, but I thought I saw a piece of paper behind the check-in counter stating hourly rates.

After taking off my jacket and my vest and hanging them in the dingy closet across from the even dingier bathroom, I peeled back the threadbare comforter on the bed, thankfully finding what appeared to be clean sheets. Finally, I sank down on the edge.

What a fucking day.

When I'd gotten the phone call from Joe, I'd been in the middle of a meeting with a client. I'd almost fallen out of my chair snatching it off the table. Back when Nora had been younger, after she'd tried to end her life, Joe had called me periodically to check in and give me updates. We didn't talk long or often, but I always smiled when his number popped up on the screen of my phone.

Not that day though. It had been too long since we'd last spoken for him to be calling for anything other than bad news.

My blood boiled as Joe filled me in on what Jonathan had done. Within an hour, I paid a small fortune for a ticket on the first flight out. There was never a question of whether I would drop everything and go to her. It was Nora; there was nothing I wouldn't do for her.

Though staying at her house would have seriously tested the limits.

Even fresh out of a jail cell, in wrinkled clothes, and with her hair a tangled mess, she was just as beautiful as she'd always been. But that wasn't why I was there. We had far bigger fish to fry than mutual and undeniable attraction.

My phone rang and I dug it out of my back pocket, groaning when I saw *Mom* flash on the screen. My mother and I had a strained relationship, but she at least attempted to keep in touch.

Falling back across the bed, I put the phone to my ear. "Hello."

"Hello, son. My one and only son, might I add."

I rolled my eyes. "Well, that sounds like the beginning of a guilt trip."

"No guilt," she said haughtily. "I just think it says a lot that I got a call from your aunt saying you were in Clovert and I am the very last person to know."

Jesus, word traveled fast in that town. "It wasn't a planned trip. Some...business came up."

"Oh, I've heard all about your *business* there, Camden. What I don't understand is why you would fly all the way across the country to get into a tuffle with Jonathan again. Can you just leave that man alone for once?"

I barked a laugh. "Is that what you think is happening, Mom? A tuffle?"

"I honestly don't know what to think. You've spent your entire life fighting with him. At some point, I just assumed you'd grow up."

Clenching my teeth, I suddenly sat up, gripping the phone so tightly my fingertips turned red. "Oh, I've grown up. I went to law school, and while I was there, they taught me that it's not okay for a cop to harass a victim's family and especially not pull her over and plant drugs in her purse."

"My God, Camden. Is this about that girl again?"

"Her name is Nora, Mom. Say it with me: *Nor-a*. And she's not some girl. In case you don't remember, dear old Auntie Caskey's son and Jonathan's prized brother *raped* her."

"Jesus, Camden. Don't be so crude."

"Oh, I'm sorry. Was that uncomfortable for you to hear? You know what else I bet is uncomfortable? Being a twelve-year-old girl and having someone force themselves on you."

She let out a loud sigh. "And here we go again. After all these years, you're still stuck on this. We don't know if he did that to her."

"I picked the splitters out of her back!" I boomed. "But fine. You want to pretend Josh didn't do anything to Nora. Let's talk about facts. We know he did do it to Thea. You can't argue with that. There are medical records that say otherwise."

She could have argued a lot of things right then. My mother was a bright, educated woman. After marrying my dad, she'd never needed to work a day in her life, but she was intelligent—albeit a little Southern Stepford at times. She could have pointed out how death had been ruled an unconstitutional punishment for rape. She could have stated Josh had deserved a fair trial before a jury of his peers. She even could have just kept her fucking mouth shut altogether.

My mother chose none of the above.

"Have you ever considered that maybe it was consensual?"

My.

Head.

Exploded.

"Are you off your fucking rocker?" I shouted, shooting to my feet.

"Camden," she hissed. "Don't you dare raise your voice at me like that."

Pinching the bridge of my nose, I began pacing the room like a caged animal. "You have no idea what you are talking about. Just when I start to think you aren't like the rest of your screwed-up family, you start spouting shit like that."

"They're your family too. And you're going to embarrass all of us if you don't drop this little grudge you have against your cousin. He's a police officer. Arresting people who break the law is his job."

"And upholding that law is mine. I don't give a shit if the person is a Caskey, a Kennedy, or Christ himself."

"You don't mean that."

I let out a humorless laugh. "You have no idea just how much I do mean it. Look, I have to go. Take care of yourself."

"Camden!" she shouted across the line, but it was too late.

I pulled the phone from my ear and hit the end button.

It wasn't two seconds before my phone started ringing again, but I did not have the time, the energy, or the patience to deal with any more bullshit. I knew better than to assume she'd give up though, I'd be lucky if she wasn't already in her car, on the way to Clovert. Whatever. My mom was the least of my worries at the moment.

I tossed it onto the bed and continued to pace, hoping to burn away enough of the adrenaline so I could actually catch a few hours of sleep and be worth a damn the next day.

And to think, I'd assumed keeping my hands off Nora was going to be the hardest part of this trip.

TWENTY-THREE

Nora

"I'm sorry. Come again," I whispered across the phone, slowly sinking down onto the couch.

My principal cleared her throat. "It's just temporary."

"You can't suspend me, Julie. I didn't do anything wrong."

"It's policy, Nora. Especially since there were drugs involved. I'm sure you'll be reinstated in no time. Pending the outcome of your, uh… Oh, dear, how do I put this? *Legal predicament*, of course."

Tears welled in my eyes as I drew in a shaky breath. "You can't do this to me. Come on, Julie. Screw policy. Those kids are my life."

"I know, and I give you my word we'll take great care of them for you. Barbara Gilbert has already agreed to come in and take your class. You like her, right?"

I bit my bottom lip and hung my head. Last I'd heard, Barbara was turning down short-term substitute work because she was holding out for a permanent position.

And clearly she'd found one.

With *my* kids.

"Yeah. She's great."

"Listen, we're all rooting for you here. If you didn't do anything wrong, you have nothing to worry about."

Yeah, right. If only that were the case. I was a Stewart and we were currently zero and one with the judicial system.

My head snapped up when there was a knock on my door. Nine o'clock. Right on time. My heart skipped a beat knowing it was Camden on the other side.

"I understand, Julie. Can I pop in after school one day and pick up a few things from my desk?"

"Absolutely. Just focus on yourself and we'll hold down the fort until you get back, okay?"

I sighed and walked to my door. "Yeah. Okay. Have a good weekend."

"You too, dear."

I ended the call and shoved my phone into the back pocket of my jeans. I paused to smooth my hair down and do a cursory sweep under my eyes just in case any of my tears had the chance to escape.

My efforts were fruitless because as soon as I opened the door and Camden's bright-blue eyes landed on me, he rushed out, "What's wrong?"

"Hi," I greeted, sick and damn tired of people asking me that. But even more sick and tired of there usually being an answer.

He extended a paper travel cup of coffee my way. "Is that a real hi? Or hi, I'm avoiding your question?"

"Both." Shoving the door wide to invite him in, I took the cup from his hand, never having needed a second dose of caffeine more.

Sexy as sin in a pair of sneakers, low-slung jeans, and a fitted black v-neck T-shirt that hugged new and mouth-watering planes his suit had hidden the night before, he stepped into my house. "Okay, then. Let me put it this way. As your attorney, is there anything I need to know about?"

I turned on a toe and walked to the kitchen, positive I was going to need to doctor the coffee with more cream and sugar. After placing my cup on the counter, I pried the top off and sighed. "My principal suspended me"—I hooked my fingers in air quotes—"pending the outcome of my legal predicament."

"Shiiit," he drawled. "I'd really hoped we could get in front of that. Have you talked to your union representative yet?"

Retrieving the milk from the fridge, I barked a laugh. "Um, I think your New York is showing. There's no teacher's union in these parts."

"Oh, right," he said then took a sip of his coffee. "So, how are you handling the news?"

I slid my teal canister over, scooped two heaping spoonfuls of sugar into my cup, and gave it a swirl. "Well, I've had about three minutes to process it, but I'm happy to report I haven't broken into the vodka or cut the brake lines on Jonathan's cruiser yet, so I'd say so far so good."

He grinned. "That's reassuring. I'm still trying to figure out how to explain away your teeth marks on Officer Rice's hand. Cut brake lines would definitely require a touch more legal finesse on my part."

I chuffed and looked down to put the top back on my coffee. "I still can't believe you're an attorney."

"Well, maybe if we'd spoken in the last five years, you'd know."

"What?" I asked, my head snapping up. It could have been an innocent prod from an old friend. Just a teasing joke. But there was something odd to the edge in his tone.

He smiled. "You ready to go? I called and impound is only open until noon."

Ooookay. Interesting subject change. But it was Camden,

and while things were certainly different between us—seriously, he hadn't pulled me into a hug once yet—I told myself that it was nothing.

"Um, yeah. Let me just grab my stuff."

While I packed a new purse and wallet with my emergency credit card that lived in my nightstand and thankfully not in my wallet currently numbered in an evidence locker, he stood in the middle of my living room, scanning the pictures on the wall. It was so incredibly surreal to see him inside my house.

Over the years, I'd spent a lot of nights imagining having him there. Just two friends catching up—at first fully clothed before spending the night doing a little naked catch-up too.

I'd never been brave enough to reach out to him though. In my head, my emotional house still needed a lot of cleaning before being ready for the likes of Camden Cole.

We drove to the impound yard together, making small talk about all the things that had changed since he'd been to Clovert last. I think he was most impressed by how we had two grocery stores now, which solidified my speculations on why he'd never come back for a visit. Buying Cheetos at two different locations only held so much travel appeal.

Things felt normal again on the car ride. We laughed and told stories about old times. When we passed the Leonards' house, I filled him in on the never-ending feud between their family and the Lewises. Mr. Leonard had been dead for over six years, but his sons and grandkids had gotten in on the action too. Thus, Leonard's Local Tackle was born, putting Clovert on the map with not only two grocery stores, but two bait shops as well.

It wasn't even ten o'clock on the morning of the day after I'd been arrested, the same morning I'd been suspended from my job, yet Camden had worked his magic so I was grinning from ear to ear when we walked into the small office at the impound yard.

"I'll be right with you," greeted a police officer with dark-brown hair who I recognized as a kid Ramsey had gone to school with, his eyes still glued to his computer.

"Hey, Nathan," I said, stopping at the counter.

He flicked his gaze to mine, his eyes flashing wide before doing a double take. I was used to that. Being the county villain, I usually elicited two responses from people. Either they hated me and went out of their way to make sure I knew it or they hated the Caskeys. And while they didn't openly support me, they just ignored the problem altogether.

"Officer Pollard," he corrected, landing himself firmly in the former category.

Okay, so clearly, Nathan Pollard's balls had dropped since I'd watched him get pantsed in front of the entire school in ninth grade.

I gritted my teeth. "Right. Sorry, *Officer Pollard*. We're here to pick up my car."

"Hmm," he hummed, his gaze drifting to Camden. "And you needed your lawyer for that?"

Jesus, the Clovert gossip train must have worked overtime for him to already know Camden was my lawyer.

Camden shot him a sardonic smile. "How about you do your damn job and hope someday you get promoted to big-boy cop status, *Nathan*."

His eyes narrowed on Camden and I had to bite the inside of my cheek to keep from laughing. Damn, it felt good to finally have backup.

Without retort, he turned back to his computer.

I bumped Camden with my shoulder and he shot me a wink, and for a brief second, I forgot I was the most hated woman in all of Clovert. And even if I was, I didn't care too much when I had Camden at my side.

"That will be six hundred and eighty-two dollars," Nathan said with a smile almost as disgusting as the number he'd just rattled off.

"Six hundred dollars? For what?"

He swayed his head from side to side. "Towing, storage, security for the lot."

"Security for the lot? You've had my car for one freaking day! I hardly think my 2005 Honda Accord needs a presidential detail."

He shrugged. "Fees add up. Now, will that be cash or credit?"

"Neither! You are out of your damn mind if you think I'm paying you almost seven hundred dollars. I know for a fact Billy Dice only charges fifty bucks to tow anywhere in the city limits. He would have towed my car to Texas for less than seven hundred bucks."

"Relax," Camden muttered, pushing a credit card across the counter. "I've got it."

I slid it right back in his direction. "Uh, no, you don't. The only thing less likely than me paying this clown six hundred bucks to get my car back is *you* paying this clown six hundred bucks *for me*."

"Nora, it's not a big deal."

"Yes, it is." I looked back at Nathan. "You know what? I want to see receipts. You're telling me you paid Billy Dice and whatever rent-a-cop you have guarding this place at night almost seven hundred dollars? Prove it. Show me the documentation and I'll gladly pay a percentage over that. The citizens of Clovert need the jobs, but six hundred dollars is highway robbery and you know it, *Officer Pollard.*"

Camden grabbed my arm and gave me a tug. "Excuse us for a moment?" he told the extortionist in a uniform then once again handed him his credit card. "Go ahead and put it on that. We'll be right back."

"Don't you dare charge that card!" I yelled as Camden dragged me outside.

"Would you stop?" he hissed as soon as the door shut behind us.

I yanked my arm from his grip, my shoulders still tender from my time in cuffs—and not in the fun way where Camden had spent the night and gotten a little kinky. "You aren't paying for it."

His expression was hard as he leaned down, getting in my face. "Yes, I am. And you're going to hush and let me. Jesus Christ, woman, you aren't helping your cause here. I know you're pissed and you have every right to be, but these charges against you are serious. Honestly, a misdemeanor for some pot is the least of your worries. Do you understand aggravated assault on an officer can hold up to twenty years in prison?"

It was safe to say I did not understand that; therefore, my back shot straight and I clamped my mouth shut.

"Yeah, I see you're getting it now." He moved in close, one of his hands going to my hip. "I talked to the prosecution this morning. Given your track record working with the kids in the community, they are willing to at least discuss the severity of the charges. But you have to cool it with the Wonder-Woman-on-steroids act. You bit an officer yesterday, Nora."

"I kicked Jonathan too," I confessed because, well…it was Camden. He was my attorney and I thought he should have all the facts before he tried to defend me from twenty years in prison.

He blinked, but I swear I saw a twitch at the corner of his mouth. "Right. Well, no more of that."

I rested my palm on his hard chest. His hand flexed at my hip the minute I made contact, but if he could touch me, I assumed I could do the same. "I'll do better, I promise."

"Less Chuck Norris and more of you being a heart-of-gold first-grade teacher who spends her spare time packing bag lunches for underprivileged kids."

"Yeah, I kn—wait. How do you know about that?"

His hand fell away from my hip so fast you'd have thought I'd caught fire. "I, um, did some digging on you last night."

I narrowed my eyes. It was a feasible explanation. Dropping my name into Google was probably the first lesson he'd been taught in *Getting To Know Your Client 101*.

But it was the "um" that piqued my suspicions.

Gorgeous, powerful, somewhat cranky attorney-at-law Camden Cole was not an "um" man. And it didn't matter if I hadn't yet spent a full twenty-four hours with him. This version of Camden carried himself with such a confidence it teetered on arrogance—sexy, mouthwatering, tingle-inducing arrogance, but arrogance no less. Sure, the nerdy boy I'd once known who'd prattled on for hours about absolutely nothing could hem and haw with the best of 'em.

But not this guy.

Between his reaction in his car the night before when I'd grabbed his hand, that strange edge to his tone when he'd made the jab back at my house, and now an "um," something was going on. What? I had no idea, but he wasn't the only one who would be doing some detective work from here on out.

"I'll behave, but I can't let you pay to get my car out of here. Teachers aren't exactly rolling in dough like fancy New York City attorneys, but I have a rainy-day-slash-Louboutin fund."

A smile stretched across his obscenely handsome face. "A rainy-day-slash-Louboutin fund?"

"Yeah, it's money I set aside every month in case of emergency…or the first-ever Louboutin clearance event. Whichever comes first." I let out a groan and looked back at stupid Nathan Pollard through the glass door. "This month, it just happens to be pouring."

Reaching out, he hooked his pinky with mine and shot me a grin. "Maybe, but we've stood in the rain together before."

And with that, a warmth rushed through my veins and he gave me back the boy who'd stolen my heart all those years earlier.

He dropped my hand in the very next beat, but together, we walked back inside.

I signed the paperwork while he typed out a text at warp speed on his phone.

And then, side by side, we walked out to an assigned parking spot number to find my car, with four flat tires and both of the side-view mirrors broken and hanging from cables.

I wanted to cry.

I wanted to go full-fledge Nora Stewart rabid-dog wild woman on the entire crooked Clovert police department.

I wanted to turn around, walk away, and never look back.

But when Camden dipped low, put his lips to my ear, and whispered, "Keep it together, Chuck," all I could do was laugh.

TWENTY-FOUR

Camden

I LAY ON MY BED IN THE HOTEL, MY CHEST HEAVING, NAKED as the day I was born, my cock pissed off and deflating against my thigh. That fucking bastard and my eyes had spent all Goddamn day trying to kill me.

Yeah, Nora was fucking sexy. This was not new information. Yet I'd spent my day trying not to stare at her ass in those tight skinny jeans—or consequently adjusting my dick when my eyes had found the task impossible.

And the touches. All the fucking touches.

Hooking her arm with mine when we'd walked into Joe's barbershop, her soft curves molding to my side.

Her thigh pressed against mine as we'd sat on the loveseat in his office, filling him in on everything from my chat with the prosecutor to which repair shop we'd had her car towed to.

Don't even get me started on the way her shirt had gaped in the front when she'd bent over her menu at the burger place we'd gone to for lunch. Her breasts were still carved into my subconscious from our one and only night together. I did not need a reminder of how perfect they were.

And because she was Nora, the living and breathing embodiment of every dream and fantasy I'd had my entire life, I could have gotten off just from sitting across the table and listening to her talk.

RECLAIM

Long story short: I was fucked and not in a good way.

My cock twitched at the memories, and I let out a groan, pressing my head back into the pillow. I'd already wrestled that son of a bitch into submission once in the shower and once not even thirty minutes later when he'd refused to chill the fuck out and tuck into a pair of pants without tenting the front.

And he was already swelling again?

How the fuck was I supposed to make it through dinner at Nora's house with my cock trying to claw his way out every five fucking minutes?

I should have canceled. We'd swapped cell numbers, so I could even just puss out and send her a text about how I was tired and couldn't make it.

But she was cooking, and when I'd dropped her off, she'd declared after the day she'd had she didn't want to do anything but have some wine and catch up with an old friend.

And I was a sucker who would have done any and every damn thing in the world to make her happy.

Fuck. Me.

I stood up, walked over to my suitcase, and dug out a pair of boxer briefs. They weren't quite the straightjacket I needed to keep myself in check, but they would have to do. My phone started ringing from the worn-out wicker nightstand next to the bed, and I hopped over, pulling my jeans on one leg at a time.

"Hello," I said, doing the button-and-zip routine.

"You have one fucked-up family," a deep voice rumbled across the line.

I planted a hand on my hip. "This is not news to me. What do you have for me, Leo?"

Leo James. Former DEA agent turned owner of Guardian Protection Agency turned jack-of-all-trades who, with the help of his team of bodyguards, security specialists, and investigators, dabbled in a little of everything in the personal protection sector. He was no nonsense and cost a fucking mint, but every single person I'd called from New York all the way to Seattle swore by him.

I'd contacted him on my way to the airport after hearing that Jonathan had Nora in lockup. I'd only gotten so far as to tell him what Josh had done to Thea and subsequently that Ramsey had spent twelve years in prison for killing him, strategically leaving out all details that could blow back on Nora, when Leo interrupted me, saying, "Fuck that motherfucker. Email me the details and I'll get Apollo on it tonight," and then hung up.

I did not know Apollo or how he was going to "get on it" from their home office seven hundred miles away in Chicago, but I'd sent him the details anyway.

"What I got is a folder full of Caskey fuckery. Where would you like to start? Your grandfather's foot fetish porn collection seems like a fun jumping-off point. Though your uncle's affair with his best friend's wife would be my second choice."

I curled my lip. "I'm gonna take a hard pass on both. Just give me what you got on Jonathan."

He chuckled. "Smart man. Unfortunately, what I have on Jonathan is not as exciting. Seems he's the only one in that muddy bloodline who knows how to lock down a damn Wi-Fi network. However, we did find one thing that might interest you. The night before your girl was arrested, Officer Caskey took down a kid named Sean Watkins on a possession charge. Nothing big, first offense, slap-on-the-wrist misdemeanor. But the interesting part is, according to police reports Caskey confiscated point eight two ounces of marijuana. Want to take a guess how much was found in your girl's purse?"

"Point eight two ounces," I mumbled.

"Bingo! Now it's not the nail in the coffin you were hoping for, but we're still working on it. In the meantime, put some pressure on him. Let him know you know about Sean Watkins. Get him on edge. He'll fuck up eventually."

I pinched the bridge of my nose. I didn't doubt he was right about that. My fear was I wouldn't still be in Clovert when Jonathan fucked up, but Nora would. "Will do. Thanks, Leo."

"No problem. We'll be in touch."

He hung up and I sank to the edge of the bed. What the hell was I going to do when I had to leave her there? Why she even still lived in Clovert was a mystery to me, but short of kidnapping her, I had no idea what else I could do about it.

After dragging a shirt on, I called up to the police station to request a copy of the Sean Watkins arrest report. Jonathan wasn't in the office, but I made sure to ask enough questions and said my name no fewer than a dozen times until I was positive word would get back to him.

I had an hour before I was supposed to be at her house, and while my cock had thankfully gone into hibernation at the thought of my almost eighty-year-old grandpa's apparent foot fetish, I still had a whole night with Nora to face.

Honestly, that might have been harder than anything else. Literally and figuratively.

TWENTY-FIVE

Nora

Ever punctual, Camden knocked on my door at seven o'clock on the dot. I drew in a deep breath and ran my fingers through my beach waves, taking a second to do one last physical inventory.

Tight, cropped skinny jeans. Check.

A pink silk camisole that was supposed to be worn under a cardigan, but it did great things for my boobs, so I did *not* want to cover that up. Check.

Black strappy heels—in my own house when I could have gone barefoot. Check.

A smoky eye that looked both seductive and effortless. Check.

A ball of nerves roughly the size of North America vibrating in my chest. Check. Check. Check.

God, why was I so damn nervous? Camden and I had had a great day together. He had been a little distant, but at lunch, it'd felt like he was slowly starting to come out of his shell. When he'd dropped me off at my house, he'd actually pulled into the driveway and walked me to my door, which I'd chalked up as a huge success after my dash at the curb the night before. He'd even given me a one-sided hug. That side not being his left or his right, but rather a hug from my side and a stiff acceptance from him. Whatever. Close enough.

RECLAIM

After that, I'd spent the rest of the afternoon cooking. Since my car wouldn't be ready for a few more days, I'd luckily gone to the grocery store semi-recently and had all the fixings for baked ham, mac and cheese, and a salad. Halfway through making the mac and cheese, I realized Camden's body didn't exactly lead me to believe he splurged on anything with carbs or cheese often, so I sautéed up asparagus. While I was doing that, I realized asparagus could be a very divisive vegetable. People either loved it or hated it, and I had no idea which side of the fence Camden landed on, so I then baked two sweet potatoes, stewed some tomatoes, air fried a zucchini, and chugged a glass of wine.

It could be said I was panicking, but it had been a while since I'd been on a date.

Not that Camden's coming over for dinner was a date or anything.

We were just two friends sharing a meal and a bottle of wine—or the three quarters of a bottle that was left, anyway.

I momentarily considered chugging another glass then talked myself out of it and headed for the door.

"Hi," I chirped entirely too high-pitched for it to have been perceived as natural on any level.

He was in jeans again, but this time, he'd paired them with a button-down, the sleeves rolled up to show off the subtle veins on his muscular forearms. Jesus, I was seriously hard up, but when had veins become so sexy?

He opened his mouth, and I was positive he'd planned for words to follow, but as his gaze raked down my body and back up again, nothing came out.

I grinned, patting myself on the back for the extra time and thought I'd put into getting ready. "You want to come in?"

"Yeah," he replied, stepping inside and robotically lifting a bottle of wine in my direction. "Here."

Wow. Two whole syllables. Oh, yeah, I'd done good getting ready for my date.

Fuck. Not a date.

Not.

A.

Date.

Though the night we'd spent together in the hot tub hadn't been a date, either, and it had turned out incredible.

"Thanks." I shut the door and took the wine from his hand. "I already opened a bottle, but I'll pop this one in the fridge." I headed for the kitchen, putting an extra sway in my hips for his benefit.

"Fuck me," he mumbled under his breath. "Fucking fuck me."

Pretending not to hear him, I took his reaction as yet another good sign for my date, non-date. After pouring him a glass of wine and topping myself off with a heavy hand, I set his in front of him on the bar dividing my kitchen from the living room. "So, how'd the rest of your afternoon go?"

Twisting the base on the counter, he spun the stem of the glass between his thumb and his forefinger but didn't take a sip. "Okay, I guess. I got a call from an investigator I hired to look into Jonathan."

I tugged at my earlobe as though the audio had deceived me. "I'm sorry. Did you say you hired a private investigator? In Clovert?"

"Technically, he's out of Chicago, but yeah. If Jonathan is pulling this kind of shit on you and your family, I'm sure he's done other stuff too. We prove he's a crooked cop and he'll lose his badge. If we're lucky, he could spend a few years behind bars. But regardless, your charges will get dropped and he won't be able to target you anymore."

RECLAIM

I blinked, my lips curling up sardonically. All of it sounded great. Like great-great. Better than great. But there was one, teeny-tiny problem.

"Are you crazy? I can't afford an investigator. Especially not one out of Chicago. I make Clovert money, Cam. Bad Clovert money at that. I know I told you about my rainy-day-slash-Louboutin fund, but I think you have vastly overestimated the contents of the account. And now that I've been suspended from work, the rainy day might turn into a rainy year. Truthfully, I don't even know if I can afford *you*. I was planning to discuss a friends-and-family discount tonight after I thoroughly plied you with food and alcohol."

"Nora, relax. I'm not expecting you to pay for anything."

I crossed my arms over my chest, and had I not been working myself into a frenzy, I would have smiled at the way his gaze dropped to my boobs. "Then who is? I don't know if you remember or not, Cam, but handouts are not my thing. Especially not from you."

His head snapped back as if I'd slapped him. "Why *especially* not from me?"

"Because that's not who we are. We're give and take. You bring a sandwich. I bring a sandwich. You already dropped everything, flew down here, and are doing your best to dig me out of this mess." I walked around the bar and stopped in front of him. Hooking my pinky with his, I swayed our arms back and forth. "I appreciate you being here more than I can ever express, but I can't in good conscience let you pay for an investigator too. You've already brought a sandwich. A big one. Like one of those yard-long submarine sandwiches that I'm going to be eating for the next month. It's my turn." I glanced over my shoulder at the smorgasbord of food splayed across my counter. "Good news, you'll probably be able to eat on it for a month too."

"I can see this," he teased. "But what if my dad wants to bring a sandwich?"

I did another round of the slow blink. "Your...*dead* dad?"

Releasing my finger, he stepped away, plucking his wine from the bar as he went. "Yep, that's the one." He walked over to my tan microfiber sectional that Thea had sold me for a steal when she'd moved and sank down right in the middle, crossing his legs knee to ankle. It was almost as sexy as the veins. "When he died, I inherited a good bit of money. My mom and I went round and round about me taking it. I have no idea why she was surprised. I'd refused to take a single penny from them when I went off to school, but she was livid when I refused an inheritance. She yelled at me that if I didn't take it she was going to give it to Jonathan's charity in Josh's name."

"Shut. Up." I walked over and sat on the cushion beside him, careful not to touch him again despite my nearly constant desire to launch myself into his arms.

"I'd never snatched a check so fast in my entire life." He took a sip. "My dad and I had a complicated relationship. He wasn't abusive—at least not physically the way yours was. But he did a number on me trying to force me into this perfect mold he had in his mind of who his son should be. Square peg, round hole and all. It didn't matter what I did. He always viewed me as a failure, and it took a long time for me to figure out that maybe I wasn't the part that was messed up."

I inched closer until my knee bumped his thigh. "He was a fool. Your square peg is better than his round hole any day of the week. And he missed out by being too damn stubborn to open his eyes."

He grinned. "Please don't say my square peg and my dad's round hole in the same sentence ever again."

RECLAIM

I barked a laugh. "Yeah, as soon as it came out of my mouth, that metaphor went sideways. But I meant it. Look at you. Smart, and kind, and funny." I batted my eyelashes. "Not too hard on the eyes, if I do say so myself."

He shook his head, but that grin stretched.

I crinkled my nose at him. "Your dad can keep the sandwich. I'd rather have you and your square peg."

It was his turn to laugh, and it was deep and rich, the soundtrack of everything I'd missed over the last five years.

"Don't speak too quickly. I pay all my own bills and the mountain of student loan debt out of principle, and I use his money for things that would piss him off but mean a lot to me." He smiled tight and gave a piece of my hair a gentle tug. "Like, say, a donation to a brown bag lunch program for the students of Clovert or maybe an investigator to take down his nephew."

I sucked in a sharp breath, and it had absolutely nothing to do with taking down Jonathan Caskey.

"You donate to my lunch program?"

He shrugged. "It's a *great* program."

"Cam," I whispered when all further words failed me.

He slid his hand over and gave my knee a squeeze. "You have no idea how proud I am of everything you've done for those kids."

A tear finally worked its way from my eye. "How?"

"A tip from an anonymous source."

"Joe." I laughed through tears.

"Or Joe." He winked. "But, now, you're going to let me pay for an investigator so, at the very least, we can get Jonathan off your back. Those kids need the sexy brown-bag lunch lady back ASAP."

"Cam," I repeated because what else was there to say?

He tipped his chin down and stared deep into my eyes.

We were close—maybe not close enough to kiss, but with a few inches, I could have remedied that.

He moved his hand to my face and traced my jaw with his thumb. My breath hitched and a mixture of clean cotton and rich musk intoxicated my senses. Pure Camden Cole erotic.

"You gotta stop calling me Cam, babe," he rasped, but he said it with his gaze trained on my mouth.

Maybe it was the moment.

Maybe it was the wine.

Maybe it was because he was so close after all those years of dreaming of him.

Whatever it was, I set aim on his mouth and threw caution to the wind.

Camden threw a proverbial bucket of ice water back.

"Nora, wait," he said, hurling himself out of the way and spilling his wine all over the carpet. He shot to his feet and planted his hands on his hips, his breathing so ragged there was a solid chance he was hyperventilating.

And wasn't that just a kick in the pants. The only man I'd ever loved, and he was on the verge of asphyxiation at the idea of kissing me. *Outstanding.*

"I'll get a towel," I announced, my face sliding through the spectrum of reds.

After lurching to my feet, I darted down the hall, passing not only the guest bathroom that had towels under the sink, but also the hall linen closet, which had several more. I was in the midst of an embarrassment overdose and my bedroom seemed like the safest retreat.

What the hell had I been thinking, trying to kiss him? Yes, he had been staring at my mouth and being generally sweet, but things had been off since he'd arrived in town. He'd rejected me almost every time I'd touch him. What part of that made me think this was ever going to end with our mouths fused together and, if I'd had anything to say about it, our clothes strewn across the floor?

I shut my bedroom door and cradled my head in my hands. What was wrong with me? He'd been nothing but good to me. Short of a steed, he'd been a white knight rushing to my aid every chance he got, and this was how I repaid him? By trying to seduce him when he so obviously wasn't interested?

Sure, it had been five years, but I'd assumed our physical connection would still be there.

God knew I still felt it.

I now knew he did not.

Awesome. Fucking awesome.

There was a rap at my door. "Nora?"

Shit.

"Just a second!" I called, walking to the mirror to see if the staggering ache in my chest showed on my face. It did, but there was only so much I could hide, so I swiped under my eyes and smoothed down a few frizzies on the top of my head. Then I hurried to the bathroom and snagged a towel off the bar before running back out and swinging the door open, avoiding eye contact as best as possible. "Sorry, I just needed to grab a towel."

He grabbed my arm before I had the chance to pass. "Nora, come on. Let's talk."

"Okay." I tugged my arm away and laughed awkwardly. "I just need to get the wine up before it has a chance to settle. White wine may not stain, but it will make a sticky mess if I'm not fast. This is a rental and I'd really rather not lose my security deposit." I tried to act chill as I sped down the hall, but did powerwalking ever really look cool?

I dropped to my knees beside the wet spot and dabbed, wondering how long I had to do it before the towel absorbed me too.

His shoes entered my line of sight. "Just stop. I'll have the carpet cleaned. It was my fault."

"It's fine. I've almost got it."

"Nora," he urged. "Stop."

I tucked my chin to my chest and told myself not to cry. I'd never truly been rejected before, mainly because I never put myself out there.

But this was Camden. And rejected kiss aside, things had been strange and uncomfortable since he'd shown up. I wanted to pretend he was still my boy from the creek, the teenager I'd kissed when I had no other way to show him how much I loved him, or the man I'd given my virginity to because I couldn't imagine ever being with anyone else.

But it was different.

He was different and it fucking sucked because I'd let my Camden disappear in the five years while I had been trying to fix myself.

With a hand under both of my arms, he lifted me with ease, wrapping me in a tight hug as soon as he had me on my feet.

"I'm sorry." I closed my eyes and buried my face in his chest. "I shouldn't have done that. And, now, it's weird. And it was already weird. I just… I've missed you. Having you here…" I groaned. "I don't know. It felt right. But clearly it wasn't, and now, I feel bad because I made you uncomfortable. And…and…"

He squeezed me tight. "Shhhh. It's okay. I'm not uncomfortable. You didn't do anything wrong. I felt it too. It's just…" He rested his chin on the top of my head. "I'm not available right now, Nora."

My lids popped open and an "O" formed on my mouth. My emotions were all over the place, so I couldn't pin down if it was the start of *Oh no*, *Oh shit*, or *Okay*.

The idea of Camden with a girlfriend burned, but it wasn't a novel concept. I'd seen pictures of him with girls online and lived to tell the tale. Honestly, it made sense. He'd been friendly and attentive since he'd arrived, but the minute I'd crossed the line, he shut down. I couldn't believe I hadn't thought of it earlier.

In a way, there was a peace that accompanied the thought of him having a girlfriend. It meant all the strange and awkward reactions he'd been having were because of her, not because our friendship had changed or after all this time I was losing him.

He simply had loyalties that lay elsewhere.

Don't get me wrong. There was a definite knife hanging out of my heart, but I respected him for the way he'd handled himself.

I gave his chest a shove and stepped out of his arms. "Jesus, Cam. Why the hell didn't you tell me?"

"I was…waiting for the right time."

"Well, I'd say you hit the nail on the head. I almost mauled you."

He looked down at his shoes. "Yeah, phew. Really dodged that bullet."

"All right, smartass. Who is she? You want to talk about her?"

He slanted his head to the side. "No?"

"Okay, good. You are my best friend, and on any other night, I am happy to listen, but maybe not on the same night I threw myself at you and got rejected."

Yeah. See? I could totally do this. Though more wine definitely wouldn't hurt.

I walked to the kitchen and grabbed my glass and then took a long drink, which made my nose burn.

Camden stood in my living room, his blue gaze locked on me, a wrinkle in the middle of his brows. "So, we're okay?"

I lifted my wine glass in the air. "Absolutely. I'm happy if you're happy."

His Adam's apple bobbed. "Right. Totally happy."

I kept busy for the next little bit, chatting and warming up the food that had cooled. After a while, his stiff shoulders relaxed and a smile returned to his handsome face. He told me all about his life in New York. Come to find out, he was a criminal defense attorney, and his eyes lit every time he talked about his career.

He was working at a busy firm with the hopes of one day becoming a partner, but he did pro-bono work on the side. He said no one had ever paid him in ham and mac and cheese though, and yes, he actually ate cheese. We sat on the couch with two spoons and shared a pint of ice cream, laughing like old times. Though I still fought the urge to kiss him almost constantly, things felt normal again, and for that, I'd never been more grateful.

He left around midnight, even giving me a hug at the door. I'm talking a good hug. A classic Camden Cole hug.

We made plans for the next day, unfortunately most of which involved a drug test he'd scheduled just to "cover my ass in case we saw the inside of a courtroom." But he also promised me brunch at my favorite diner in Thomaston, so I didn't complain.

All in all, it was a fantastic evening of good food, good wine, and good company.

Even if I did cry myself to sleep.

TWENTY-SIX

Camden

THE DEAFENING RING OF MY CELL PHONE ON THE nightstand shocked me awake. Between listening to the couple in the room next door argue and thinking about Nora's oh-so-calm reaction when I'd told her I wasn't available, it had taken forever for me to fall asleep.

I had no idea what specific time it was at the moment, but based on the dim light cascading through the curtains, it was too damn early to be receiving phone calls.

An unknown number flashed on the screen, and against my better judgment, I picked it up. "Hello."

"You stupid fuck. Are you kidding me with this shit?" Jonathan snapped.

Smiling, I shifted up in the bed, propping my back on the headboard. He must have heard about my interest in the Sean Watkins arrest. This would be fun. "Good morning, cuz."

"Fuck you! You think you can put a tail on me and I wouldn't notice? You have no idea who you're dealing with here. I don't give a shit if you're family. I will put you in the ground before I let you jeopardize my career."

A tail? I hadn't put a tail on him, and as far as I knew, Leo hadn't, either. But I sure as shit wasn't going to tell him that.

"Okay, you want it gone? Talk to the prosecutor, tell them you fucked up, get the charges against Nora dropped."

He barked a laugh. "You're delusional."

"Am I? Because, right now, I have evidence to support how you not only planted evidence, but also tampered with evidence, falsified a police report, and that doesn't include the property damage and harassment. Sounds to me like I'm not the one jeopardizing your career. You're doing a fine job of taking care of that all on your own."

"Call off your dogs!" he boomed.

"Drop the charges against Nora!" I shot right back.

"Oh, I'm gonna drop something on that bitch. Little throwback to when she liked it hard and rough. She give it to you like that, Camden? Is that why you're all pussy-whipped, flying down here, and shoving your nose into shit you have no fucking clue about?"

I sat straight up in bed, the hairs on my arms standing on end. "What the fuck is that supposed to mean?"

"You should try taking her to the old dugout. I've seen a few videos where she comes alive like a fucking wildcat."

My stomach soured and bile clawed up the back of my throat. A thought so vile that I'd never even considered it scorched my neurons. "You kept Josh's videos of her?"

"You never know when shit like that might come in handy. Like, say, when your cousin is trying to ruin you over some bitch and those tapes anonymously find their way to the internet for the whole world to see."

I stood up and balled my fist at my side, a blistering rage igniting in my veins. "You son of a bitch. You wouldn't fucking dare. Josh is on those tapes too. You're not going to rake your precious little brother through the mud like that."

"You know, I'm not real worried about his reputation as long as it keeps me out of the grave next to him. Call off your

RECLAIM

dogs, get off my ass, go back to New York, and never show your face again. Or get ready for war. Your choice."

The line went dead and I stood there with the phone to my ear, trying to make sense of what the hell had just happened.

He had the videos.

He had a tail who was not mine, and therefore, I couldn't call them off even if I wanted to.

And, for some reason, he thought he might end up in a grave next to Josh.

What the *fuck* was happening?

There was only one person I could think of who might be able to piece this clusterfuck together.

"Swear to God, this better be good," Leo said when he answered the phone. "Boy, my eyes aren't even open yet. What time is it?"

"It about five your time, but I need help and I didn't want to wait."

He let out a groan, which sounded more like he was climbing out of bed than frustrated. "Go ahead. I'm listening."

I spent the next few minutes filling him in on my call with Jonathan. As I'd expected, the tail was not ours. Which meant Jonathan had far bigger problems than harassing the Stewarts. When I told him about the tapes of Nora, he appropriately lost his shit, spiraling into a tornado of curses and death threats that matched the fury bubbling inside me.

"All right," he clipped. "Here's how this shit is going down. First off, you need to get to your girl and tell her these tapes still exist. That shit isn't going to be easy on her, especially if he manages to release them and she gets blindsided. Second, I'm gonna send a guy your way. If Cousin Cocksucker is getting desperate, there is no telling what he's going to do. I'd rather have feet on the ground and you not need them than be underprepared. Lastly, I'll make some calls and see if I can figure out what the hell kind of trouble this asshat has gotten himself into. If he's got as much pull in this small town as you say he does, he's not going to waste his time working with off-the-grid small-timers. If he's running scared, someone will know why."

I let out a sigh, reconsidering the whole kidnapping-Nora thing, but at this rate, New York wasn't even far enough away from Caskey to keep her safe. "Thanks, Leo. I appreciate it."

"Not a problem. Take care of your girl and we'll be square."

She wasn't my girl. Well, not exactly. Not in the way that meant I got to keep her when this was all said and done.

But she was still mine.

Or at least I was hers.

"Keep me in the loop," I said to Leo.

"Will do."

We both hung up, and I walked straight to the shower. I was quick, not even my cock objecting as I did the world's fastest lather-and-rinse routine. I spun around the room, dragging on a pair of jeans and a gray T-shirt, and then moved to the nightstand and grabbed my keys. My wallet wasn't sitting there, so I searched through the pants I'd taken off the night before and dug it out of the back pocket.

Our ten-dollar bill came tumbling out with it. I froze, staring down at it. When the hell had she given it back to me?

While the ten had been in my possession for the last half a decade, it wasn't often I allowed myself to handle it. For over a year after our night at my dad's hunting cabin, I'd carried it with me everywhere, never knowing when I'd see her next, and always hoping it would be soon. As time passed, though, and the dream of her finding her way back to me started to disappear, I began leaving it in my dresser at home. I tortured myself with a lot of things, but the memories that bill held were often more than I could take.

Bending over, I plucked it off the carpet, a wave of nostalgia assaulting me.

Snapshots of our past together came back to me in a rush.

Nora laughing as she'd swung from the rope into the creek.

Nora racing away from me, her hair flowing behind her, a smile aimed over her shoulder.

Nora's eyes as she'd stared at me, her hand poised over mine in the middle of a high-intensity game of Slapjack.

Nora.

Nora.

Nora.

I'd spent five years missing her.

Five years waiting for her to come back to me.

Five years giving her the time and space I'd promised so we could both get our lives together.

In the end, it was Joe who had called me though. Not her reaching out because she wanted me in her life. Not her pining for the last five years, desperate to reconnect. Just…Joe.

Of course, I was going to be here for her. We were friends—first and foremost. But we'd also been more, and learning how to move on without her had almost destroyed me.

After tucking the bill into my pocket, I grabbed my phone and headed out the door.

As much as I would have loved to lose myself in Nora Stewart for whatever time I had left with her, there was no way I was signing myself back up for the heartache that accompanied another goodbye.

I stopped by the Clovert Bakery on my way to her place, hoping to soften the blow with donuts and a coffee. It wasn't quite seven when I arrived, and her house was still dark, so rather than scaring the hell out of her by knocking, I dialed her number.

She answered on the third ring, sleep still clinging to her voice. "Wow, you're up early."

"Actually, I'm outside. Can you let me in so we can talk?"

There was a rustling on her end. "Depends. Is it a good talk or bad talk?"

"Uhh, I brought you donuts and a coffee with enough cream and sugar to kill a horse."

"So a bad talk then. *Great*." Her front door suddenly opened, and she appeared on the other side, her hair pulled back into a ponytail, the phone still held to her ear. She was adorable, all mussed from sleep.

But that wasn't why my mouth dried.

Or my heart stopped.

Or my cock twitched.

Nora Stewart was standing on the other side of the threshold in the sexiest outfit I'd ever seen. It wasn't tight, revealing, or anything men usually found inherently sexy. But, to me, it was only one shade below her opening the door stark naked.

She was wearing my sweats—the ones she'd unabashedly stolen from me when she'd snuck out of my bed the one and only time we'd been together. They were my favorites despite the small bleach stain on the left thigh—an accident from when my roommate had taught me to do my own laundry. The bottoms were now frayed and there was a threadbare hole in the right knee, but they were mine.

And she was wearing them.

Five years later.

I couldn't be as positive if the plain white T-shirt was mine, but based on the way it swallowed her, I thought there was a good chance.

And fuck me if it didn't do some serious things inside my chest.

Following my stunned gaze, she looked at her clothes. Her head popped right back up. "I'm not giving them back."

I had to clear my throat before I could reply. "I didn't ask you to."

"Well, as long as we're on the same page." She swung the door open in silent invitation.

I miraculously managed to put one foot in front of the other without falling and walked into her house. Jesus, this woman was going to be the death of me.

Taking the coffee and donuts from my hand, she carried them to the kitchen counter. "Now, how bad are we talking, Cam? Glazed bad? Or chocolate-sprinkles bad?" She pried open the top on the donuts. "Fuck. A dozen assorted. I'm dying, aren't I?"

I stared at her. She wasn't dying, but with what I had to tell her, it might feel like she was. And it was my responsibility to deliver the news, knowing that it was going to throw her back into the pit of demons she'd spent the majority of her adolescence trying to crawl her way out of. She'd come so far and yet another fucking Caskey was going to pull the rug out from under her again—and there was not one damn thing I could do to shield her from it.

Concern flashed across her face, and she abandoned the donuts and walked over to me. "Jeez, I was just kidding. Why are you looking at me like that?"

My throat got thick. Damn, this was going to be like burning at the stake. But it had to be done. She deserved to know. "I got a call from Caskey this morning."

"Oh, God," she groaned while staring up at me with bright-eyed anticipation.

Snaking a hand out, I gripped her hip and pulled her in close. "Apparently, someone is following him. He thinks it's someone I hired, but my guy knows nothing about it."

"Ohhhhhkay," she drawled curiously. "So, somebody else hates him too. How is this bad news for me?"

I moved my hand up to her neck, cupping the back and giving her a reassuring squeeze. Fuck, I hated the Caskeys. "He has the videos, Nora. Josh's videos."

She blinked, processing and formulating. And I waited for the fallout, ready to be there when she fell.

"And?" she said matter-of-factly.

"And…he's threatening to release them if I don't call the mystery man off."

She blinked.

Once.

Twice.

Thrice.

Like a time bomb ticking down to detonation.

I gave her neck another squeeze. "Nora, babe, I'm here to help, okay? We're going to figure this out."

She blew out a controlled exhale. "Okay. Have you ever defended someone in the mob?"

I cocked an eyebrow. "No."

She nodded short and slow. "Albanian Mafia? I hear they're pretty powerful."

"Can't say I have."

"Do you have any connection to organized crime at all?"

More than just a little confused, I shook my head. "Not that I know of. Why?"

Tick. Tick. Tick.

All at once, she exploded. "Because I need a hitman!" Spinning out of my grip, she took several steps away. "Oh my God. What the hell is wrong with that family?" She paused. "Present company excluded. But holy shit, Cam. Those people are insane."

"I know," I replied because, well…she wasn't wrong.

She started to pace. "I was twelve, and I know I didn't look twelve, but I sure as shit didn't look eighteen, either. What the hell does he think he's going to do with that video? It would literally be a federal offense if he uploaded it anywhere. Actually, you know what? Let's see if he needs to borrow my computer. A federal prison might do him some good." She stopped and crossed her arms over her chest. "I need you to find out who's following him. And then we need to pay them double to become *our* tail, because if it is pissing Jonathan off enough for him to be making threats, I want to be the one responsible for it. I want that joy, Cam."

A lot of things were happening at that moment. She was making wild and quasi-amusing statements involving a hitman, Albanian Mafia, and joy.

But I was more focused on what she *wasn't* doing.

She wasn't unraveling.

She hadn't fallen into a pile of broken pieces.

She wasn't in that pit of demons at all.

My Nora was standing tall, her shoulders back, pissed all to hell and back—rightly so. And I was so fucking proud of her there wasn't a parallel universe or alternate dimension out there in which I would have been able to suppress my smile.

My legs devoured the distance between us, and I wrapped her up in a bear hug, leaning back to lift her off her feet. "You are fucking incredible. Do you know that?"

"Put me down! I'm in the middle of a rant."

I laughed—which, given the subject and situation, shouldn't have been possible. But, then again, I'd seriously underestimated the power of Nora Stewart.

Setting her back on her feet, I waved an arm out. "By all means, carry on."

And carry on she did. She cussed and raved, plotting out at least seven different elaborate plans to get rid of Jonathan Caskey.

And I sat on the stool, eating a cruller, grinning like a fool, and sipping on my coffee. All the while having no fucking clue how I could ever go back to a life without her.

TWENTY-SEVEN

Nora

DEEP BREATH IN.
Soft snore out.
Deep breath in.
Soft—

His arm twitched around my middle. I froze, holding my breath so as not to wake him.

I had no idea how we'd ended up in that position. On the couch. Me the small spoon. Camden curled behind me. However, I was in no rush to get out of it, either.

After I'd stopped ranting enough to hold a conversation, Camden and I had moved to the couch. I'd settled into my favorite corner with my legs stretched out across the neighboring cushion, and he'd sat on the opposite end, as far away from me as humanly possible. We came to the conclusion that Jonathan sucked, and I was thankful his investigator was looking into things. I was not in any way happy or comfortable knowing Jonathan had those tapes, but I wasn't a scared and alone little girl anymore, so I took it in stride. It would definitely be the hot topic with my therapist over the following weeks though.

I'd turned on the morning news for background noise and it had seemed to immediately ensnare Camden. Though it had bored me to sleep. Literally. What? He'd woken me up early. A mid-morning nap had never been more necessary.

I had no idea how long I'd been asleep or how I'd woken up in the cuddly version of *The Twilight Zone*, but I was not complaining.

Or moving.

Or breathing at the moment.

His twitchy hand stilled.

And I let out a quiet sigh of relief.

"How long have you been awake?" he asked, his voice gravelly and sexy from sleep.

Busted.

"Um...long enough to know you're a mouth-breather."

He barked a laugh and sat up, forcing me up with him. "It's better than being a drooler like you."

I slapped him with one of the throw pillows. "Lies."

He stood up and stretched, his T-shirt lifting just enough to reveal a deep V of chiseled muscles disappearing into his waistband. I told myself not to stare.

Then I promptly stared.

And because it was my life and I seriously could not catch a break, he caught me.

"Eyes up here, Stewart."

I flashed him a tight smile. "Sorry. Maybe leave this part out when you tell your girlfriend about me. Probably the spooning too. I've grown quite attached to my eyes and would hate to have her fly down here just to claw them out."

"Oooh, a catfight. Will there be Jell-O involved?"

"Psh, in your dreams, buddy."

He laughed, shaking his head. "Your eyes are safe. I don't have a girlfriend, Nora."

"What? Yes, you do."

His brows popped up. "You know something I don't?"

"You told me last night you have a girlfriend."

"Uh, no. I told you I wasn't available. You assumed I had a girlfriend and I didn't correct you. Big difference."

For the way my jaw dropped, I probably looked like Wile E. Coyote. "So you lied to me instead of just telling me you weren't interested."

"No. I told you the truth. If I had told you I wasn't interested, it would have been a lie."

I prided myself in being a smart woman. Growing up the way I had, I'd been a critical thinker since I'd exited the womb. But I could honestly say I had not one fucking idea what the hell Camden was talking about.

"That makes zero sense."

"Says the person who clearly hasn't spent five years waiting for the woman they love to actually show up or reach out."

"What?" I gasped, the pain obvious even to my own ears.

He waved me off. "Wipe that look off your face. It's fine. I'm not trying to make this a big deal. It's a self-preservation thing. You're gorgeous. Of course I'm interested, but I can't go down this road with you again, knowing it only leads in one direction. We're friends. I've accepted it. It's not like I'm sitting around, beating myself up over it anymore."

I shot to my feet. "Oh, so it's just me, then?"

His whole body blanched. "What the hell is that supposed to mean?"

"I cried myself to sleep last night because I finally got a chance to see you again and I thought you were already taken."

It was the wrong thing to say.

So, so, so the wrong thing to say.

"You *finally* got the chance?" he snapped, and from the way it sounded, so did his patience. "You've had five years of chances to see me. Every fucking day has been a chance for you to see me. But you took none of them."

What in the actual fuck was happening?

Camden did not have a girlfriend.

Camden was interested.

Yet Camden was currently yelling at me because *I* hadn't reached out to *him* in five years.

I cocked my head to the side. "Oh, I'm sorry. I must have missed all five years' worth of phone calls where *you* took the chance to see *me*."

"I was giving you space. The last thing you told me was you were working on yourself and healing your head and your heart. You said you were too selfish to let me off your hook. Well, guess what? I fucking suffocated on the hook."

"You told me not to let you go!"

"Because I thought you'd come back!" He thrust a hand into the top of his hair, his chest heaving. He let out a loud groan and tipped his head back to stare at the ceiling. "Maybe I was just young and dumb, but when you left that day, I thought it was temporary. I loved you. You loved me. The timing was wrong. I understood. We both needed to get our shit taken care of so we could be together. But I thought *we* were the end game, Nora."

"We are," I breathed, reaching out to rest a hand on his chest, but he backed away.

"When?" he thundered, staring me right in the eye, the most agonizing heartbreak carved into his face. "Five years of my life have passed by without you. I graduated from college, law school, started a career, celebrated birthdays and holidays. I went to weddings and watched my friends vow to spend forever with the ones they loved. I took up running, Nora. Come to find out I actually love it. For two years, I gave up meat. Just cold turkey became a vegetarian. Then, on year three, I remembered I really fucking love steak, so that flew out the window. I watched movies and read books I loved and had a six-month showdown with my neighbor because they always vacuumed at three in the morning and it drove me insane. And you weren't there for any of it."

My nose stung, and tears welled in my eyes. "I was trying get better for you—for *us*. I'm still trying to get there."

"And that's the problem. You think that a *there* exists, Nora. Some mythical final destination where we can be together. Meanwhile, our entire lives are passing us by."

I wrung my hands in front of me. "You deserve someone who's perfect, Cam."

"Perfect doesn't exist! What I deserve is someone who wants to be with me. Not because I'm here. Not because it's convenient. Not because you need something or I need something. I'm talking someone who cannot physically stay away for one day, much less five fucking years."

I took a giant step toward him, challenge mounting in my veins. "You think I didn't *want* to be with you? You think I didn't die inside every time I saw a picture of you with some woman on Instagram?"

He let out a humorless laugh and planted his hands on his hips. "What women, Nora? I'm one rung on the ladder away from being a monk."

"Oh, please. I see the pictures you're tagged in… Pencil Skirt Barbie, Ski Slope Sally, and my personal favorite: Tattoo Tammy. Come on, Cam. Pick a type!"

"I would if I was dating any of them. But considering Paula is my cousin on my dad's side, and the girl from the ski slope is married to my friend from college, and Tammy is in a committed relationship with my other friend—*Angela*—I think it would be in seriously bad form to date any of them. But if you would like to talk about Instagram, I am *here* for it. I really enjoyed watching your relationship with Forehead Freddy from the IG bench."

My head snapped back. "Who?"

"The guy with the big forehead who always puts his arms around you and I can never see his fucking hand so I have no idea where he's grabbing you and it literally devoured me every time you posted a picture of the two of you."

"You mean Charles?"

He threw his arms out to the sides, slapping them against his thighs. "I don't know!"

"Oh, good Lord, Cam. Charles is a very, very married art teacher at my school. He helps with the bag lunch program, likes to take pictures, and brings me succulent clippings once a month. That is the extent of our relationship."

He shut his mouth and cut his gaze off to the side. "Well… that is…good to know."

An unlikely smile curled my lips. "You stalk my Instagram?"

He rolled his eyes. "Don't give me shit. It's part of being on the hook."

We stood there in silence for a long minute.

Camden caught his breath, fascinated with his shoes.

I felt like a heel, but I was utterly enthralled by how he was one rung on the ladder away from being a monk.

"Why haven't you ever been with anyone else?"

His head popped up, his gaze incredulous. "Because I want you! Why is this such a difficult concept?" His long legs swallowed the distance between us. Grabbing my hand, he pressed it into his chest, his heart pounding beneath it. "Five years, five hundred years—it doesn't matter. I want *you*, Nora. In my life. In my bed. At my side. Any and every way I can have you. I only want *you*. I don't care if it's messy or complicated. I don't care if you are still working through the shit-hand life dealt you. I don't care how it comes or what it looks like. I only want *you*." He paused to take a breath, but I'd heard enough.

I wanted all those things too. No, I wasn't perfect—and messy and complicated were literally the definition of my life.

But I loved him.

My entire life, I had loved Freaking Camden Cole. That had never changed.

I didn't just press my lips to his; my mouth collided with his like a hurricane hitting the coast. He groaned into my mouth, his tongue tangling with mine, desperate and commanding. I pressed up onto my toes and circled my arms around his neck, but I couldn't get close enough and I ended up crawling up his strong body.

His hands immediately went to my ass. He ground his cock into me through the confines of his jeans.

"Fuck," he hissed.

"Bed. Room," I panted between kisses.

With heavy steps that were somehow frenzied yet purposeful, he carried me down the hall, straight to my bed. As if taking me to bed were old hat and not only the second time he'd done it, he acted with intention and grace. How was it even possible that, with such limited experience, our bodies recognized the desire they had for one another without much thought or concentration at all?

"Every day. Every night. This need for you never stops," he rumbled, moving his attention to my neck, sucking and licking until chills exploded across my skin. "You're mine."

"I've always been yours," I whispered. "Only yours."

Leaning to one side, his wandering hand lifted my shirt, the one I'd stolen from him all those years ago. The black bralette I'd tugged on before letting him in didn't hide much.

But I didn't want to hide from Camden.

Not anymore.

Not ever again.

Crisscrossing my arms, I tore both the shirt and the bra off in one swoop.

He hissed through his teeth and bit his lower lip, a fire sparking in his blue eyes.

Then I lost sight of them altogether as his head dipped low and he sealed his warm mouth over my nipple.

"Oh, God!" I cried, thrusting a hand into the top of his hair.

"Don't you ever fucking tell me you aren't perfect," he rumbled.

With Camden, I'd always felt perfect. It was when we were apart that my mind would make up stories and scenarios where I wasn't good enough or couldn't ever be who he deserved.

Realization hit me. The walls I'd built around my heart crumbled around us one by one.

"Cam, please," I choked.

He kept his head down, dividing his sensual attention between my breasts. Nipping and sucking, teasing and kneading. "Swear to me this is it. I can't take another fucking goodbye. Never again. Do you understand me?"

"Yes," I breathed.

He suddenly sat up. "Say it, Nora. Say you're really mine."

It required exactly no thought to answer. "I've always belonged to you, the same way you belong to me."

An inferno ignited in his eyes as he hooked two fingers

under the waistband of my sweats, tugging them down. My panties followed just as quickly, and in the next blink, his shirt joined them on the floor.

Naked, I sat up and traced the ridges of his abs up to his pecs. He stared down at me, his lusty gaze tracking my every movement.

I kissed my way down his stomach to the sexy V. His breath hitched when I popped open the button on his jeans.

"Make love to me, Cam."

A growl vibrated in his chest as he kicked his jeans off. When his lips found mine again, the frenzy returned tenfold.

He kissed me hard and his hands roamed my soft curves while I raked my nails down his back, exploring the rigid planes.

Coaxing me to the edge, his long fingers played between my legs until I was breathless with urgency. But, no matter how I begged, Camden took his time, circling my clit between feathery strokes. My climax came in devastating waves with his name clinging to my lips.

"Fucking incredible," he moaned, swallowing my pleasure as I rode out the wake.

Only then did Camden move on top of me. Those blue eyes that had claimed me when I was only a girl stared down at me, blazing with more love than I'd ever dreamed was possible.

But that was my Cam.

In that moment, I knew I would spend the rest of my life doing whatever it took to give that love back to him.

He entered me with a devastating control, the muscles on his back flexing with every thrust. It wasn't long before he found a rhythm that drove us both wild. He uttered gravelly words into my neck, my name punctuating all of them, and I clung to him, ripples of pleasure building within me.

Unsure how much longer I could hold on, I locked my legs around his hips and urged him deeper. "Oh, God, I'm close."

"Give it to me, Nora," he ordered, his rhythm quickening.

My resolve snapped, and with a shattering climax, I unraveled beneath him.

"Yesss," he hissed. "That's it, baby. Oh, fuck, that's it."

One last drive and he seated himself to the hilt and emptied inside me.

We both lay there for several minutes, a tangled heap of arms and legs, chests heaving and hearts racing.

"Can you breathe?" he asked, his face hidden in the curve of my neck.

"Yeah."

"Okay, good, because it's going to be a while before I can move."

I laughed, and his head popped up, a goofy smile doing nothing to hinder the sexiness that was Camden Cole disheveled post-orgasm.

"Hey, you," he whispered.

I smoothed down his short, brown locks. "Hi."

"I'm going to say something, and it might not sound like a compliment, but trust me. It is the highest praise I can give. Holy fuck. Being with you is infinitely better than the last five years I've spent with my hand."

I lifted my palm into his line of sight and gave him a finger wave. "Don't I know it."

His grin was so wide it looked like a toothpaste commercial. "I love you so fucking much."

"Thank God, because you're stuck with me now. And you should know I am currently suspended from my job, have a soon-to-be very empty rainy-day-slash-Louboutin fund, and I am out on bail with pending drug charges. So, congratulations."

RECLAIM

He chuckled. "If it means I'm lucky enough to keep you, I'll take my chances."

But as I lay there staring at him, sated and languid, my heart so full of love, I didn't know if I'd ever be able to process it all, because he was wrong.

I was the lucky one.

TWENTY-EIGHT

Nora

"Come on, Nora. You've gotta have a preference," he said, standing in my bedroom, a towel wrapped around his hips, his glorious abs on display, little droplets of water dripping from his hair. Plus, he had this irresistible glimmer in his bright-blue eyes.

It was early morning and I still hadn't mustered the strength to get out of bed, though Camden in a towel was sparking some energy for other things.

After Camden had made love to me, we'd spent the day in bed—talking and laughing, kissing and touching. We never made it to get my drug test or to the brunch he'd promised me, but as the sun sank beneath the horizon and Camden's mouth trailed down my body for the third time, I couldn't bring myself to be concerned with anything else.

We were ravenous by dinner time, so we had pizza delivered and ate it around my coffee table in various degrees of undress. After that, we shifted to the sofa to cuddle for a change of pace. I laid my head on his shoulder and trailed my fingertips up and down his naked torso while he played with a strand of my hair. Every so often, he'd dip his head, press his lips to mine, and murmur, "We're finally gonna to do this, right? Me and you?"

Every single time, I answered, "Forever, Cam."

RECLAIM

I hated how he still had doubts, but I understood. In the past, our times together were always punctuated with long goodbyes. He wasn't wrong. I did think *there* was a physical and emotional destination. Like maybe I'd wake up one morning and everything would finally feel right. The brick wall of my past would melt away to reveal Camden and a golden path to our future.

But too much time had already been wasted.

I'd always been such a burden on the people who loved me. I didn't want to put that on Camden's shoulders too. I'd dreamed of being whole and having the ability to offer him something more than trouble for once.

But maybe the things I wanted to offer him weren't the things he needed.

Choices. Everyone makes them.

But not all of them should be yours to make alone.

Which was exactly why, as I stared at him in that towel, the bright morning sun illuminating the room, as he impatiently waited for me to give him feedback on where we would be settling as a couple, I replied, "You are my preference, Cam. Where do you want to live?"

He prowled over to me, putting his knee to the bed before bending over for an entirely too chaste kiss. "I don't know if you'd even like New York. We could always move out of the city, but even the suburbs are a whole different world than Clovert."

I circled my arms around his neck and dragged him down for a lingering kiss. My body was sore from his constant attention the night before but it began to hum back to life. "You're in New York though."

He settled on his side and cradled his head in his hand, his elbow on the bed, and slid the blanket back to reveal my breasts. Tracing his finger around my nipple, he replied, "I am right now, but I only have a tiny studio apartment and it doesn't even have a stove."

After gliding my palm down his stomach, I tugged at the tucked fabric on his towel, popping it open. "I don't need a stove. I need you."

Smiling, he grabbed my wrist. "You're not going to distract me from this conversation. We need to figure it out. Assuming we can get things settled this week with your case, I'll need to get back to the city. Now, whether it's to put in my notice and pack my stuff or to take a few days to scope out a house for us before you follow me is up to you. But I'm not leaving until we have a plan of action."

"Then hurry up and make a plan so I can"—there was a damn blanket dividing us, but I scooted closer and rolled my hip, not surprisingly finding him hard and ready—"get back to other plans."

He hummed deep in his throat. "Okay. So you'll come with me to New York, then. What about your students? And your summer lunch program? And Joe? You know, Thea and Ramsey might decide to move back one day, but even if they don't, New York is a long way from Georgia."

Damn. He had a point.

And I really fucking hated that he had a point while I was so close to having him inside me again. "You are taking all the fun out of this with your rational questions."

"Trust me. Nobody hates being rational right now more than I do."

I sagged into the bed. "I haven't really considered it all yet. As far as my family goes, I'll miss them, but Joe has Misty and her kids around him, and we could always come back for visits, right?"

He kissed the tip of my nose. "Of course."

"It might take a while, but I could probably get a job teaching in New York. Some of the other teachers at school might be willing to take over the lunch program."

"Is that what you want?"

I shrugged. "I don't know, but after everything we've been through, I can't ask you to give up your entire life and move back to Clovert. You've worked too hard to build your life—even while suffocating on my hook. I don't want to be the hook anymore, Cam. I want to be a team for once."

With an arm around my hips, he rolled me to my side, my chest coming flush with his. "Okay. We'll figure it out. Maybe I can look around Clovert for opportunities. Then you can come up to New York and see if it's even someplace you could see yourself being happy. Hell, maybe we compromise and move to somewhere totally different. My roots have only ever been with you."

God, how was he so sweet?

"I'm not sure if you're aware or not, but you, Camden Cole, are pretty damn amazing." I tipped my head up to ask for a kiss and he didn't keep me waiting long.

"Good. Then we're even," he murmured, his hand snaking under the covers, headed straight for my ass.

The sound of my doorbell pulled him up short.

"Ignore it," I urged.

"What if it's Joe?"

"Then we'll be doing him a favor by not letting him in right before you do wicked things to his daughter."

The side of his mouth curled. "I thought she was about to do wicked things to me."

I raked my teeth over my bottom lip. "We could do both."

The doorbell rang again.

"Noooooooo," I groaned.

He chuckled. "Just go answer it. It might be import—"

That was all he got out before Thea's voice came from my living room. "Wake up. Wake up. Breakfast has arrived, and you've got some explaining to do."

I sat straight up in bed, nearly knocking Cam off the side.

"Do you have any cream cheese? A half dozen bagels and they didn't put any in the damn bag," Ramsey called out as though he and his maniac wife had not just broken into my house.

Though I did love that maniac and her crazy husband. And while I didn't get to see them nearly as much as I would have liked, interrupting me when I was in bed with a gorgeous man was not ideal timing. But I wasn't going to send them away, either.

"Who is that?" Cam asked, his brows furrowed.

I scrambled from the bed and went to my dresser to drag on a pair of jeans and a T-shirt. "Ramsey and Thea. I guess it's meet-the-family day. You should probably get dressed."

His eyes flared and it made me laugh.

Still tugging my shirt down, I sauntered over to him and bent for a quick kiss. "Relax. They'll love you, but hurry up. A half dozen bagels isn't going to last long with Ramsey."

With that, I was out the door, carefully shutting it behind me so he had privacy to get dressed. "Well, well, well. Look what the cat dragged in. I see you found my hide-a-key."

"Who needs a hide-a-key? I made a copy of that thing," Thea teased.

Ramsey's whole face lit when he saw me. Abandoning his bagel on the plate, he headed straight for me and wrapped me up in a bear hug. "Jesus, Nora. Why the hell didn't you call?"

Because Ramsey would have felt guilty for having moved

away. Thea would have gotten pissed and raised immortal hell at the police station.

And, well, they had just gotten married and started a life together. I really liked the idea of not dragging them into more of my mess again. But, most of all, with Camden at my side, I really felt like we had things under control.

I stepped out of my brother's hold and crossed my arms over my chest. "I've been...busy."

"Doing what?" Thea asked, sliding the tub of cream cheese she'd found in my fridge toward Ramsey. "You were *arrested*, Nora. By a freaking Caskey. We would have been here sooner but we had to get special permission to come down for the day. Dad tried to tell me you were in good hands, but honestly—" Her shoulders snapped back as her gaze lifted over my shoulder.

"Hi," Camden said, his front hitting my back, his hand going to my hip.

"Oh my God," Thea whispered.

Her eyes bounced from me to Camden and back again. While Thea didn't understand the depths of my relationship with Camden, she'd heard me talk about him over the years. Being that her soul mate had been incarcerated for the majority of her adult life, I'd tried not to rub it in on the few occasions I had gotten to spend time with Camden. Though, one night, after a few too many glasses of wine, I'd spilled all about our night in and out of the hot tub. I'd even shown her a picture of him from Instagram once too. But as far as she knew, Camden Cole was the one who got away.

"Are you..." She flicked her gaze back to me. "Is that..."

Shocking the hell out of me, it was Ramsey who finished her stammered question. "Mr. Cole." He wiped his hand on the thigh of his jeans twice before extending it for a shake.

Cam took it immediately. "Please. For the hundredth time, call me Camden."

Mr. Cole?

For the hundredth time?

What the hell?

It seemed I was not the only one on the train to Confusion Junction.

"Do you two know each other?" Thea asked.

Ramsey laughed and continued shaking Camden's hand, going so far as to cup it between both of his palms. "This is Mr. Cole. The attorney I told you about who helped at my parole hearing."

"Just Camden. Mr. Cole was my dad," the obvious *stranger*—the one I was planning a life with—said behind me.

Wait…

Oh my God.

"No way!" Thea gasped, stealing the exact words from my mouth. She came unstuck and hurried around the counter. Then she thrust a hand out, and Ramsey let go long enough for her to get a shake in too. "It's so nice to finally meet you. Ramsey told me you were incredible speaking to the board on his behalf. He doesn't think they would have released him without you."

"Happy to help," Camden said.

Had I been able to form coherent sentences at a decibel that would not leave all the dogs in Clovert deaf, I would have taken that route. But finding out the love of my life—who had just come back into my life *days* earlier, who'd then planted his foot in the ground that we were no longer doing goodbyes and fewer than five minutes earlier had been debating where we were going to live—had somehow gotten my brother out on parole for a crime he had not committed after we'd all given up hope and had never so much as mentioned it, did not lend itself to those kind of rational reactions. Therefore, my only response was to crane my head back and stare up at him.

Blinking. Lost for words.

His blue gaze met mine and he must have caught the gist of panic in my eyes, because he released Thea's shake, wrapped his palm around my hand, and inquired to my family, "Can you excuse us for a moment?"

"Yeah, totally," Thea chirped.

While Ramsey's, "Sure," held a confused reluctance.

Camden gave my hand a tug and guided me down the hall. As we went, Ramsey and Thea continued to talk, their hushed whispers not nearly quiet enough for my small house.

"How do they know each other?" my brother asked.

"Are you kidding me? He's the kid she's been in love with since, like, middle school," Thea replied. "He's so much hotter than the pictures."

"Sparrow, I am standing right here. Can you quit panting for a second and explain to me what the hell is going on?"

Thea laughed, and Camden must have heard their exchange too, because he grinned before shutting the door.

When he released my hand, I took a step away, needing a second to catch my breath.

"I was going to tell you," he stated immediately. "I wasn't hiding it or anything. I thought you might have already known, but then you didn't say anything and so much has been going on between us."

"That's why you have your license to practice law in Georgia," I whispered, puzzle pieces snapping into place.

"That's one of them."

My nose started to sting as I stood there staring at him, over a dozen emotions swirling inside me. "We weren't even speaking when he got out," I croaked.

He shrugged with one shoulder. "So? We haven't been speaking for half our lives and I still love you."

"Cam," I breathed.

"Look, a big part of the reason I went into law in the first place was because of you. You talk about devoting your time to the students at your school so they don't have to go through the hardships you did. Well, I've always felt like, maybe if I'd been older or able to help when everything happened with you and Josh and Ramsey, maybe all our lives could have been a little easier. So the minute I was able, I did something about it. He didn't deserve to be in there. And you didn't deserve to live in a prison outside those bars, either. I just wanted you—hell, all of us—to finally be free."

Rivers dripped from my chin. "You make me feel free."

He smiled, slowly walked toward me, and then gathered me in his arms. "Then why are you crying, crazy?"

"Because I just realized I may have gotten in over my head with you. I'll have to spend the rest of my life making sandwiches to repay you for this."

He chuckled. "What if we just stop keeping score from here on out? No more you bringing a sandwich or me bringing a sandwich. Just us, working together for the best lives possible."

I stared up at him, love and acceptance that I'd never feel with another human being seeping into my bones. The constant ache inside me ebbed into nothingness.

Life wouldn't be perfect with Camden. My life would be a never-ending work in progress, but with him at my side, it didn't seem so damn daunting anymore. We could take it slow and get to know each other again. Things like fighting over who took the

RECLAIM

trash out last and why he squeezed the toothpaste from the middle of the tube were a rite of passage for couples. And I was ready.

Finally.

Because with Camden, I was ready for anything.

Lifting up onto my toes, I pressed a gentle kiss to his mouth. "Thank you for being you. And for taking care of me all these years. I don't know how, but I promise I'll make it worth it for you."

He smiled and deepened the kiss, taking a breath only long enough to say, "You already have."

TWENTY-NINE

Camden

"You're a Caskey?" Ramsey asked, aggressively chewing a piece of gum as we sat around Nora's dining room table, bagel crumbs and empty coffee cups long since forgotten.

I sighed and gave Nora's thigh a squeeze under the table. "Technically. Though I don't advertise it."

Thea leaned forward and her green eyes searched my face. "Fascinating. I thought you were required to be a douchebag with those genetics."

"Thankfully, the douchebag gene skipped me." Popping my eyebrows, I looked to Nora. "Or at least I think it did."

She shrugged. "You *were* wearing penny loafers the first time we met at the creek. I don't think it skipped you as much as you fought it off."

"Hey," I said, feigning offense and shifting my hand down to chomp at the ticklish spot above her knee. "Take it back."

She laughed, prying my fingers away one by one. "Fine. You just have extra-pretentious taste in shoes."

Wrapping my hand around hers, I lifted it to my mouth and kissed the back. "Fair enough."

When I looked up, Ramsey and Thea were leaning back in their chairs, holding hands, and grinning like a pair of Cheshire cats.

Nora rolled her eyes at their love-struck stares. "So, anyway, I think Camden and I are moving to New York."

"What?" Thea exclaimed.

My body tensed. "Well, we haven't made any final plans yet."

"But it's happening," Nora stated. "And I don't want to hear a peep about it from either one of you. As soon as you're allowed, you two will be off traveling the world together. Maybe you can stop by our place in the city sometime."

"Oh, thank fuck." Ramsey let out a loud belly laugh. "Leaving you alone in Clovert has been a nightmare. Now, if we could only figure out how to get Joe and Misty out of here too."

"Shit," Thea said, jumping to her feet, causing her husband to jump with her. "We promised Dad we'd be at his house a half hour ago. Misty is making some kind of casserole for lunch and we need to stop and grab something to eat in the car on the way over." She shot me a tight smile. "Word to the wise, never eat anything that woman cooks."

"Especially not the pot roast," Thea and Nora stated in unison before dissolving into a fit of laughter.

"Duly noted." I nodded, rising to start cleaning up.

Nora's eyes lit as she stood and wrapped her arms around my waist. "Hey, why don't we go over there too? I could formally introduce my boyfriend to the family."

Fuck me. I was a grown ass-man with a career and a car payment the way God intended, but I was damn near giddy at the idea of being Nora's boyfriend.

I waggled my eyebrows. "Your boyfriend, huh? Sounds like a promotion."

"Long overdue." She patted my chest and then pursed her lips, asking for a kiss.

Who was I to deny such a request?

While Ramsey and I cleared the table, our women huddled together, sharing whispers and giggles. I was in the same clothes I'd worn to Nora's house the morning before—although I hadn't been wearing them for the majority of our activities—but I liked the idea of changing into something clean before heading to her dad's for lunch. We agreed to meet at Joe's after Nora and I swung by the Clovert Inn so I could change and check out. Hellhole hotel aside, I wasn't spending another night without Nora.

We all walked out the front door and started down the sidewalk to our respective vehicles. Four people smiling and laughing genuinely happy for the first time in, well, possibly ever. It should have been my first clue that all hell was about to break loose.

"You son of a bitch!" Jonathan Caskey roared as he came storming through Nora's front lawn. He was in plain clothes, but his cruiser was pulled up on the curb, two tires parked in the grass.

My whole body went on alert, and in the next second, Ramsey was at my side, Thea and Nora forced behind us. While I had every bit of faith that Ramsey could hold his own, I'd worked my ass off to get him out of prison and not for another damn Caskey to send him back.

"Take the girls inside," I said.

"Fuck that!" Thea shouted, fighting to step around her husband.

"Don't make this worse, Sparrow," Ramsey rumbled as Jonathan continued to advance.

"You've got to be kidding me," Nora chimed in, stepping around *me*.

Which was fan-fucking-tastic. *No one* had gone inside. Mr. Out On Parole, Miss Out On Bail, and Mrs. Flat-Out Pissed-Off were all at risk of getting tangled in this clusterfuck.

"Just stay here and let me handle this." I walked away from the group, meeting Jonathan in the middle of the yard with plans to send him right back in the direction he'd come. "Nope. We are not doing this here. Not today. Fuck…maybe not ever."

"I told you to call off your goddamn dog!" he yelled, spit spraying onto my face.

I gritted my teeth. "And I said drop the charges against Nora."

Narrowing my eyes, I took a second to really take Jonathan in. Unkempt clothes hung on a frame that was far thinner than it had appeared when he had been in uniform. His hands shook, and his dark, sunken eyes continuously scanned the yard, never lingering for longer than a beat.

"This is not a fucking negotiation!" he boomed. "You have no motherfucking idea who the hell you are dealing with right now."

I laughed humorlessly. "I think you've made it pretty clear that I'm dealing with a crooked cop who gets his rocks off playing God with innocent people's lives."

"You think I give one single fuck about your whore or her cock-sucking family?"

My vision flashed red for an instant before time suddenly slowed to a crawl.

Everyone moved at once, the explosion of chaos rocking me back onto my heels.

Thea shouted something behind me, and on instinct, I turned at the sound.

Ramsey hooked her around the stomach before she had a chance to get more than a few steps away from him.

Nora burst forward at the same time, pure rage cloaking her beautiful face.

But it was the cold tip of a gun slamming against my temple that halted the melee.

There was a round of gasps punctuated by a shrill scream tearing from Nora's throat.

"Cam!"

"Back up!" Jonathan yelled, wrapping an arm around my neck and dragging my back to his front. The barrel of his weapon dug into my head. "All of you. Back the fuck up."

"Easy. Easy," Ramsey said, stepping in front of Thea, one hand in the air and the other reaching for his sister. "We don't want any problems."

"Get them in the house!" I barked.

"One fucking move, I will put a bullet between your eyes."

Ramsey gave the illusion of stilling, but he continued inching closer to Nora—my beautiful, terrified Nora, her brown eyes wide, tears already streaking her cheeks. Jesus, she'd been through enough.

We'd all been through enough.

A ball of fire grew in my chest as I held her panicked stare. "Put the gun down," I snarled over my shoulder.

Jonathan's voice was cold and cruel. "If your guy doesn't lay off, I'm as good as dead. I have no problem taking you down with me."

"I have no idea what the fuck you are talking about, okay? Whoever is following you isn't working for me."

"Liar!" he yelled, his unsteady hand shaking so violently that the gun rattled against my head. "You've always had it out for me. You like the idea of putting me in the ground next to my brother, huh? I don't know why I'm surprised you're fucking your way into the family who did it. You think if I'm out of the way all the Caskey money will be yours? Is that what you're after?" He laughed, loud and maniacal. "Well, bad news, Cole. It's gone. All of it. Fucking *gone*."

Shit.

There it was. Whatever was happening. Whatever Jonathan had gotten himself into. It all boiled down to my archnemesis: money.

I had not one clue how it was even possible for his family to have burned through a fortune like the Caskeys were believed to have. But, then again, maybe *believe* was the operative word in that statement.

I glanced back at Nora—my strong, beautiful girl. Ramsey had managed to get his hand around her wrist, but she refused to budge. Funny, I'd spent my whole life trying to keep her and the one time I wished she'd leave, her feet were rooted in the ground.

I should've been terrified. I should have taken a deep breath and offered him the entire contents of my bank account. But not twenty-four hours earlier, I'd finally gotten the girl. We were planning a life together, a future, and a forever. For an instant, I was the kid carrying a bowl of banana pudding again, desperate to get back to Nora at the creek. There was no fucking way I was going to let Jonathan Caskey steal her from me again.

Shifting back, I got low, ready to duck out of his grip, and seethed, "I'm going to fucking bury you."

In one fluid movement, he swung the gun from my temple and trained the barrel on my entire world. "Not if I bury her first."

"No!" I yelled just as a bullet exploded from his gun. A crippling pain erupted in my ear, but it was nothing compared to the agony slashing through my chest. "Nora!" I screamed as she fell backward, Thea and Ramsey diving after her.

Panic slayed me, a visceral fury flooded my veins, and a crash of adrenaline ignited my system.

I needed to get to her. I needed to gather her in my arms and tell her it was all going to be okay.

But, first, I had to end this once and for all.

Spinning out of his hold, I slammed a fist into his face. Bones crunching and blood spraying, I showed him no mercy. He fell back and I followed him down, raining punch after violent punch. As long as his heart was beating, I would never feel an ounce of satisfaction.

I sat up, straddling his motionless body, my fist reared back, ready to land another devastating blow, when suddenly a mountain of a man tackled me from behind.

Immediately lurching to my feet, I was stopped by a tattooed hand landing square in the center of my chest.

"Relax, Cole. I got this." After roughly rolling Jonathan's unconscious body to his stomach, he gathered his wrists in one hand and planted a knee into his back. With his free hand, he grabbed the gun off the grass and shoved it into the back of his jeans.

Confusion snapped me from my frenzy as I stared down at a man with dark hair, a thick beard, and black ink crawling across his skin. I'd never seen him a day in my life, but somehow, he knew me. "Who the hell are you?"

"I'm the guy saving your ass from a murder charge." He jerked his chin. "I'm Aiden Johnson. Leo sent me."

I had a dozen questions, but all of them could wait.

"Nora!" I shouted, sprinting past him.

I couldn't have been more than a few yards away, but it felt like it took an eternity to reach her. My heart pounded, and every inhale felt like jagged razors in my lungs. Ramsey and Thea were crouched down around her, blocking my view, and I bulldozed through them.

"Move!" I roared.

I wouldn't survive this.

I wouldn't survive losing her.

Not after I'd just gotten her back.

Ramsey moved out of my way, his face pale, his phone already to his ear. "We need an ambulance. I think she's okay, but I don't know for sure."

Dropping to my knees, I began frantically searching her body, patting down everywhere I could reach. "Where do you hurt? Are you bleeding? Talk to me."

"I…um. I don't think he hit me."

"Are you sure?" I continued with the pat-down, inspecting her arms and legs for any sign of trauma.

Her trembling hand came up to cup my jaw, forcing my eyes back to hers. "What the hell just happened? Are you okay?"

No. It was safe to say I would never be okay again after watching him pull the trigger, knowing she was on the other end. But as long as she was safe and at my side, I would find a way to breathe again.

"Come here," I forced out around a lump of emotion lodged in my throat, falling back on my ass as the adrenaline began to ebb from my system.

Sirens screamed in the distance as she wasted no time crawling into my lap and burying her face in my neck. "Oh, God, Cam."

"I'm right here," I murmured, smoothing her hair down. "Just breathe."

Motion over my shoulder caught my attention and I swiveled around to find at least a dozen men covering the lawn.

All of them in suits, not a single Clovert police uniform in the bunch. A few of them were surrounding Jonathan, who was now cuffed but still lying facedown.

"Sir, are you injured?" a woman asked.

"No," I breathed, my head swirling as I tried to figure out what the hell was going on. The ambulance wasn't even there yet, but there was somehow a row of unmarked cars lining the street.

"What about you, ma'am?"

Dazed, Nora shook her head. "I'm fine."

"Okay, well, hang tight. We have medical on the way, just in case."

Ramsey was off to the side, talking to a man I didn't recognize. He was still visibly shaken but comfortable with the conversation, Thea tucked under his arm.

Aiden Johnson caught my eye and left his conversation with yet another suit to head my way. "He hit the window," he said when he got close, pointing at Nora's house. "You'll need to get that fixed tonight."

"I don't give a fuck about a window. What the hell happened here?" Nora moved off my lap and we stood up together. She instantly wrapped herself around my side.

Aiden's eyes dropped to her. "You good, babe? Luckily, he was too freaked to have had any aim, but you took a nasty spill on the sidewalk." He grinned, and up until that point, I'd doubted he possessed the facial muscles to pull off such a gentle feat.

Leo had been smart when he'd hired this guy; Aiden Johnson was intimidating as hell.

"I'm okay," she whispered, shifting impossibly closer.

I gave her a reassuring squeeze. "Who the hell are all these people?"

His dark eyes came back to me. "Oh, right. First off, we

figured out who was tailing your cousin. It took a little while because the feds aren't usually real excited to discuss an open investigation, but Leo called in some favors."

"What?" I snapped, Nora parroting the same sentiment beside me.

"And they weren't even the only ones." He crossed his arms over his barrel chest. "Seems your boy owed some bad fucking people a lot of cash. When he didn't have it, he made a deal to oversee a handoff of some product, which eventually turned into him escorting drugs through the county on their way to Atlanta and down to Florida. Problem was, feds caught word and started digging. This set off all kind of alarms for the cartel and they came to the conclusion that Caskey had flipped and was setting them up with the authorities. Based on the timing of your return to Clovert, Caskey's dumb ass thought this was all somehow your fault, even though he had one foot in the grave long before he arrested your girl here." He shrugged. "I'm guessing he was never the brains in the family."

I blinked, trying to process all the flaming shit he had just thrown into the already raging Caskey dumpster fire. Some of it made sense. Some of it was unbelievable. Some of it made my fists ache for another piece of him.

But it was the promise of one thing that put a shit-eating grin on my face.

"He's done," I stated. "There is no coming back from all of that. He'll be lucky if he ever gets out of prison, and messing with the cartel like he has won't make his stay very comfortable, either."

He deserved everything that was coming to him and more.

Aiden barked a laugh. "That man is lucky he's still breathing. An order was given to take him out last night. Long story short, you beating the shit out of him back there might have saved his life. Don't let the motherfucker say you never gave him anything."

Nora tilted her head back. "It's over?"

"It is."

She beamed up at me, the return of her smile—although wobbly—breathing new life into my soul. "Like, really over?"

"Yeah, babe."

And it was.

All our pain.

All our suffering.

All our heartache.

With Jonathan behind bars, it was finally fucking over.

My head snapped up. "I want his computer seized. He has videos—"

Aiden lifted his paw in the air. "Way ahead of you. Apollo is over at his place now. Nothing he has will ever see the light of day again."

I dipped my head with gratitude, and about that time, Ramsey and Thea came walking back over. Thea appeared slightly calmer; meanwhile, Ramsey still looked like he might puke at any second.

"Hey," he breathed, giving his sister a head-to-toe. "Are you sure you're all right?"

Nora flashed him a smile. "I promise." She lifted a pinky in his direction, and he fought some serious emotions back before hooking his finger with hers.

After Aiden excused himself, the four of us stood there. Ramsey and I were like bookends while Nora and Thea hooked their arms in the middle.

That day could have ended in disaster. One slip of his finger,

RECLAIM

one wrong move, and all of our lives would have been irrevocably changed.

But, every now and again, something good comes from all the bad.

Arm in arm, we watched Jonathan Caskey kick and cuss as they loaded him into the back of a police car.

With the click of the door behind him, four people who had crawled through hell on their hands and knees were finally set free.

THIRTY

Nora

I clung to Camden's arm as he tried to get out of bed. "Don't go."

He laughed and stood up despite my best efforts. It wasn't often when I missed the days of him being scrawny and clumsy, but being able to overpower him long enough to tie him to my bed so he could never leave held a lot of promise.

"Trust me," he said. "This isn't my idea of a good time, either. But if we don't hurry, I'll miss my flight."

I sat up, crisscrossed my legs in front of me, and pouted. "You said no more goodbyes."

"I did. But then someone who shall remain nameless decided they wanted to finish the last two months of the school year before moving. And I realized my cruel and unreasonable boss won't pay me to lie on her couch, waiting listlessly for her to come home and get naked." Resting his palms on the bed, he bent and kissed my nose. "Relax. I'll be back next weekend and then you're coming to New York the following and so on and so forth. By the time June hits, you'll be sick of me and begging for a goodbye."

I tugged on the front of his shirt, dragging him back down. "Blasphemy. I'll never get sick of you." My lips twisted. "The leaving-the-toilet-seat-up thing though…"

RECLAIM

He smiled, wide and life-changing—or at least it was for me. "I'd apologize, but I have a very riveting game of Is-that-a-dead-rat-or-just-the-hair-Nora-left-in-the-drain to play before we can leave." He pecked me again, this time on the mouth, and I reluctantly let him go.

"I hope it's a rat this time!" I called as he disappeared into the bathroom.

It had only been two weeks since Jonathan Caskey was arrested, and while it seemed like the days had flown by, we'd crammed a lot into that time.

As soon as news of Jonathan's arrest broke, Clovert's gossip mill exploded. Partially because, within a matter of hours, his father was taken into custody on embezzlement charges after Jonathan had sung like a bird on the entire family. Seriously, the Caskey family was a shit storm, but for once, it wasn't raining down on me. By the end of the week, Camden's grandparents had pulled up roots and moved to Florida, and despite the dozen shrieking threats she'd left on his voicemail, Camden's mom steered clear of Clovert too.

With help from a sexy attorney who I later stripped out of a tailored, navy suit to show my undying gratitude, the prosecution dropped all charges against me. My principal canceled my suspension, but I took a week of personal leave anyway, because.... Well, I deserved it. Also see the aforementioned part about the sexy attorney who was no longer in the navy suit but still working remotely from my dining room table.

It had been a whirlwind of getting to know each other again, but Camden and I had made great strides in our relationship. And by this, I just meant we spent every waking minute together, bickering or laughing. Sometimes laughing and bickering at the same time.

One day for lunch, I made him a chicken salad sandwich. They were, after all, his favorite. Ham, pickle, and mustard being his second choice. His face when he realized I'd remembered was priceless. The only thing better was when he dragged me onto his lap, tore the sandwich in half, and insisted we share. Shortly after, he closed his laptop and peeled my shirt off so we could share a few other things as well.

I'd only had him back for a little over two weeks and I had no idea how I'd survived the last five years without him. He was only going to be gone for a few days and I was already dreading every single minute of it.

This time, he was coming back.

Then, the next weekend, I was going to him.

The way it always should have been.

On that thought, I climbed out of bed and made fast work of getting dressed.

After a quick breakfast and two travel mugs of coffee, Camden and I left for the airport. We'd returned his rental a week earlier, so he was behind the wheel of my Honda—a car he hated but I secretly loved seeing him drive because, well, it was mine and it was his now too.

"Now, listen," Camden said as we drove through town. "I need you to tell Forehead Freddy you're taken as soon as you get back to school. I don't like the way he looks at you in pictures."

I thought he was probably kidding, but it still made that Camden Cole warmth seep into my chest. "I'm sure he'll be devastated."

"As he should be." His hand had been anchored to my thigh since we'd backed out of the driveway and he gave me a squeeze.

I tapped my finger against the window. "You should have turned there. Juniper is going to be super backed up with all the road work."

Another squeeze. "Maybe."

RECLAIM

"No maybe about it. They've had one man single-handedly repaving that road for two years. You have to sit and wait until—" The words died on my tongue when he slowed and hit the blinker right in front of the Leonards' house. "What are you doing?"

"We just need to make a quick stop. It won't take but a minute." He pulled into the long driveway leading up to the brick ranch-style home where Mr. Leonard's elderly son, Sam, now lived.

"What for?"

He grinned. "You'll see."

My pulse quickened even if I didn't understand why. He was up to something.

He stopped and put the car into park in front of the two-car garage. Still sporting a massive grin, he lifted my hand to his mouth, kissed the back of it, and said, "Come on. I want to show you something."

There was nothing at the creek he could have shown me that I hadn't already seen, but my stomach still dipped with excitement.

After we both climbed out, he waited for me at the front of the car and laced his fingers with mine. It had been years since I'd gone out to the Leonards', but as Camden led me around the back of the house, childhood memories came rushing back.

Our creek had been my safe haven. The quiet lull of water had drowned out the chaos in my mind. The cute boy who'd played Slapjack with me under the trees. A friend when I'd needed one more than ever. It was my escape from reality when life became more than I could bear.

Things looked different now. The grass in the field had grown and some of the banks had washed away in a flood a few years back, but our sacred spot of dirt and beach were still there as though no more than a few days had passed since we'd last visited.

We stopped next to his favorite rock, and I could almost still see him wearing those penny loafers and perched on top of it the first day. I'd loved that boy with my whole heart even before I had known what love truly was, but the man standing in front of me now was better—so much better.

"God, I missed this place," he whispered, hooking an arm around my hips and pulling me in for a hug.

"Me too." Smiling, I drew in a deep breath that was equal parts fresh water, trees, and Camden Cole. The perfect scent in my opinion.

"You know, for a lot of years, I never understood why you didn't move away from Clovert. I couldn't fathom that you had a lot of positive memories rooting you to this place. But then, when we're here, all the good times come flooding back."

"Get out of my head, Cam. I was literally just thinking that."

He chuckled, but his smile quickly fell. "I don't want to lose it. In New York, it's different. It's busy and chaotic. We'd have to travel for hours to find a place like this. When I moved away from Alberton, this kind of life was exactly what I was trying to escape. I needed to get away from the memories clinging to these trees or there was a solid chance I'd still be sitting at this creek, waiting for you to come back."

My stomach knotted. It was both super sweet and crazy sad, and it made me feel wicked guilty. I slid my hands up his chest and circled my arms around his neck. "I'm sorry."

"Don't you dare apologize. It took a while, but we got here eventually. The problem is, while I was trying to get away, I ended up creating a whole new life that can't really be done in Clovert. I worked my ass off for a lot of years, and while I'm sure there are plenty of people who need an attorney for public intoxication after the Fall Festival, they aren't exactly my target clientele."

I giggled. "Oh, come on, Ed Lewis could keep you in business year-round all on his own."

"Probably. But that's not what I want, babe. And I also don't want to strip all of this from you, either."

"You aren't stripping—"

"I am. You have family here. Friends and students who love you. A summer lunch program that, honestly… It fucking kills me to think you won't be here to watch it thrive. I need you. I need you in every single facet of my life, but not if it means giving up your own. I want the best of both worlds, Nora. A few days ago, I finally figured out how we can make this work, but I need your help."

"Anything."

He chewed on his bottom lip for a second, his blue eyes locked on mine, and then finally announced, "I want to buy the creek."

"I'm sorry, what?"

He chuckled. "I want to buy it. Come on. This is *our* creek. It might as well be named the Stewart and Cole Worm Farm. The house is shit. I did a walk-through with Sam a few days ago. I swear it hasn't been updated since the seventies. But we have time to do a remodel. Make it ours too."

I blinked. "Um, wait. I'm confused. Didn't you just say you can't do your job in Clovert?"

"I did. But my boss has a summer house in Maine. He takes his whole family and goes there June through August. We could do that, Nora. We'll get something small in the suburbs and then we can come back here for the summer. I'd still have to work and maybe fly back a few times a month, but you could still oversee your lunch program."

He released me and walked over to two trees, his voice filling with almost as much excitement as his face. "But, at night, we could hang a hammock up out here." He swung his arm down to the deep end of the water. "And on the weekends, we can have Joe and Misty over for cookouts and go swimming. I know we've talked about taking things slow and getting to know each other again, but maybe one day we could raise our kids here—happy kids, kids who will never have to deal with the hell we went through. We can make new memories until this becomes their creek too." He hurried back over in front of me. "I get it. It's going to take compromise from both of us, and it's not always going to be easy. But, for the right price, Sam said he'd be willing to sell us this place. And I don't give a damn what the right price is. I want this, Nora. I want it with you."

He finally stopped talking and stared at me expectantly, but I couldn't breathe much less string together a complete sentence.

Me. Camden. Kids. Our creek. A lifetime of laughter and happiness. I'd never even dreamed that big before.

Sweet Jesus, Freaking Camden Cole was still the genius of all geniuses from all those years ago.

"Say something," he whispered.

I nodded a dozen times.

His smile grew with each one.

"I'm in, Cam. All in. Just tell me what you need me to do," I choked out, fighting an onslaught of emotion back.

He rested his hands on my hips and playfully rocked me from side to side. "I need help paying the down payment."

RECLAIM

"Uh, I'm not sure the rainy-day-slash-Louboutin fund is big enough for it, but I could save up or take out a loan."

He laughed and shook his head. "No, crazy. I need the ten in your back pocket. I think it's time we put the original Stewart and Cole Worm Farm money to good use."

Our ten-dollar bill had not been in my back pocket when I'd gotten dressed that morning, but based solely on the pride in his eyes, I was positive it was there now.

Dipping low, he brushed his nose with mine. "That ten has always been a safety net for us. A way we could find each other and a reason to come back. It was what bound us to one another when we couldn't be together in reality. We don't need it anymore, Nora. This is real now. It's you and me forever. From here on out. Every day. No searching for just-in-case moments. No fallback plans or fail-safes. If I need you, you'll only be in the other room. When you need me, I'll be just outside. What better way to use that money than to put it down as the first building block on our future together?"

I dove into his arms, tears spilling from my eyes. "I love you so much, and I love every single thing about the words you just said too. I will happily give you ten dollars as soon as we get back to the car. But you have lost your mind if you think I am ever getting rid of our ten-dollar bill. That is mine. Do you hear me? You gave it to me, and I'm finally ready to accept it."

"Well, it took you long enough." He laughed deep and rich, cocooning me in his strong arms, which had been holding me up even from a distance for the majority of my life. Arms that I had no doubt would hold me close, through good times and bad, every day for the rest of my life.

God, I loved this man.

I didn't deserve Camden Cole, and I never would, but I

wasn't entirely sure anyone on the planet was good enough for a soul like his.

Choices. Everyone makes them.

And by some miracle I would never understand, Camden chose me.

EPILOGUE

Camden

Ten years later...

"Nora!" I called, using my foot to shove the front door open, my hands—and face—filled with Fraser fir needles. "Where do you want this?"

"Do not ask her that. She'll have us toting it all over the house," Ramsey grunted, supporting the back end of the biggest Christmas tree I had ever seen.

Nora and Thea had tagged it with a sold ticket earlier in the day while volunteering at the tree sale to benefit the ever-growing bag lunch program. It was a good-looking tree, but they had failed to mention its enormity when they'd sent Ramsey and me in a damn sedan to go pick it up. Joe had come to our rescue with his buddy's truck then promptly disappeared when it had come time to load it up.

"In the living room," Nora replied. "Wait. Unless you think it would look better at the top of the stairs so you can see it from the window?"

"See?" Ramsey hissed and then called back to his sister. "Living room it is!"

I was all about filling the house with happiness and joy every chance I got, but a fourteen-foot Christmas tree that was almost as wide as it was tall was seriously pushing the limits.

After Nora and I had bought the creek, we'd gotten to work on the home renovations immediately. This had led to us finding termites in almost every wall, a crack in the foundation, and electrical work that was held together by tape and a prayer.

We had a long talk one night while going over the estimates to make the necessary repairs, including a frank discussion about our finances. Nora was planning to teach after we moved to New York, but finding a job straightaway was going to be difficult. I made good money, so we would have been fine without her income, but not if we were paying on two homes, one of which we wanted to completely overhaul. In true Nora fashion, she hugged me tight and told me the creek house could wait until we had time to save up for it. All she needed was me.

I understood exactly what she was saying because all I needed was her. Yes, we could have waited and made improvements little by little on a house that would work and be *fine* for us. But *fine* was not what I wanted for Nora Stewart ever again.

I wanted her to smile every morning when she woke up.

I wanted her to feel safe and proud each time she walked in the door.

I wanted her to have something that was even half as beautiful as she would always be to me.

So I presented her with a proposal. No, not *that* kind of proposal—yet. But rather, what better way to get back at my dad than to live happily ever after? I had my inheritance tucked in a bank account out of my sight, doing nothing productive other than reminding me of how worthless he'd made me feel growing up. I saved it for things I knew he'd hate but things that meant a lot to me. And trust me—nothing would have pissed him off more than to see me tearing down a house in order to build a new one when I was already going to be upside down

RECLAIM

on the land, all so I could live in sin with a woman—a *Stewart* woman at that.

It would have been wasteful, stupid, and flat-out disrespectful to the Lord.

And. I. Was. *Stoked.*

Nora shrugged and told me to follow my heart.

I bulldozed the house by the end of the week. It took six months to build our new four-bedroom, three-bath two-story, complete with wraparound porches on both levels and our very own hot tub out back. But when it was done, the awe on Nora's face as she walked through the door for the first time made it the best money I'd ever spent.

"Whoa," Thea breathed as Ramsey and I made it to the living room. "Is that thing going to fit in here?"

"It better," I replied. "Otherwise, we're laying it on its side and having a Christmas log this year."

"It'll fit. I measured," Nora said, walking into the room, her hair a mess, flour covering her black-and-pink apron.

I cocked an eyebrow at her. "What happened to you? Did you lose another fight with the new mixer?"

"Ha. Ha. Ha," she deadpanned. "And also yes. I knew I should have brought mine down with us. Next year, remind me."

"Right. I'll add it to next year's mental packing list right now." I smiled.

She stuck her tongue out at me. "Just put the tree in the corner, smartass."

Nora and I still lived in New York most of the year. Much to my surprise, she loved the big-city life. Well, strike that—she loved *visiting* the city. We lived in a sleepy suburb of New Jersey where she taught at an elementary school not far from our house. I might have been biased, but I'd always thought the kids who ended up in Miss Stewart's—eventually Mrs. Cole's—class won the lottery of sorts.

Nora and I had taken our time building our relationship—*a lot of time*. As much as I would love to say it was all hearts and flowers, that would be a lie. Like most things in life, we were a constant work in progress—changing and evolving faster than the seasons. But through it all, we held on to each other, leaned on each other, and loved each other without condition or restraint.

Around the five-year mark, time sped up for us. People had been asking us for years when we were going to settle down and get married. We always laughed because we were as settled as two people could get. It was just without a ring on her finger, which somehow made it less permanent. We didn't need a ring or a piece of paper though. Nora and I were happy.

Until Thea had a baby.

Joseph James Stewart changed our lives all over again.

With Ramsey and Thea living in Washington State, we didn't get to see them as often as any of us would have liked, but for Joseph's first Thanksgiving, the whole Stewart/Hull/Cole family flew out.

Watching Nora's blinding smile as she smothered that baby in kisses breathed an urgency into my veins that was somehow as primal as it was romantic.

We'd talked about kids. We both wanted them. It just never seemed like the right time.

But hadn't I been the one to once tell her that time was wasting?

We were lying in bed later that night when she announced, "I want a baby."

"Oh, thank God," I breathed, slapping a hand over my

heart. "I've been sitting here for the last three hours trying to figure out how to ask you for a baby when I haven't even proposed yet."

She laughed. "You don't have to propose. I locked you down years ago."

Rolling onto my side, I brushed the hair off her face and asked, "Okay, but what if I want to get married? And not just because I want babies, but also because I want a baby and have loved you my entire life and, while our love has never been anything other than forever, maybe it's time we let the world in on that?"

She leaned in and brushed her nose with mine, murmuring, "Then let's get married."

It wasn't exactly a proposal, but it was us.

We went ring shopping as soon as we got home, where she picked out a modest diamond that made me roll my eyes. It was safe to say it was not the rock I slid onto her finger when I got down on one knee later that night after a candlelit dinner that, while cliché, also made her cry, so I took it as a win.

We might have dated for five years, but Nora and I went from zero to sixty in a matter of weeks after that. Not even a month later, we surprised the whole family with a beach wedding in Jamaica. It was something fun and different for us, even if Thea was pissed we hadn't let her plan the trip. It also served as something Nora would later call a *babymoon* because Owen Ramsey Cole was born nine months later.

That little boy immediately became our entire world. As I'd expected, Nora was an incredible mom, and to hear her tell it, I was doing a damn good job breaking the mold from my childhood too.

Ramsey and I gently set the giant Christmas tree down, the

tree stand making it even taller, but with mere inches to spare, it cleared the ceiling. Collectively, we all blew out a sigh of relief.

"All right." I clapped. "Ladies, let the decorating begin. Ramsey and I will be—"

"Oh, no you don't. We have lights to hang and popcorn to thread. Boys!" she called. "Time to decorate!"

A stampede of kids came barreling from the playroom. Ramsey and Thea had welcomed Andrew a few months before Owen was born, so along with Joseph, those three were like a pack of wolves destroying everything in their path.

Owen slammed on the brakes the minute he saw me, skidding across the wood floor on socked feet. "Daddy!" he yelled as though I'd just come back from war and not a twenty-minute trip to pick up the tree. He was a daddy's boy.

And yeah, I fucking loved it.

It was scary how much he looked like me. His hair was darker, but the blue eyes were mine—something that thrilled his mother.

My mother, on the other hand, had never come around to the idea of me being with Nora. We hadn't spoken in years, but after Owen was born, I'd thought she'd at least want to know she had a grandson. She hung up on me. And to be honest, it was startling how much I did not give one flying fuck.

I loved my life.

I loved my wife.

I loved my kid.

As far as I was concerned, I had it all.

If she didn't want to factor into that happiness, it was for the best she stayed gone.

Besides, Owen had some pretty great grandparents on Nora's side.

"Ho! Ho! Ho!" Joe said as he came through the front door, a massive stack of presents cradled in his arms.

"Papa!" all the kids yelled, racing toward him.

Misty was right behind him, unfortunately holding a Crockpot. "Hot plate coming through."

Being the gentleman I was—and also needing to steel my stomach for whatever was inside—I walked over and took it from her hands.

"Oh, wow. Pot roast," I announced.

She patted me on the chest. "I know the girls are cooking tonight, but I couldn't resist making your favorite. I threw in a few extra artichoke hearts, so there should be plenty for you to have leftovers."

"Mmmm," I hummed, internally gagging. Yes, she put artichokes in her pot roast. Sadly, that was not the worst part. "You are too good to me. I'll just put this in the kitchen."

Nora followed behind me, giggling with every step.

Setting the pot on the counter, I glanced around the corner to be sure Misty was out of earshot. Then I turned on my evil wife. "You told her it was my favorite, didn't you?"

"Uh, technically, it was Thea." She bit her bottom lip. "But I didn't correct her."

Grabbing her hand, I gave her a tug, pulling her against me. "If you weren't carrying my daughter, I'd—"

"Shhhh!" She slapped a hand over my mouth. "We aren't telling them until after dinner."

I tilted my head, freeing my mouth. "You mean if I make it through dinner."

"Does it help if I tell you I made banana pudding for dessert?"

"Maybe." I leaned over and caught her mouth in a kiss.

"Or maybe you can make it up to me later tonight down by the creek."

"Awesome. So I can catch pneumonia?"

I scoffed. "You're not going to catch pneumonia. We've never caught anything down by that creek."

She peered up at me, her golden-brown eyes sparkling with more love than I ever knew possible, and smirked. "I caught you, didn't I?"

The End

OTHER BOOKS

The Difference Trilogy
The Difference Between Somebody and Someone
The Difference Between Somehow and Someway
The Difference Between Someday and Forever

From the Embers

Release
Reclaim

The Retrieval Duet
Retrieval
Transfer

Guardian Protection Agency
Singe
Thrive

The Fall Up Series
The Fall Up
The Spiral Down

The Darkest Sunrise Series
The Darkest Sunrise
The Brightest Sunset
Across the Horizon

The Truth Duet
The Truth About Lies
The Truth About Us

The Regret Duet
Written with Regret
Written with You

The Wrecked and Ruined Series
Changing Course
Stolen Course
Broken Course
Among the Echoes

On the Ropes
Fighting Silence
Fighting Shadows
Fighting Solitude

Co-Written Romantic Comedy
When the Walls Come Down
When the Time is Right

ABOUT THE AUTHOR

Originally from Savannah, Georgia, *USA Today* bestselling author Aly Martinez now lives in South Carolina with her husband and four young children.

Never one to take herself too seriously, she enjoys cheap wine, mystery leggings, and baked feta. It should be known, however, that she hates pizza and ice cream, almost as much as writing her bio in the third person.

She passes what little free time she has reading anything and everything she can get her hands on, preferably with a super-sized tumbler of wine by her side.

Facebook: www.facebook.com/AuthorAlyMartinez

Facebook Group: www.facebook.com/groups/TheWinery

Twitter: twitter.com/AlyMartinezAuth

Goodreads: www.goodreads.com/AlyMartinez

www.alymartinez.com

Made in the USA
Columbia, SC
25 May 2024

fab2f081-30a5-4953-97ab-bd54e32cf16aR01